TIERNEY JAMES

DARK SIDE OF NOON

Publishing Coordinator – Sharon Kizziah-Holmes
Cover Design – Jaycee DeLorenzo

L & D PRESS
Owasso, OK

ISBN-13: 978-1-965460-12-2 (Paperback)
ISBN-13: 978-1-965460-13-9 (eBook)

DEDICATION

To the Pawnee and Pueblo people who have enriched my life
with their amazing culture.

ACKNOWLEDGMENTS

Kate Richards of Decadent Publishing – My amazing editor who never tires of my mistakes and questions. Thank you for making me a better writer on each project I send you.

Nan Sipe – Thank you for always making me think I have a chance at this writing life by requesting to see my next manuscript from Kate Richards.

Sharon Kizziah Holmes of Paperback Press – You are the best hand holder I know. I appreciate you getting my manuscript formatted and ready to upload each time I create a new world.

Jaycee DeLorenzo of Sweet & Spicey Designs – You always come up with an amazing book cover for me.

My husband who has decided I'm not giving up and supports me in this crazy writing journey.

CHAPTER 1

She ran. Even though she couldn't see it, she had no doubt it hunted her. Something. The sounds of whispers, the smell of sweet breath and smoke, engulfed her when she stopped to stare from the overlook to the valley below. Spinning around, she could feel its presence. Waiting. The hair on her neck stood up, and goose bumps formed down her body covered in perspiration from the strenuous hike. She noticed nothing but the tops of the pine trees bending, as if someone might be parting them to glare down at her.

A light touch landed on her shoulder. She spun around and found herself alone. A flock of birds flew up from the ridge behind the trees, screaming a warning. A breeze swept in and toyed with her ponytail as she pivoted toward the trail. Then it appeared, standing in the trees. A shadow moved forward the moment she decided it was time to try and escape.

No matter how hard she ran, it followed. If she stopped, so did the unknown presence. The whispers of a language she couldn't understand began, and the invisible touch of caution slipped icy fingers of possession around her throat to cut off the scream she tried to force from deep inside her.

The trailhead came into view, giving her hope her final sprint might be enough to survive. Her labored breath drowned out the rolling thunder echoing throughout the forest she'd left behind. She splashed through a mud puddle as the trail dipped, throwing her balance off, causing her to spill face-first through scattered gravel often found in the area. Blood trickled down the side of her face and out of her nose. Her palms burned from the implanted gravel pieces. Jumping up, a glance over her shoulder determined the strange thing that pursued her had evaporated.

Sucking in the last gulp of air she'd take, she turned and ran into the body of a creature she'd never have a chance to describe to authorities.

~ ~ ~ ~

Wind Dancer stared out the windshield of Jacque Marquette's slightly used SUV. He remained rigid and embodied the image of a wooden Indian Jacque had seen at a rib-and-fries joint in Oklahoma City a day earlier. He hadn't said a word since breakfast. There were times, like now, when his Pawnee friend creeped the hell out of him.

Jacque reached across and touched the seat-belt lock to make sure it was secure. "You okay, buddy?"

Wind Dancer turned an icy glare on him and nodded. "Okay, buddy." He returned to staring into the mile after mile of desert.

A little over a year earlier, Jacque discovered there really were boogeymen, ghosts, and a parallel universe where a Pawnee could slip across into the twenty-first century. He'd been followed by an Osage bent on revenge. A pretty doctor named Cleopatra Sommers stood between Chicago being wiped out by smallpox and a skinwalker who tried to kill him. Thanks to Wind Dancer, and a large dose of mumbo-jumbo spiritual traditions, he tricked the scariest things he'd ever known into returning to the hell from where they came.

Acclimating a person from the 1800s to modern life would be hard on anyone. Make that person an American Indian who had enough superstitions and practices to scare even Stephen King, and a small grasp of the English language, and Jacque found himself torn between laughing his head off or trying to keep his friend from getting into trouble. Sometimes it felt like he babysat a toddler who had a propensity to want to play in traffic.

Jacque pulled into a gas station. The gauge said half full but, out here, who knew when there would be anothers chance to fill up?

"Want to take a break?" Jacque opened the car door and eased out to stretch stiff legs.

"What do you want me to break for you, Jacque?" Wind Dancer pulled at his seat belt.

Jacque groaned, reached in, and pressed the release. "Click this next time. I told you that yesterday."

"I am sorry. I will remember." He exited the car and stood motionless for a few seconds.

"That's what you said yesterday and the day before."

"Jacque, does your car have magic to protect us?" He stuck his head inside then out several times. "Your car feels like the cave where I crossed over to this time. But I see no open holes to travel."

He felt amusement playing at the corners of his mouth but decided not to toy with the Pawnee. "It's the air-conditioning. I turn it on, and we keep cool. Part of the car. Not magic. I didn't have to use it until today. If you see one of those holes, you're always talking about, it better not be in this car. I spent way too much money on it. I'll want a refund if that happens."

"Refund. Does that mean you will have fun for another time?"

"No. It means they will return my money."

Wind Dancer raised his chin in understanding before shutting the car door. "Understand. Now, what did you want me to break?"

Jacque waved him away as he began to pump gas. "Never mind. Go take a leak or something." He could see a question forming in the confused Pawnee's face. Jacque moved to the front of the car to point down at his privates. "Understand?"

"Understand—buddy."

The pump failed to print a receipt, sending Jacque inside the small convenience store to get one. He scanned the store, trying to locate Wind Dancer. When he didn't see him, he turned in a complete circle and moved to areas he couldn't see from the front.

"Ah. My friend came in here to use the men's room. Tall. Native American?"

The chubby woman with a full head of hair the color of a fire engine leveled an arthritic finger toward a side door. "He didn't pay for the drinks."

He spotted Wind Dancer standing on the edge of the parking

area, staring toward the mountains. "How much?" Taking his observation off the Pawnee wasn't an option. The whole toddler thing always loomed in his subconscious. If anything happened to him on this trip, Dr. Sommers might decide to administer an untraceable poison to Jacque's coffee. A man in his line of work could drop with a heart attack at any minute.

"Eight dollars," she said flatly.

Jacque jerked around and frowned at the woman who had already started to watch *The Price Is Right* on her small TV, propped over the cigarette shelves. "Just how many drinks did he buy?" He fished out his credit card, and the woman quickly completed the transaction then licked her fingers after taking a bite of a jelly donut. A dribble of red filling clung to the corner of her chapped lips.

"Have a nice day." She had already focused on the TV again when he started out the door.

"Wind Dancer," he growled. "What the hell are you doing? Where are the drinks?" Wind Dancer continued to concentrate on the vastness of New Mexico. "Hey. Are you listening to me?" Jacque stormed up within a foot from the Pawnee. "What's up with you anyway?"

The Pawnee spoke in a whisper, "Let them pass, and all will be as it should be."

His body froze in place then he registered the rattle. A four-foot-long snake curled around one of Wind Dancer's boots. As another rattlesnake slithered away and toward Jacque, he yelled out and hopped backward. He stepped on a pebble sending him in a downward spiral to the ground. The snake pursued him.

He tried to scamper up but slipped once more as the Pawnee reached down and grabbed the snake on his boot and pulled its head off. He stepped lightly and calmly toward the advancing snake and snatched him up in a manner similar to an Afghan tribesman grabbing a headless goat in a game of Buzkashi. With one twist of the snake's head, it was no longer a threat. Another plus to having a Pawnee with super strength.

"Holy Mother of God, Joseph!" he yelled as the Pawnee took his hand and pulled him up. Jacque pivoted away from him and headed to the car, mumbling curse words he'd probably have to explain later. A sudden gust of wind sent a cloud of brown road dust into his face. "That's just great," he fumed, squeezing his eyes shut as the particles covered his clothes. "Now I'm dirty."

"We go now." Wind Dancer brushed past him and opened the hatch.

"Whoa. What are you doing? Don't put those rattlesnakes in my car," he warned.

"We can eat the meat tonight over our first campfire. I will use the skins later."

"No." Jacque slammed the hatch shut. "I'm not eating anything that got us thrown out of the Garden of Eden." He shooed him toward the trash can that appeared about to burst with debris. When he complied, Jacque returned to the driver's side and opened the door.

"Where is this garden? We should get vegetables. Cleopatra says we need to eat more vegetables and less meat. I want to please her."

They got in and started the car. "Yeah. Well, by the expression on her face the other morning when I picked you up, I'd say you're doing okay in the pleasing department. Now, where are those drinks?"

"I poured them on my boots. The snakes didn't like it."

Jacque pulled out onto the highway after a semi roared by. "You didn't use any of that animal whisperer stuff?"

"No. Snakes do not have ears." Wind Dancer clicked his seat belt then landed a fist against Jacque's arm. "I guess Chicago detectives don't interrogate many snakes." He laughed. A rare occurrence.

"Easy, buddy. You don't know your own strength." When Wind Dancer crossed over from the 1800s, his strength and hearing had increased. Add in his ability to communicate with animals and other weird behaviors, and Jacque spent a lot of time trying to figure his partner out.

"Some of your friends must know we are here."

"Huh?" Jacque adjusted the mirror and noticed flashing red lights. He pulled the car over, hoping the police car would keep going, but it pulled up behind them.

"Hello, officer," Jacque said with driver's license in hand. "What seems to be the problem?"

"You were speeding." The officer took the card then leaned down and appeared to evaluate Wind Dancer who had taken to staring out the windshield again. "Who's he?"

"Ah, this is Joseph Wind Dancer. He works at the Field Museum in Chicago. On a little vacation."

"Mr. Wind Dancer?" the officer asked. "Are you okay?"

He nodded and poked Jacque. "Yes. Jacque is a detective. He is my friend."

"A cop?" The officer examined the license again. "Sorry about this."

Wind Dancer withdrew his hand, now covered with dust. "Jacque is a dirty cop."

The officer observed Jacque and used his index finger to move his cowboy hat off his forehead. "Is that right?"

Several hours passed in police headquarters in the town of Sunset Rock, New Mexico. The smell of a pine air freshener mixed with stale coffee and body odor irritated the already disgruntled Chicago detective with an upset stomach. He and Wind Dancer had been escorted in by two squad cars without flashing lights to have a friendly conversation about their vacation plans. Jacque understood they were only being cautious and figured they got a lot of strange types coming through here with drugs as well as questionable characters trying to live off the grid.

Considering the way Wind Dancer had introduced them, they were lucky they hadn't been told to assume the position. That could have gone sideways pretty fast considering his Pawnee friend would have taken offense and turned into something akin to the Incredible Hulk. He was pretty protective of him and Dr. Sommers. Protecting the doctor, he understood, but there were times he felt a little embarrassed at how he stepped in to keep danger at bay.

A woman appeared at the front desk and spoke quietly to a young officer. After she sent a glance his way, Jacque decided maybe having to sit here for two hours would turn out to be a plus. Dressed in a dark suit and white tank top, she reminded him more of FBI than local PD, but what did he know? New Mexico wasn't Chicago. A few hairs freed themselves from the bun on her neck to frame her oval face. She appeared to be Hispanic or maybe Native American.

"She smells good, like Cleopatra." Wind Dancer elbowed him and smiled. He'd barely spoken since they arrived. He'd taken to evaluating new situations in silence. Most people took offense at his inappropriate comments or observations.

"You can smell her from here?" Jacque whispered out of the corner of his mouth.

"And everyone else. I think the woman over there, the one with snakeskin boots, has not stood in the bathroom waterfall in a while."

"We call it a shower, Joseph."

"Yes. A shower. I think maybe she doesn't know about how to get one."

"Quiet." Jacque stood as the woman in the suit moved in their direction. Her chocolate-colored eyes, shaped like large teardrops, paralyzed him with indecision. Should he be cavalier and witty with their first introduction. Or aloof and macho?

"Detective Marquette." Her red lips parted into a friendly smile he guessed to be a rehearsed expression. She extended a slender hand which he took, surprised at her grip. "I'm sorry you had to wait. I'm Police Chief Perez."

"I have not met a woman chief," Wind Dancer announced as he walked around her for his inspection.

"Sit down, Mr. Wind Dancer, so I can talk to your partner." Her eyebrows were arched and her voice icy. "I'll deal with you in a minute." She switched to a language Jacque didn't understand, but Wind Dancer sat down and crossed his arms across his chest. "Thank you."

He nodded and commenced with the frown of a man who'd been put in his place.

"Sorry. He doesn't understand a lot of our ways. He's been—"

Perez held up her hand to stop his attempt at making a good impression. "I know all about you and Mr. Joseph Wind Dancer."

"Is that right?" Jacque chewed on his words, trying to sound more like John Wayne than a Chicago cop with an attitude.

"You two were involved in the terrorist attack on Chicago."

Jacque pursed his lips, deciding it was better to listen at this point. He doubted she knew the depth of that nightmare.

Her attention shifted from Jacque to Wind Dancer for a few seconds before returning to him. "Care to take a ride?" She tilted her chin up and sounded like he might not have a choice.

"What did you say to him?" Jacque asked, concerned the Pawnee might not like taking orders from someone he thought was a female chief.

"I told him in the Zuni language to wait his turn. You didn't know he understood Zuni?"

Jacque rolled his shoulders and fended off the appearance of surprise. "Of course I did. Wasn't sure anyone around here spoke it, though, especially you."

"Let's head out." She didn't wait for an answer. "If you don't mind, you can drive. I left my car there earlier."

Jacque tugged on the Pawnee's shirt and tilted his head toward the door. "Don't screw this up," he warned and slapped the Pawnee's chest. It only mildly concerned him when he received a thumbs-up. "I didn't know you spoke other languages."

"Much you don't know about me, buddy."

Jacque made sure Wind Dancer got in the back seat of his SUV so Perez could ride up front. He pulled out onto the highway before starting to talk.

"I'd like you to take a look at this for me." Perez clicked her seat belt then glanced at the detective.

"Sure. What's this about?" Jacque answered.

"When I checked you out online a warning appeared, so I called my contact at the FBI in Albuquerque." She glanced over at him then to the road. "He suggested I contact a friend of yours by the name of Agent Farrentino."

"Well, it might surprise you, but I don't have any friends at the FBI, so whoever you talked to is probably yanking your chain."

"Yeah. He thought you might say that. Hey, I'm jammed up. With the government shutdown, we have been playing catch-up with things around here."

He pulled into a paved parking lot, the first one he'd seen since Santa Fe.

Perez said, "This is our crime lab and morgue." The building appeared modern rather than the pueblo style like everything else for hundreds of miles.

When he'd parked and powered the windows down, Perez turned in the seat to face Jacque. "Two weeks ago, a woman went missing in Kewa National Park, same area as Carson National

Forest. Her roommate reported her missing when she didn't return from a scheduled two-day hike."

"She did this alone?" He never understood why people would go off alone without leaving a detailed plan in case they didn't return. "Just a hunch, but I'm guessing since we're here, it didn't turn out well.

"Right. There were actually three other grad students with her. That morning they headed out and this girl, Karla, decided she wanted to remain there for a couple of hours to write in her journal and enjoy the last few hours alone."

"Did they check out?"

"Yes. Even had a few texts and a video she posted on social media before she started the last few miles out. The other three drove to Santa Fe and let the roommate know the change in plans. I figure if they killed her, they wouldn't have bothered to tell the roommate. Give the wild animals a chance to take care of any evidence."

"What happened?"

"I also thought maybe Mr. Wind Dancer might share his intuition about this kind of thing."

They exited the car and headed inside. What the outside of the building lacked in Western décor, the inside more than made up for. Turquoise mosaics of turtles and lizards dressed the walls, along with a shadowy person playing a flute. Pictures of pueblos and Native Americans hung on the lobby walls, and cowhide chairs sat empty with only a receptionist waiting to help them.

No one checked badges, IDs, or anything to ensure protocol and security was followed. If this were Chicago, by now they would have been in lockdown mode for entering a restricted area.

"I had Karla's body moved out of her locker so you could see for yourself." Perez opened the door and let them enter.

A young girl with short brown hair lay ghost-like on a metal table. It never got easy for him. A kind of rage always welled up inside him when he knew a life had been cut short in someone so young and full of promise. He moved toward the table and noticed Wind Dancer standing near the door. "Everything okay?"

Wind Dancer frowned and rushed to pull him and Perez away from the table. "She has been touched by the man who walks tall with long steps." He tugged harder on Perez's arm, which she jerked free. "You are in danger."

CHAPTER 2

"**W**hat the hell, Joseph?" The detective slammed a fist at his friend's chest then pulled Perez in closer before addressing his friend. "You're not saying the girl is now a skinwalker, are you?"

"A skinwalker?" Perez's voice sounded like glass breaking. Those beautiful brown eyes widened with concern as her forehead furrowed.

"No. She dead a long time to be skinwalker. But evil touched her. I can feel it."

Perez squared her shoulders and stiffened the soft lines of her jaw to appear severe. "Are you some kind of medicine man?" Was she accusing him of something?

"Exactly what did the FBI tell you about us, Chief Perez, and what makes you think we can help you? We're here on vacation."

"Yes. I know. A camping trip." She eyed him with a little too much contempt for his liking. "Mr. Wind Dancer appears as if he can take care of himself in the wilds of rugged country, but you resemble a city slicker with dreams of being a character from the Gunfight at the O.K. Corral."

"I'm not sure how we can help you." He curled his lip up in a snarl. He felt as if his masculinity might be in danger from a small-town cop whose job probably consisted of arresting teenage boys for cow tipping. "Let's wrap this up. We were hoping to set up camp tonight. Maybe do a little fishing."

A snide smirk toyed with the edge of her mouth, making Jacque focus on her red lips and regret sounding like a jerk. She fanned her palm toward the body. "Mr. Wind Dancer, I am carrying a gun that could bring down a buffalo at a dead run. I assure you I will be fine and so will your friend. I suspect"—she shifted her attention to Jacque—"he is carrying something similar."

Jacque resisted explaining the weapon remained packed in his luggage in the SUV parked in the morgue lot. "Damn straight," he offered, jamming his hands on his waist.

"Damn straight," Wind Dancer echoed. It was a nice touch when his nostrils flared and those intimidating eyes narrowed at the detective. Jacque took a more relaxed stance by dropping his hands to his sides before stepping closer to Chief Perez.

"Let's get on with it." He read a printout handed to him by a lab tech. "What is this about marks on the face and hands?"

"Search parties were out searching for her within hours of the roommate's call," she began. "Twenty-four hours, we were in there with horses. Forty-eight hours, we had drones in the air."

Jacque wondered why they didn't start with that, but she held her hand up. "Before you ask, we had to send for the drones. Our little town doesn't have the resources to purchase then train anyone to use them. Because of the government shutdown issues, we couldn't connect with the forestry department or the Bureau of Land Management to get help. Ended up having a few high school students from Taos come in to use theirs."

"What is a drone?" Wind Dancer asked. "Is this more white-man magic they call science?"

Perez shot him a disgruntled frown.

"I'll explain later. But yes. It is." Jacque moved up alongside the table. It was easier telling him magic and science coexisted in this parallel universe. Wind Dancer shifted his weight and doubled his fists. "It's okay, buddy. I'm not going to touch her. Is that good?"

"Yes. Good. No touching."

Perez stepped closer. "We found her on day five."

"How deep in did you have to go before you found her?"

"Well, that's the thing," she said quietly. "She was found ten feet off the trail about a five-minute walk from the trailhead." She continued after Jacque leaned in for closer inspection. "We searched earlier, even had the rescue dogs in there. No sign of her."

"The evil one brought her back." Wind Dancer crossed his arms.

Jacque addressed Perez. "How long had she been dead?"

"Estimated about ten hours, but the nights were cold, and we'd had rain. Our hope had been she'd gotten lost and might have climbed higher to get her bearings. We were coming out and spotted vultures circling. Took us right to where we'd started."

"So, you found her on day five, but time of death was ten hours?" He scratched his head. "Cause of death?"

"Exposure didn't help the situation. Her medical history suggested she'd had a heart murmur since she was a kid. Doc here"—she lifted her chin toward a man sitting at his desk—"believed she probably had a heart attack. But even he admitted it was only a guess. The death certificate says cause of death was undetermined."

"She scared to death," Wind Dancer offered.

"Any signs of..." He put himself between Wind Dancer and Perez and spoke under his breath. "Any signs of sexual assault?"

"No. Some of her clothes were missing: shoes, socks, a flannel shirt she wore in the video she sent to her friends. She still wore a tee shirt, underwear, and jeans."

Jacque noticed strange scratches. "What are these marks on her face?"

"There was a cut on her cheek and one over her eye. Small scratches like she plowed up the ground with her face. Since the knees of her jeans were ripped, we figured she fell running from whatever spooked her. Her nose, as you can tell, is damaged. That, too, might be from a fall."

"So, what are you thinking here? Maybe, out there all alone, her imagination started working overtime. Spotted a bear or mountain lion. Ran. Got lost—"

"The evil one brought her back," Wind Dancer repeated.

"Joseph, please—"

Perez sucked in her breath and continued to stare at the body. "He may be right. When we found her, she was laid out on a bed of pine boughs, arms at her side. She wasn't there earlier in the day. I know this because it is close to an overlook where several volunteers drank their morning coffee, getting ready to go out again. It is wide open there."

"What do you want from me?" Jacque rubbed his chin. This did puzzle him.

"I thought since you and Mr. Wind Dancer managed to stop a serious incident involving—"

"No," Jacque said, heading for the door.

Perez cut him off, but Wind Dancer stepped around them and opened the door for them.

"No. No. No," Jacque said.

"What are you afraid of?" Her voice held the tone of a playground bully calling him a scaredy-cat.

Jacque felt his face flush with anger. "I'll tell you what I'm afraid of—stuff I don't understand, like something called a skinwalker who takes over a dead body, or a crazy Pawnee." He glanced at the Pawnee whose mouth turned down in a frown. "No offense, buddy."

Wind Dancer gave him a thumbs-up.

"I don't understand my friend here who shows up at a Pawnee earth lodge in downtown Chicago, claiming to be from another time," Jacque explained. "Parallel universes, smallpox, and why this guy can understand what animals are thinking are just some of the things I can't figure out."

Perez eyed Wind Dancer, and he returned the icy contempt with narrowed eyes.

"Except snakes," Wind Dancer offered casually. "I can't understand them."

"You see, Chief Perez? Those are the things I'm scared of. Give me an old-fashioned serial killer any day. At least they make sense, and they screw up, so they eventually get caught." Jacque skirted past her. "Let's go, Joseph." The two men headed out into the lobby then the parking lot.

Perez hurried after them. "She wasn't the first one, you know."

Jacque paused with his hand on the door handle of the car. "How many?"

"Four that we know of."

"There will be more," Wind Dancer said drily.

Perez cocked her head. "And how do you know that?"

Jacque pinched the top of his nose and shook his head. "You had to ask, didn't you?"

"The hawk told me." His eyes followed the flight of the bird across the sky. "Four is a scared number to us. Now the evil one will start over, in a new place."

Perez glared at him for a few seconds then shifted her attention to Jacque. "Is he for real?"

"I am real." Wind Dancer used his finger to poke his arm then shoulder. "Real."

Perez stepped away from the car as Jacque opened door and forced a narrowed smile that chilled him.

"I'll find my own way back. You have a nice trip, gentlemen. There's a small grocery store just before you get to the park. Check in there for a camping permit. They have gas available. I wouldn't let your tank get too low."

Jacque slid into the seat and pulled the door shut. When the engine turned over, he powered the window down. "Good luck, Chief Perez. Hope you find what you're looking for."

Wind Dancer leaned over toward Jacque to make eye contact with the officer. "I do not hope this. You cannot catch the evil one alone or with your buffalo gun. The hawk says it is so."

She squinted contempt as her hand went to her sidearm and patted the car. "Be sure to give your friend his medication today," she said, pointing to Wind Dancer.

"Yeah. I hear ya." He put the car in gear and pulled onto the highway. Gritting his teeth, he shoved at Wind Dancer's arm, aware once more how strong the man was. "Do you always have to be so asinine?"

"I do not know this word, Jacque." He buckled the seat belt. "I think it might not be good."

CHAPTER 3

Dr. Cleopatra Sommers finished her presentations on gang violence and medical care in the ER. Both sessions were packed with young doctors and nurses. The conference brochure referred to her involvement during the smallpox outbreak in Chicago several years earlier and how she'd been on the frontlines of solving the mystery of its origination.

Only a few people actually knew the mystery came from a parallel universe and had jumped through time, landing in Chicago. That person was Neosho, an Osage Indian from the 1800s, infected with smallpox. He crossed over in search of her. He'd watched her grow up in the Field Museum where her father worked.

The Native American exhibit had been her favorite place to study, play, and dream. Full of display cases with mannequins dressed in tribal costumes, one stood out above the others. He was a Pawnee she'd named Wind Dancer. All her dreams, disappointments, and fears were shared with him as she grew up. There was no way she could have known he might be listening.

The Osage had been in the case next to Wind Dancer. He, too, listened and learned from her world. The night he came for her, Wind Dancer followed to save her. The next few days had been an adventure wrapped in a horror story. Larger than life, Wind Dancer had swept her off her feet and given her a love she never imagined.

Besides the Field Museum knowing about the transformation that occurred in their Native American Exhibit, the Pentagon, high-ranking government officials, DARPA, FBI, and the Center for Disease Control kept the information a closely guarded secret. Mistakes had been made and no one wanted that kind of threat to generate a national panic among the masses. Research continued and Wind Dancer now enjoyed working at the Field Museum with the best scientists in the country.

The downside of falling in love with a man from the 1800s and an entirely different culture than you, meant explaining a great many things, like microwave ovens, why the lights came on with a switch, cars, television, and war. One of the hardest things for him to grasp was why people didn't grow their own food or hunt.

"What if your stores close or run out of food?" he'd asked with such curiosity, it made her laugh until Chicago was shut off from a lot of deliveries for a time during the smallpox explosion.

Everyone was quarantined, and martial law activated to keep the outside world safe. People whined and complained like spoiled brats for months. Children had to be homeschooled, and parents found themselves having to actually work at being a good parent. There were so many hurdles to jump, Cleo wondered if this was the beginning of the end. But they survived and came out stronger and wiser for it.

Wind Dancer, once he crossed over into this world, found he had super-sensitive hearing, increased strength, more stamina and agility, and could actually understand animals. Yet, with all those special gifts, he remained humble and kind. He hated injustice and bullies. Jacque Marquette played referee on several occasions to ensure the Pawnee remained out of jail.

The two men formed a strong bond of friendship Cleo found endearing. However, there were times she felt like a stern parent who needed to discipline her children's bad behavior. Jacque was the older brother who dared his sibling to try new things even though he already knew the outcome would lead to trouble. In spite of those pranks, Jacque became a kind of caretaker for his unusual friend and tried to protect him from the new world he found himself in. The Pawnee really was a stranger in a strange land.

In order to protect future generations from the horrors of

modern civilization, Wind Dancer returned to his land the same way he'd come. Cleo wasn't sure she'd ever be able to see him again. During that span of time, she and Jacque had become close friends, wondering and waiting for Wind Dancer to return. Despite her objections, Jacque had promised Wind Dancer he would take care of her until he could return. She reminded him often she was more than capable of taking care of herself. This made him list all the ways she'd gotten into trouble when the whole crisis began.

There had been several times when she'd had dinner with a male friend, and Jacque appeared at the same place.

Finally, tired of the "coincidences," she stomped over to his table while her friend went to pay the bill. "What are you doing here?" she growled at him like a pit bull. "Are you following me, or what?"

Jacque blinked innocently and shrugged. "I stopped in for a drink. Who's the guy?"

"None of your business."

Unfortunately, the dinner companion walked over to the table and stuck out his hand.

"Hi. I'm Clive Atkinson."

Jacque stood, to tower over him. Cleo knew he did it for the sake of intimidation when he took the outstretched hand with a vise grip. They exchanged pleasantries before Clive turned to Cleo.

"Marta has gone into labor. Thankfully, her mother was with her. She just got to the hospital. Let me put you in a cab so I won't worry about you. Or do you want to come, too? I'm sure Marta will be a lot calmer with you than me. I'm a basket case."

Cleo smiled at Jacque's bewildered face. "Clive is a pediatrician at the hospital. I introduced him to his wife, Marta. He's on his dinner break."

"First baby, and I'll tell you I'm scared to death. So much for being a pediatrician," he laughed.

"Could be a long night, Clive. I'll see you in the morning. I'm sure you'll do fine. Call me if anything happens tonight. Promise me."

"Promise. Now about the cab."

Jacque laid a protective hand on Cleo's shoulder. "I'll see that she gets home. She loves riding in the squad car."

"No, I don't," she said.

"Okay. Thanks, Jacque. Great meeting you. Didn't know Cleo had any guy friends besides at work."

"Oh yeah. We're buds," he declared and gave a thumbs-up. "Good luck," he called as the man exited the restaurant.

"Buds?" She plopped down in a chair at his table. "I need dessert."

"The guy too cheap to buy you dessert?"

Cleo remembered the scene fondly now, although it had taken time for her to realize Jacque was following through on his promise to Wind Dancer. A few times it felt like they might be headed toward a more-than-friends relationship, but nothing happened other than dinner once a week, an occasional movie, and workouts at the gym. Being a doctor took a great deal of her time, and his job as a police detective was consuming as well.

She missed both Jacque and Wind Dancer. It had been less than a week, and she couldn't wait to be near all the macho, overprotective baloney and pranks they pulled.

A warning light on the car dash flashed five miles past a small community. By the time she'd turned around and gotten to a garage, the car was jerking and making noise that reminded her she hadn't let Jacque know she was on her way. She'd wanted to surprise them.

"You're kidding me? The fuel pump? I don't even know what that means. Just fix it. I'll call the rental company."

But the mechanic took the name of the company and said he'd call them and make sure they knew how serious it was. "They'll send you another car, although it might be tomorrow before anyone can bring it. Probably send one from Santa Fe." He smiled. "I'll insist."

She remembered a small inn on the way through and found the phone number. The owner came to pick her up and took down information from the mechanic as to when the car would be ready the following day. There was always a chance the rental company would have him repair it if it would be faster than they could get a replacement. The inn keeper managed to talk her ear off as he drove her to the inn.

"How far am I from Sunset Rock?"

"Maybe twenty to thirty minutes," Mansi Garcia, owner of the Whispering Pines Inn, guessed as he pulled into the circular drive.

"Not far at all." He jumped out of the car and retrieved her luggage. "Come on. You're our only guest, so you'll have the run of the place. It's lasagna night." He appeared near retirement age. In spite of being round bellied, he had the quick step of a man much younger. "Nothing fancy. Usually, we have a few folks from town stop in for dinner."

After checking in and finding her cabin, Cleo decided a little downtime might be a good idea before joining Wind Dancer and Jacque. She loved having her own coffeemaker and refrigerator. Since dinner wasn't for a few hours, she decided to make a glass of iced tea and sit on the deck to admire the valley with a backdrop of hazy mountains in the distance. From here, it felt like her accommodation was more of a treehouse than a tiny cabin.

Her mind wandered in the manner she used to shut down the stress of everyday life. Although attending a conference couldn't compare with the ER, the nonstop chatter, workshops, and networking were exhausting.

A crow flew from a pine tree followed by several more, making enough racket she set down her tea and went to the railing to see what might have frightened them. Could there be a mountain lion or maybe a bobcat passing through in search of food or a bear hunting for respite from the heat? She spotted a couple of chipmunks scampering between the rocks below.

A shadow amongst the trees caught her attention. She cocked her head and squinted as her hands touched the railing. Whatever she'd seen had stopped moving and blended in with the forest enough to become invisible. Yet, whatever it was watched her, appraising her, like a mountain lion or wolf might do to evaluate the enemy or their next meal. She could feel its eyes exploring her body.

A sudden chill swept over her. She ducked inside and grabbed a pair of binoculars next to the door. By the time she got them into focus, the image had disappeared. It reminded her of those Bev Doolittle paintings she'd seen as a child where the landscape appeared to be one thing, but when you stood across the room, there was an animal or person staring right at you. She used to love to study those. This didn't feel the same. Whatever tried to hide was big and unafraid.

~ ~ ~ ~

"Need seconds on anything? We fixed enough for an army, I think." The innkeeper waved at a couple sitting in the middle of the dining room. A family of five were dining near the door, and two older couples sat outside on the patio with their dessert.

"No thanks," Cleo said, reaching for her iced tea. "It was all delicious. I'm not sure I have room for dessert, but I do love tiramisu."

"There's a nice breeze on the patio. Beautiful view. Why don't you go out there, and I'll bring you coffee and a small helping of dessert? The fresh air will change your mind. Besides, you could use more meat on those bones."

Cleo caved to his suggestion and joined the others on the patio. She'd barely sat down before the two local couples introduced themselves and peppered her with questions about where she lived and why such a pretty thing would travel alone.

The woman, dressed in a leopard top, reapplied her red lipstick as she talked. She reminded Cleo of Jacque and how he managed to get people to spill their guts to him.

"I'm Dr. Cleopatra Sommers from Chicago. I spoke at a conference in Albuquerque, and now I'm on my way to Sunset Rock to meet friends. We're going to camp in Kewa Park."

"Well, good luck with that. Been a lot of strange things going on up there," Leopard Shirt warned. "I wouldn't want to be spending the night there."

"Don't be scaring her," her husband scolded. "A girl went missing while hiking. They found her a couple of days later. Apparently, she had a medical condition and died. No big mystery."

"Well, it would be scary to die alone in a wild place when you needed help. That's really too bad," Cleo said, remembering a number of scary things in Chicago over the last couple of years.

Mansi arrived with the tiramisu and coffee. "There you go, young lady."

"Ask him. Mansi keeps up on all the weird things that happen in the area. Right, Mansi?" the heavyset man with the bald head asked.

Red Lips rolled her eyes skyward before speaking. "I was just saying I wouldn't want to be camping in Kewa for a while until they knew exactly what happened to the girl they found."

Mansi's smile faded even though he seemed to try and stretch it out to appear pleasant. "Accident, I hear. Anytime you go in the wilds alone, you run the risk of things going wrong. Don't think there's anything suspicious."

When Mansi returned inside, Red Lips leaned toward her. "He's lying. Don't you go up there alone."

"One of my friends is in law enforcement and the other…" Cleo wondered how to describe Wind Dancer. "He's one of those warrior guys."

"Oh! Like the ninja show on TV?" Bald Guy asked. "You should be fine."

They soon said their goodbyes, and Cleo took the last sip of her coffee. She was glad she'd decided on dessert. Walking down the path to her cabin, she heard Mansi arguing with someone inside the inn. The windows were open for the cool mountain breezes, and the noise spilled out into the evening.

"I said no more hunting," yelled Mansi. "You know what will happen. It will be just like last time. This has got to stop." Whoever else was inside, Cleo couldn't make out their response. Mansi continued, "What if someone sees you? Then what?"

The argument continued as she hurried to her cabin. One thing she couldn't stand by was a poacher. What animals were in season to hunt was not her area of expertise. A number of wildlife areas all over the country had park rangers and wildlife officials who tended to keep an eye on that sort of thing. Besides, it wasn't like she could do anything about whomever Mansi was warning.

CHAPTER 4

Together the two men set up their camp. Wind Dancer, for once, appeared to be comfortable doing tasks: building a campfire to cook, arranging the supplies for easy access, and helping Jacque make sense of assembling the tent. With a picnic table at each site, it provided another spot to set up the small two-burner gas stove Jacque purchased for the trip. Apparently, a waste of money, since his partner insisted they cook over an open fire. He guessed they were going caveman for this trip.

He'd pretended to know what he was doing for the sake of saving face with Wind Dancer. But the truth remained, he'd had Cleo Sommers give him a list of what he needed, and she had even tutored him in a few things. Although an ER doctor, she'd spent summers camping and discovering historical finds with her father, a famed archeologist. Growing up without a mother turned her into a tomboy and pretty handy with things most little girls showed no interest in.

This whole camping idea had been her idea to get Wind Dancer out of her hair so she could prepare without explaining every little thing. She accepted an invitation to speak at a medical conference in Albuquerque. The plan involved her flying in for the conference then driving up to meet them for a few days of back-to-nature relaxation.

Jacque admitted it sounded good to him, too, until he'd spent several days on the road explaining appropriate behavior, why people didn't hunt their food, and why weren't there any buffalo. When the Pawnee did finally stop talking and focused his attention out the windshield, it made him nervous.

Did he spot holes in the parallel universe? Were monsters following them? How many enemies did the Pawnee have in the world he traveled from? How much did he want to know about all this supernatural, voodoo, hocus-pocus crazy crap? That question wasn't hard to answer—none of it. He didn't even like that creepy little cartoon character called Casper the Ghost.

At least he'd have Cleo to keep him out of trouble on the way home. She served as translator for a lot of Wind Dancer's nonsense like skinwalkers, talking animals, evil ones, holes in a parallel universe, and customs a variety of tribes still practiced. It was the little bombshell she dropped on him when they were loaded up ready to go that worried him.

"Oh, Jacque, just a heads-up. While we're gone there will be a total eclipse of the sun. I should be there by then, but if I'm not, remember this may have great meaning to Wind Dancer and well, you know how superstitious he can be."

"Now you tell me," he said as he slammed the car door. "He might call out a kind of magic mojo that will make murder hornets look like ladybugs."

"Here he comes, so don't mention the eclipse. I'll take care of it when I get there." She patted his arm and smiled. "You'll be fine."

Three days from now. He felt his blood pressure spike at thinking about it. In the meantime, they could do a little fishing, exploring the trails, and more fishing. No drama. No murdered-hiker mystery to solve. No evil one to spy on them.

Darkness fell much too quickly for Jacque's liking, but he had to admit the night sky took his breath away. The camp next to them was about fifty feet away, separated by a small stand of trees. He could hear a child and adults laughing. If they weren't nervous about all this empty space, why should he be? Maybe he'd lived in the city too long, and breathing fresh air had made him a little light-headed.

The neighbors came calling with a pan of brownies and introduced themselves. Ellie and Ty were from Austin, Texas and came here every year. Now they had their little boy, Liam, to introduce to the miracles of nature. He was a happy kid and smiled nonstop.

"How old are you, Liam?" Jacque asked when the little guy stuck his hand out to shake.

"Five." His speech was a bit slurred. The mom told him to hold up his fingers to show how many. He realized the child had Down syndrome.

Jacque worried Wind Dancer would say something inappropriate or shy away, making the situation awkward, but instead he squatted down and motioned for the child.

"This is Joseph Wind Dancer, Liam. He's my friend." He invited the couple to join them as he waved toward several camp stools.

Liam moved to the Pawnee and reached for the angled face. Wind Dancer closed his eyes for the child at first and let him touch his face, long hair, and the beads he wore around his neck. When he opened his dark eyes and focused on the child, Liam stepped away, as if he were afraid. Very quietly, and gently, Wind Dancer began speaking to him in his native tongue, and the child stepped forward and wrapped his arms around the Pawnee's neck. The hug was reciprocated as he sat on the ground and pulled the boy into his lap.

"I've never seen anything like that," Liam's father said. "Usually, he's more cautious around strangers. What did he say to him?"

Jacque shrugged. "Hell, if I know. The man is a Pawnee and never ceases to amaze me. He's this way with animals, too."

The mother hugged her arms against the cold and smiled. "Look at them. He's telling him about the stars. Liam loves anything to do with space, stars—"

"Probably because of *Star Wars*," his father laughed. "But your friend is speaking in his language, not English, and Liam seems to understand every word."

"Your boy very smart. He understands much. Never doubt that." Wind Dancer frowned at the parents as if they had insulted the child. "In my home, we honor children who are blessed with this gift. You are lucky."

The father put an arm around his wife and nodded. "Yes. We

think so, too, Wind Dancer. Not everyone sees that. I'm glad you can. You have made him extremely happy."

Wind Dancer helped the boy to stand as his parents announced it was time to go. "Say good night to our new friends, Liam."

"Um, there aren't any wild animals around here, are there?" Jacque inquired with all the bravery he could muster.

"Jacque afraid." Wind Dancer smiled and fist-bumped his friend in the arm, causing him to stagger.

Everyone laughed, and Ty offered a little information. "This time of year, you might hear a few yips of coyotes or maybe owls. They can be spooky. We did see a few mountain lion tracks on one of our hikes yesterday, but they were pretty old. The ranger we encountered at the store outside the park said they'd caught that one and hauled it off to an isolated spot in Carson National Forest. It was a rare sighting."

Jacque shook the man's hand and patted Liam's head as they left and headed to their camp, using a flashlight as the moon rose over the treetops. He noticed how Wind Dancer stared after them and felt a kind of pride that he made such an effort with the boy. However, the creepy expression the Pawnee often got in those black eyes of his, now focused on something in the dark that only he could see.

"What?" Jacque came to stand by the Pawnee and tried to find whatever he could see. "Liam's family has returned to their camp. No worries."

"No. Something else." Wind Dancer's voice grew deep and slow, like breathing in your sleep.

"A bear?" Nothing. "Another mountain lion? They said there had been a mountain lion. Could be another one. Where's my gun?"

Wind Dancer jumped sideways, throwing up his hands. "Boo!"

Jacque grabbed his chest and nearly fell into the campfire. "Hells bells, Joseph," he yelled. "Not funny." As the firelight danced on his friend's face, he caught sight of a grin. "Okay. Maybe a little funny. Don't do it again. I might accidently shoot you."

"Okay, buddy. No scare again." Then he jerked around and squinted toward the water as the hoot of an owl echoed across the lake. "But there is something evil out there. I can smell it."

This time Jacque knew his friend was serious. The Pawnee stiffened, dropped his hands to his side, then tightened and released his jaw over and over. His nostrils flared as he tilted his head as if listening.

Once more, Jacque came to stand next to him.

"Human or animal?"

Wind Dancer turned to him. "Both."

CHAPTER 5

After five minutes, Wind Dancer backed toward the campfire and grabbed a stool to sit on. He turned to watch the flames, poking it with a stick from time to time. Jacque observed him from a distance and wondered what went on in his head most of the time. Whatever had been out there made the Pawnee uncomfortable.

"You come to the fire, Jacque. The unknown gone now."

"Just like that? It left." Jacque came over to sit at the fire and leaned forward, to place his elbows on his knees. "Are you spookin' me again, or was something out there?"

"I promise, no more spook you. There is danger here, but it's mostly animals."

Jacque imagined Bigfoot or a giant bear that hadn't eaten in days. "What kind of animals?"

"Snakes. Bobcat. Black bear but not near. The family was wrong about the mountain lion. Mother with two cubs, half mile over the ridge. She has already hunted. No problem."

"Then what made you nervous a few minutes ago?"

Wind Dancer tossed the stick into the fire. "I do not know. It stalked us. Big. Fast."

"Maybe a mule deer."

"Do they have two legs?"

Jacque felt a chill caress his body. "No."

Wind Dancer shrugged. "It go away when he knew I might see him. Did not like it."

"And it was big?" Wind Dancer nodded and stood.

"You should sleep now. Good night, buddy. I stand guard for little while."

"It's safe to go to bed?" Jacque stood and grabbed a bucket of water to pour on the fire.

Wind Dancer stopped him.

Jacque shrugged his hand off his arm. "We can't leave it burning. Pour this on the fire when you're ready to go to bed. I charged up a couple of solar lanterns. We'll put those outside the tents."

"Solar?"

Jacque took a deep breath. "Trust me. It will be okay. Go to bed."

In spite of being uneasy, Jacque succumbed to exhaustion and fell asleep after only a few minutes. Whispers of the wind through the treetops and the songs of crickets lulled him into a comfort zone he rarely experienced. The air felt cool and void of the hot smells of pollution, garbage, and grime found in Chicago where he'd served for more years than he cared to admit.

As he sank deeper into a rest cycle, he dismissed the superstitious Pawnee, at least until the screaming started. He sat up and pulled his gun out from the backpack lying beside him.

Wind Dancer unzipped the flap on the front of the tent and poked his head in. "Trouble, Jacque. You must come."

Jacque had slept in his clothes in case to make a quick exit if things got weird. If he was going to be carried off by Bigfoot or an alien invasion, he wanted his pants on. When he exited the tent, Wind Dancer stood at the edge of camp, staring toward the neighbors with the little boy. Flashlight beams created giant patterns that appeared to dance in jerky movements at their camp.

"The little boy, Liam, is gone." Wind Dancer stared in the direction without the light. "Come."

"Hold on, Joseph. We need to announce ourselves. They might have a gun for protection." Jacque called out and said they were coming in and waited until they were encouraged to join them.

The hysterical mother cried and ran to the edge of the camp, calling for Liam. The father rubbed a hand through his hair. "He's gone. Disappeared in an instant."

"What happened?" Jacque asked, shifting attention from the Pawnee for a few seconds. He wanted to make sure another person didn't disappear.

The man stuttered in fear. "I-I don't know. We were in bed. Something outside woke me. I thought I saw a shadow. Big. Like a deer. By the time I grabbed my flashlight to check it out, it was gone. I checked on Liam, and he was gone, too," he choked. "He's a curious little guy. I thought maybe he went outside."

"Would he do that?"

"Not usually. He's afraid of the dark. He even sleeps with a flashlight or his glowworm to keep him company. Both are still here." He pointed to their campfire. "We let it burn down after we left your camp. Liam kept talking nonstop about Wind Dancer. Most of it we couldn't understand, but we listened with interest like we knew exactly what he meant."

"He told you about the Indian folktale, 'Her Seven Brothers.' It's about the big dipper in the sky," the Pawnee said matter-of-factly as he turned his attention toward the woods.

Ellie came to stand next to her husband. "How do you know that?"

"I could hear him. I understand."

They stiffened and grabbed each other's hands before shifting their concern to Jacque. He moved closer to them and lowered his voice, although he knew from experience Wind Dancer could still hear him if he paid attention.

"Wind Dancer is very special. Not so different than your Liam. He has this supersonic-hearing thing going on. No one seems to know why. He has a lot of special gifts that make him—peculiar. Nothing to be afraid of. If Liam is close, he'll be able to hear him."

"The boy cries." Wind Dancer turned around. "I go for him."

Ellie burst into tears. "He's lost," she moaned, falling into her husband's arms.

"Not lost. Taken."

"What?" Ty gasped. "How do you know?"

"I feel it," he said. "I say truth, Jacque. You know I do. We must get him. If he goes to water, I cannot hear."

"What the hell does that mean?" Ty choked on his words. "Shouldn't we call the police, the park rangers, or something?"

"We need to go now, Jacque," the Pawnee insisted.

He pulled out his phone and realized he had no bars. "Are you sure about this, Joseph?"

"Yes. I need light." The Pawnee nodded to the flashlight. "I go faster alone."

"I'm going, too." Ty gently led Ellie to a stool near the fire pit. The Pawnee had already disappeared into the darkness.

Jacque grabbed the man's arm. "You won't be able to keep up. You stay here. I'll go for help. I know someone at the police department in Sunset Rock who can help. I don't think Ellie should be alone since we still don't know what happened. I might have better reception outside the park." He eyed the dying embers. "Build that fire up. Wind Dancer will be able to use it as a beacon when he comes back. He'll smell it and see it from a long way off."

Ellie shook her head. "I don't understand, Jacque. How?"

"It's a really long story. Do you have a weapon, Ty?"

"I have a pistol I keep locked up. Was afraid Liam would find it."

"Get it out and load it. If anything comes into the camp, you can scare it off with it."

"You talk like there are monsters out there." Ellie shivered, rubbing her arms as tears cascaded down her cheeks.

This was one of those moments when he wished he hadn't been exposed to the ugly side of man. He also wished he'd not seen the woman named Karla laid out on a slab with her face scratched up.

"I'm sorry. Being a Chicago detective, I just naturally expect the worse. I bet Wind Dancer comes carrying Liam in on his shoulders before you know it. Stay close to the fire. If you get spooked, get in your car. That might not be a bad idea anyway." He patted Ellie's arm and nodded to Ty. "It's several miles out of here, but at least I'll be on higher ground. Darkness will slow me down, but I'll do my best to hurry."

The first mile of road was mostly gravel and dirt, making a speedy exit impossible. It also twisted back and forth, avoiding boulder outcroppings. He wondered why the powers that be hadn't removed the boulders. Some eco-maniac engineer must have decided natural might be considered more pleasing. Once he hit paved road, his speed increased but only slightly. It, too, curved with trees that grew too close to the road and created the appearance of someone trying to hide. He laid a hand on the Glock he'd stuck in the holster he'd rigged between the seat and console then returned his hand to the steering wheel.

Ten minutes were lost by taking a wrong turn down a road that led to another empty campground. It would be full soon with the eclipse drawing campers from everywhere. Once he returned to where he first got lost, a mule deer ran in front of the car, causing him to slam on the brakes. The animal paused on the edge of the road and looked around cautiously then into the headlights.

Before he could move forward, a dark object pounced on the hood of the SUV and blocked his line of sight for a few seconds. It was the size of a bear with spikes on its spine. He grabbed the flashlight to get a better look. When he directed the light out the windshield, it turned glowing eyes his way and let out a blood-curdling scream. The sound startled Jacque enough, he dropped the light. He reached for his gun as the thing rolled off the hood and ran at where the mule deer had stood seconds earlier. He sat frozen by the encounter until he heard the terrified cry of a wounded animal. This time, he floored the car and drove recklessly until he reached the park entrance.

He put the car in park and shone a flashlight on the hood of the car. No dents were visible from this perspective. The bright moon appeared to bounce among the clouds as a light wind moved them across the night sky. Pulling out his phone, he realized how hard he was breathing and that his heart hammered in his chest, so he took a few seconds to calm down. He double-checked the door locks after turning off the engine, careful to keep an eye on the rearview mirrors for any movement.

"I need to speak to Chief Perez," he said, swallowing hard to make his voice sound normal.

"Sir, if this is an emergency, you should call—"

"You're damn straight it's an emergency," he barked. "This is Detective Marquette from Chicago PD. I spoke to her earlier today. There's a missing child up here at Kewa National Park. We need your help now." The irritated-detective side of him took over, causing his momentary fear of the boogeyman to evaporate. He gave the person on the other end his phone number. "Have the chief call me ASAP. And since I don't know who to call concerning park rangers, search and rescue, I'm leaving that in your hands. You got that?"

"Yes, sir. Are you at the campground now?"

"I'm at the entrance. No reception down by the lake."

"Stay where you are. I'll call the chief and the other people needed for this."

Jacque clicked off and checked his weapon. A large cloud slid over the face of the moon, leaving a halo around the edges. He decided to turn the car around in order to return to the camp. The thought of Liam, alone in the woods, with a killer or a wild animal, gave him pause. The digital clock showed 3:45 a.m. Not quite two hours since he first heard Ellie's screams.

How did Wind Dancer get to him that quickly, yet he slept so soundly he didn't hear the commotion in the camp next to them? Was it a cry of terror or Ellie screaming the little boy's name? Why didn't Wind Dancer go immediately after whatever it was in the woods? Maybe the Pawnee didn't know what was happening until he heard Ellie.

His phone hummed the ringtone song from the television show *Law and Order*. "Marquette."

"Jacque? Chief Perez. What's going on?" The words flowed through a yawn.

He caught her up to speed as much as possible without sounding like a hysterical little child who'd lost her pacifier. "I need to get back. I've been up here too long."

"Give me your exact location, including, which entrance to the park you used. That place is a maze if you don't know where you're going. Got state troopers on the way and search and rescue. Might be another twenty minutes before anyone shows up. I'm closer. Maybe ten minutes. Wait for me."

When she clicked off, he realized she demanded rather than asked he wait. One of the things he'd wanted on this trip was not taking orders or listening to unreasonable demands he behave in a certain way. After turning the key in the ignition, he put the SUV in gear and headed back to camp. He'd deal with Perez later if need be. For now, he wanted to check on the distraught family he left alone and hoped Wind Dancer had returned with the little guy in tow. Or on his shoulders.

When he pulled into the neighbors' camp, the fire had died

down to a small blaze, but he could still see the smashed tent, supplies strewed everywhere, and equipment upended. Where were Ty and Ellie?

CHAPTER 6

Jacque eased out of his SUV, gun in hand, and paused to listen. Evaluating the surroundings had served him well on the mean streets of Chicago, but out here, the sounds compromised his ability to put the chance of danger in perspective. The snap of a twig or the sudden absence of a bullfrog's croak set his nerves on edge.

An unexpected breeze sent sparks skyward at the same time the flap of owl wings soared over the flickering remnants of the campfire. Seconds later, his hoot mixed with the soft waves of water cascading over stones along the shoreline of the lake.

The moon continued to dodge in and out among the clouds as he moved toward Ty and Ellie's car. The driver's side door appeared to have been shoved inward. Jacque flashed his penlight along the entire side of the vehicle and noticed deep scratches. At this distance, he couldn't determine if the couple had made it to the car after he'd suggested it would be safer. He couldn't bring himself to call their names, in case something or someone else lurked in the trees at the edge of the camp.

Circling around to the rear, he spotted the trunk of the sedan had an object wedged haphazardly under the bumper and guessed an attempt at opening it had failed, since it remained closed. He made his way to the passenger side and pressed his face against the glass to see inside. Ellie popped up and screamed, sending Jacque backward in shock.

"Ellie, it's me. Jacque Marquette." He eased closer, remembering Ty had a pistol. Now he could also see the outline of Ty who leaned against the door and covered his face with both hands. "Are you all right?"

They nodded.

"Stay here. I'm going to check things out then I'll come get you. The police are on their way, along with first responders. Okay?"

Ellie forced a smile and laid a palm on the window. Her eyes bore a sadness that reminded him of the little boy, now gone.

After a quick check of the campsite, he returned to the car. Both Ty and Ellie watched him with expectation.

"You can come out now." He tried Ellie's door, but it remained locked. "Do you want to stay there?"

Ty said something to Ellie he couldn't hear, but the click of the lock, followed by the door being cracked open, revealed a terrified woman.

"Let me help you, Ellie." He extended a hand, and she clamped onto it as she managed to wiggle herself out. "Ty, I'm not sure you can open the door on your side. Pretty smashed in. Want me to try and give it a yank and you put your shoulder to it, or do you want to climb over the console?"

Before Jacque got a response, Ty scooted over the top of the console and climbed out. His slow movements resembled a sloth. Ellie assisted at the last second.

"Heck of a night, Jacque," Ty said, trying to right himself, once on the ground.

Jacque reached for the man and slipped an arm around his waist to steady him. "What the hell happened here?"

"Not sure. Something rushed in and started throwing things around, growling, and then headed toward us. I made Ellie get on the floorboard the best she could and I laid over a bit to try and be out of sight. Guess I hurt my back again. Had surgery six months ago."

"What was it?"

Ty shook his head then turned his eyes skyward. Light from the campfire caught the glint of tears in his eyes. "I just don't know. It leaped across the hood like some kind of gazelle then began slamming into the door, like it wanted to get to us."

"I don't see any bullet holes, so I'm guessing you didn't use that pea-shooter of yours."

"No. Not so sure it would have done any good. I think you'll find a dent in the roof, too. It jumped up there and pounced a few times before taking off. I tried to take a peek at whatever it was, but all I saw was a large shadow as it passed near the campfire."

"Maybe a bear?" Ellie's voice quivered.

"Maybe." But Jacque doubted it. "Come on. It's gone now."

"It could still be there," Ellie sniffled.

"Ellie, I've got a gun that will bring down a bull elephant at a dead run. I'm the best marksman in our precinct, too. I worked for S.W.A.T for a while before I became a full-time detective. Rest assured, if anything comes around, it's a goner. Okay?"

"Okay." She tried to smile, but it came across like someone who was constipated.

He led them to the fire, built it up then found some overturned lawn chairs for them. The clues would be fresh, provided there were any. He flashed the penlight around the area in hopes of seeing any evidence of what had come into camp. Better to wait until help came before he started poking around.

Once more, the imagine of the girl, Karla, lying on a slab, flashed in his mind. Scratches on her face, broken nose, possibly from a fall, but not much else. Was she scared to death?

He turned his attention toward the frightened couple who huddled together, holding onto each other's hands. Jacque wondered about the little boy and the Pawnee who went in search of him. He tossed another couple of logs on the fire to build it up. Hopefully, the blaze or the smell of smoke could be used to lead him back if his friend needed help. Would Wind Dancer meet his match with whatever lurked in the dense forests surrounding them?

Red strobes appeared as pinpoints of light in the distance and grew larger with each second the search and rescue vehicles neared. Jacque moved toward the police car to intercept Chief Perez.

"Chief. Thanks for coming so quickly." He nodded toward the couple who rose from their seats near the fire, still clinging to each other.

She reached into the car and pulled out a caddy of four cups of coffee. Handing it off to him, she focused on the couple who now spoke to a paramedic.

"Thought everyone might need some wake-up juice." She switched her gaze to Jacque who felt confused at how she'd had the time to pick up coffee. As she walked toward the couple, she laid the question to rest. "Convenience store on the way. Called ahead. Done this before in emergencies. Ran it out to my car when I pulled in. It's a little thing, but sometimes just holding a cup of warm coffee can settle folks down enough to give us a clear picture of what went on."

Perez stopped and eyed the car then turned to Jacque for clarification.

"No idea what did that. Neither do they. Better have your medical team check them over." He just wanted to get the coffee passed out so he could have his cup. Warming his hands was a waste of time. He needed the caffeine to think straight.

The couple was led to the ambulance truck and checked out while Perez took a stroll around the camp. By now, floodlights had been set up, and the area resembled the middle of the day. Jacque followed and observed how she zeroed in on the smallest detail, like a snapped branch or rock. But for the life of him, he didn't see any footprints. He retold the couple's story of what came into camp and wondered why there were no footprints.

"Bears are big, curious, and disrespectful of property. Until recently, the season has been pretty dry. Might not have left a print. I'll have forensics out in the morning to go over the car and other things in the camp."

"Morning?" he fumed. "Dew, wind, anything could compromise this place."

Perez stopped and turned to level a hard stare at him as she put her hands on her hips. "This ain't Chicago, Detective Marquette. We have one guy working several counties. I'm not about to get on his bad side in the middle of the night when nothing can be done anyway. Our primary concern right now is the little boy. All this"—she faced the campsite— "can wait."

"You're right," he huffed.

"Where's your sidekick?" She pivoted as if trying to locate him.

Jacque avoided the question. "By the way, the little guy has

Down syndrome."

"Well, that could be a good thing. The first report of a missing person in these parts was a forty-year-old man who was mentally challenged. Went hiking with his parents and two other siblings. He twisted his ankle and couldn't walk. The brother and sister returned to the car to get a first aid kit. When they got back, the parents said the man had disappeared."

"Disappeared? You mean like before-their-very-eyes kind of thing?"

"Not exactly." Perez took a deep breath and focused on the couple moving toward the fire again. "There was a scenic overlook. They went to see where they might be in relation to where they were staying. Maybe twenty feet or less from their son. Turned around, and he was gone."

"Maybe he wandered off." Jacque could feel the hair stand up on his neck.

"Not according to the parents or the siblings. Even if he could, it would have been only a few steps."

"Did you find him?"

"That evening. Safe and sound." Perez stepped toward the couple waiting by the campfire. "He was sitting on a boulder about a half mile from where he disappeared. Scared out of his mind."

"How did he get there?"

"No clue. The doctor on the scene said the ankle was in such bad shape, he couldn't have gotten there by himself. No shoes or socks. Funny thing is, there were no scratches or marks on his feet as if he'd walked there, either. No twigs, snags, or debris on his clothes. As you probably noticed, there are signs everywhere about staying on the trail. It's rough terrain."

"Were you able to get any information from him at all?"

Perez stopped and puckered her mouth into a pooched expression. "Said a giant got him or something like that. He was pretty nonverbal, and his parents interpreted for us. But overall, he was unharmed."

"How does that relate to the little boy?"

"About ten years ago, a little girl with cerebral palsy went missing from a school outing about ten miles from here. Picnic area. Playground. Family place. End-of-school-year trip for three classes of fourth graders. Plenty of parents there, but the little girl disappeared."

"Did they find her?"

"Yes, only this time, the child appeared to have been injured because she'd had her leg braces removed. Evidence showed she'd fallen down a creek bank into the water and drowned. Whoever took her pulled her from the water and laid her on a large boulder where she'd be spotted. Her braces were next to her."

"No way she could have climbed that boulder." Jacque spoke out of the corner of his mouth in a low tone.

"Nope. An effort had been made to remove sticks and leaves caught in her hair and clothes when she fell. The case was never solved. Those two cases suggested they were taken, but they would have been unreliable witnesses." She did a visual scan over the campsite again and leveled a hard gaze his way. "You never answered me about your stranger-than-fiction friend. Where is he? Hiding in your tent because the boogeyman is out there?"

"He went after the boy," Jacque admitted.

She snapped her head around and frowned at him. "And you let him go?"

They were in front of Ty and Ellie now, and they gazed at them in some kind of hope and expectation.

"I'm Ty Kendal and this my wife, Ellie. Our little boy is Liam."

Perez appeared to soften as she shook their hands and took the edge out of her voice. "I know this is tough. Let's get some information from you two, and our guys will head out. Okay with you?"

Jacque stayed close enough to be able to listen to everything going on around the camp. Ellie retrieved a jacket that Liam had left behind and held it out to a member of the rescue team. She tried to explain how special it was to him and would never go anywhere without it. They remained respectful and tried to reassure her as they gently pulled it from her hands. A bloodhound appeared from one of the vehicles and was encouraged to sniff the jacket.

The search and rescue team huddled up and spoke in calm voices. Everyone appeared to have a job, needing only bits of information to get the business of finding the child underway. Two-way radios were checked, along with the time, before they slipped into their backpacks and headed off into the darkness.

"How long will this take?" asked Ty as the team disappeared into the night. "I mean, to find Liam?" He reached for Ellie's hand before turning to the chief.

"There's no way to know for sure, Mr. Kendal. I'm sorry. I know that isn't much comfort. What is lucky, however, is that Detective Marquette was close by and could notify me quickly." The couple smiled at him. "The sooner we get the whole process activated the better the outcome."

Before Perez could continue, Ellie burst into tears again. "He was so happy after we left your camp, Jacque." The mother sniffed. "All he could talk about was Wind Dancer. Kept calling him his buddy."

Perez perked up and cocked her head with interest. "Really? Why is that?"

Jacque rubbed his chin and chuckled. "He told the boy a story about—"

"I didn't ask you, Detective," the chief said casually. "I want to hear what they have to say."

Jacque bit the inside of his lip hard enough, he was sure he tasted blood. "By all means, Chief Perez."

"Wind Dancer made friends with Liam right away. Seemed to understand everything he said, which is really unusual." Ty took a deep breath. "It was heartwarming how quickly they bonded."

Perez frowned at Jacque, suspicion written all over her face mixed with an icy dose of "well, well, well" contempt. She turned to Jacque. "You guys turn in for the night at the same time?"

A trap, he decided. "No. I went first. I told him to but...he thought there was something prowling around across the lake. That narrow part on the east side." He pointed to the spot, although it couldn't be seen from this campsite. "I poured water on the fire then went to bed when he said it was gone."

"Did he say what it might be?"

Jacque didn't like where this was headed. "He wasn't sure. Just that it was gone."

"Does he always take up with little boys so fast?"

Jacque shoved his finger toward her like it was a loaded gun. "Now, wait a minute. Liam came to him, not the other way around."

Perez shifted her penetrating gaze to the Kendals. They nodded.

"But he was still moving about your camp when you went to bed," she stated matter-of-factly.

"Yes. What's the big deal?" Jacque asked.

The chief motioned for him to move away from the anxious couple and walk with her.

"When did you know there was a problem?"

"I heard a scream and bolted straight up out of a deep sleep."

"And when did you encounter Wind Dancer?"

"He stuck his head in my tent as I was trying to get up. Told me something was wrong."

"So, it's possible he had never been to bed," she mused. "And isn't it possible your friend took the little boy?"

Jacque remained quiet because the same idea had occurred to him.

CHAPTER 7

The blast of gunshots echoed through the forests, causing the first responders and Kendals to direct their attention toward the darkness. One by one, they moved closer to the campfire. A wind blew across the top of the trees, making them creak and pop as an owl flew through the camp.

One of the first responders, a Native American, followed the flight of the bird before elbowing his partner. "That can't be good."

Jacque moved up next to him. "What the hell does that mean? Are you talking about the gunshots?"

The first responder doubled his arms across his bulky chest after toying with a kind of charm around his neck. "No, man. The owl."

"It's a damn bird," Jacque mumbled.

"The Pueblo people think the owl is Skeleton Man, a god who has power over death and fertility. Owls were also thought to steal souls and work through bad medicine men to sicken and kill the owl's enemies."

The partner of the Indian leveled a serious expression at the detective. "You're not from around here, are you?"

"No. Chicago." Jacque took a deep breath. "Are those owls anything like a skinwalker?"

Now both men stared at him. "Skinwalker?" The two

paramedics exchanged looks with each other then back toward the darkness. "Don't be sayin' that word here. You don't know what they can do," the man warned.

"Like hell I don't." Jacque pulled out his weapon and checked it. The two men raised their eyebrows as if concerned. "I know all kinds of creepy shit."

The story of how a skinwalker had nearly taken him to the afterlife in Chicago during the whole smallpox-parallel universe disaster was not one he liked to explain or share. It sounded crazy, and he feared telling the wrong person might get him thrown in the looney bin. But Wind Dancer knew the truth, and so did Cleo. They were there with him. A chill ran over his entire body as he thought about it again.

He caught a glimpse of Perez using her two-way radio as she moved closer to the paramedics.

"You guys check to see if you can get anyone out in the field. I want to know what's going on. I've got static." She reminded them of the frequency they had agreed on earlier to stay in touch then they moved to their truck.

"Is it unusual to not be able to reach your people on those things." He nodded toward the radio she held in her hand.

"Not really. They're good, but in this part of the park, the hills covered in forest and boulders, Mother Nature in general can often block signals. If you'd like to climb one of those trees, I bet we'd get a better signal," she said drily.

He appraised her bland facial expression to decide if she was poking fun at him. "Funny."

Perez shrugged. "Probably wouldn't work anyway. I got them earlier. After the gunshot, nothing."

The radio crackled to life. "Help. Comin'. Big."

"Come back," Perez ordered as the radio crackled again.

The two paramedics retrieved a second set of radios.

"Nothing on the truck radio. Brought these." The responder held up his then his partner did the same.

The wind that had bent the trees earlier, stopped, leaving an eerie calm. Clouds rolled across the moonlit sky until they extinguished the light completely. Lightning spiderwebbed across the sky, followed by thunder.

"Could this get any weirder?" Jacque said as he watched the

Kendals sit down and begin to lose themselves in the dancing flames of the fire. He pretended to study the night sky again, where fingers of lightning flashed. Even this carried a kind of eerie beauty that made him shake his head.

"What?" Perez said. "Just heat lightning. No big deal. Are you usually so skittish?"

"When there's talk of Skeleton Man, gunshots, a kidnapping, my partner missing, and something that beat the hell out of a car, yeah, I'd say I get a little skittish. Give me a good old-fashioned gang fight or a terrorist anytime. At least I understand that and can shoot it."

"Shoot it? That's how you big-city cops work, isn't it?" Perez taunted.

"Damn straight."

"That's the problem today. People don't understand how the world works in the spiritual realm or with Mother Earth."

Jacque couldn't help but chuckle at her remarks. "Lord help me," he moaned. "You're one of those new-age hippy types, aren't you? I bet you're a vegetarian, too."

"As a matter of fact, I am. Vegetarian, I mean." She tried to call her people in the field again, without any luck. "I'm just saying, out here, life is different. Our culture is thousands of years old and some of the old ways still serve us well. Don't knock things you don't understand. I asked you to help me earlier, at the morgue, to get some street-smart opinions that would help with Karla's case. But no. You and your friend couldn't leave fast enough to start your vacation. And just so you know, I find your partner suspicious in all of this."

"And just so you know, I'd put my life in his hands any day of the week." Noises came from the darkness, causing both Perez and Jacque to pull their weapons.

"Something out there, Chief Perez," one of the paramedics yelled as he and his partner went to stand next to the Kendals.

Perez lifted her radio and called her people in the field. There was no response until heavy breathing came through.

"Hello. Hello. Identify yourself. This is Chief Perez."

The radio crackled with static then as clear as day, the heavy breathing was followed by growling. No one in the camp made a sound. Even Chief Perez's face contorted in confusion.

Whatever trampled through the woods yelled for help, followed by gunshots.

Both Perez and Jacque pulled out their weapons and took up positions near the ambulance. The paramedics waved the couple to get inside Jacque's SUV parked nearby, before taking up positions near the Kendal vehicle.

Several lights emerged, swinging erratically, as the sound of crunching twigs and voices carried on the still night air.

"Comin' in," a man's voice yelled several times.

Moments later, four men staggered out of the woods, one being helped to walk. The paramedics rushed to assist them as Jacque and Perez ran forward to cover their retreat. Both stepped backward toward the others after a few minutes then returned their weapons to holsters.

The men's faces were scratched and bleeding. Jacque couldn't tell if it was due to some kind of encounter, running through underbrush, or falls taken during their escape. Their eyes kept darting to the line of trees at the edge of camp. The slightest sound startled them.

Perez put her hands on her hips. "What the hell happened out there?"

"I don't know." This search and rescue guy was older, maybe forty-five. He kept trying to say words of encouragement to the other three, giving Jacque the impression he might be the team leader. "One minute we were doing our thing, and the next, something came at us."

"Where's Tonya?" Perez asked.

One of the rescuers shook his head and rubbed his face as if he hid tears. "One minute she was next to me, and the next, she disappeared. Just like that. Not a scream. Cry for help. Nothing."

"Was this before the attack or during?" Jacque asked.

"During, I guess," the partner said. "I mean, I don't know. We were swinging at something big, no time to think. Then it was gone." He shoved the hands of the paramedic away and jumped off the bottom step of the ambulance. "We gotta go find her. Maybe she's lost. That thing is out there."

Then a shaky voice broke their concentration.

"Thing?" They turned around to see Ellie Kendal standing rigid and wide-eyed.

Jacque stepped to her side and led her to a stool by the fire. "When you're attacked in the dark, your mind plays tricks on you, Ellie. It does seem monstrous, even for an experienced detective like me. And I've seen plenty. Wind Dancer is searching for your boy now. Maybe he'll find Tonya, too. Okay?"

She nodded like a toddler and folded her hands in her lap. The woman was shutting down, mentally and physically.

"Keep your voices down," Jacque warned. He noticed Ty sit next to Ellie and try to talk to her. "Chief Perez, do you care if I ask a few questions?"

"Go ahead. I'm sure a clearer head would be best right now. Tonya was, I mean is a good egg. We can't lose her."

Jacque took a deep breath. "Where's the dog?"

The handler stared up at the sky and puffed out his cheeks. "He took off, howling like he'd been shot. I'm hoping he'll follow us here. I called at first but…"

"I told him to shut up. We needed to get out of there and didn't want whatever that thing was to follow us," the team leader snapped.

"My dog is out there," the handler said and doubled his fists. Jacque guessed he was feeling messed up for leaving his partner. Handlers get pretty attached to their canines.

"How far from here were you when the attack occurred?"

"Mile and a half. Maybe two," the leader guessed.

"Did you find any tracks of anyone along the way? Maybe the boy or something he dropped?"

"No, sir," the handler admitted. "My dog got spooked just before the attack and tried to get away from me, whining, even tried to bite me when I reached to pet him. This is the sweetest animal. He wouldn't hurt nobody. But he was scared and wanted loose. I thought he picked up the scent so I removed the leash for him to run. He's good about that."

"But he didn't?"

"No, sir. He tucked his tail and headed this way, or so I thought. Then, out of nowhere, a large creature or man jumped us."

Jacque paused to think a second before continuing. "So, was it a man or an animal?"

They all remained quiet, shrugged, appeared to wait on each other to speak up. He wondered about the thing that tore up camp and whatever he encountered up the road, chasing a deer.

The team leader let the paramedic bandage his head. "Keep in mind we were spread out, maybe ten feet apart. Well, until the attack. Then we all rushed in to help each other."

"Can any of you describe what this thing looked like? Any smells or textures?"

"My flashlight picked up something tall, wide, but it was from behind. It held a stick, maybe a club, and knocked it out of my hand." The youngest of the team finally spoke up.

"Same for all of us. It moved fast. Long hair, I think."

"Bushy? Straight? Color?"

The team exchanged glances and shrugged.

"The Kendals said an animal came into camp and did all this damage you see." Jacque made a circle with his hand to encompass the chaos. "Bear-like but wasn't. I spotted a similar thing earlier chasing a deer. Reminded me of a hairy dragon with big teeth. And before you ask, I haven't been drinking." He grinned. But they remained straight-faced and shivered.

"Anything else?" Jacque knew that in moments of surprise attacks, the details often got lost or mixed up.

"One thing I noticed when it knocked the flashlight out of my hand. Just a whiff maybe. Probably wrong."

"What?"

"I thought I smelled pasta. You know, like lasagna or pizza maybe?"

"So, we've got a hairy, club-wielding giant, who may or may not have a pet bear and has a taste for Italian food." Jacque shook his head and moved closer to the fire. "This just keeps getting better and better."

CHAPTER 8

A light tap came at Cleo's door as she poured her first cup of coffee. She set the mug of hot brew on the table and drew back the curtain on the door.

A smiling Mansi lifted a chubby hand in greeting. "Morning, Ms. Sommers. I brought you a basket with a few things for your breakfast. Usually, I fix a big breakfast for guests, but today you are the only one. I thought maybe you would enjoy the view from your deck instead of at the dining room." He sidestepped her and walked to the table where a curl of steam lifted from her coffee.

"There was no need to go to so much trouble, Mansi. Thank you though. I appreciate it." Cleo peeked into the basket and lifted an apple and sniffed it. She loved fresh fruit more than anything. "Do you happen to know when the garage opens up? I need to check on my rental car."

He checked his watch. "Not for another hour."

"I'm anxious to get going."

"That Floyd Miller doesn't get in any hurry. He knows there isn't anyone else around here to do what he does." Mansi chuckled. "Anything else I can do for you?"

"Oh. One more thing. Last night before dinner, I thought someone was in the woods below my room. Frightened me."

Mansi's face turned solemn and his brow furrowed. He batted

his eyes a little more than would be considered normal.

"Can you show me?" He moved to the balcony door and opened it.

Cleo followed him onto the deck. She moved to the railing. "Near that stand of thick pines. It seemed unusually tall."

"Are you sure it wasn't a bear? Mule deer come around all the time." Mansi spoke carefully and surveyed the spot in question.

"Not a deer. Moved slow like a bear though. Big. But walked on two legs."

"There's a lot of berry bushes down there. Might have been Old Moses."

"Old Moses?" Cleo leaned against the rail.

"Big black bear that roams around. Haven't seen him in a couple of years, at least here. A few folks say he's probably four hundred pounds now."

"But I think it was human."

Mansi twisted his mouth into a skeptical expression. "I'll go down and check things out. Hunters, maybe, or some kids trying to spook the tourists. We have a lot coming in for the solar eclipse today and tomorrow. It happens. We don't get much excitement around here. Even the bears don't come around much." He chuckled and waved as he backed inside then turned toward the exterior door. "I'll give the garage a call in an hour to see if your car is ready. I can run you over there."

"Thank you. Oh, and thanks again for the lovely basket of goodies." Cleo couldn't wait for him to be gone. "I'll see if my phone works better this morning."

"Cell phone coverage is hit and miss. Sorry." He waved again and whistled an eerie tune as he disappeared up the path leading to the inn.

She'd never liked whistling. Watching too many spooky movies where the antagonist decides to show up in a clown suit carrying an ax reminded her a lot of them whistled.

Cleo relaxed as she took her breakfast of sweet breads, yogurt, and a bowl of melon pieces to the deck to enjoy. A second cup of coffee warmed her hands as she studied the mountains in the distance. New Mexico truly was a magical and beautiful state.

Her thoughts turned to Wind Dancer and wondered what he might be thinking of this land so different than his native Nebraska and certainly from Chicago. The warm memories reminded her of the love that sprang up between them. The journey of their strange and wonderful history together had been woven into a story you might find in romance novels. No one had ever affected her the way he had. Together, they continued to navigate the pitfalls and joy of living in another place and time. Even a few days apart, like now, created an emptiness inside her that begged to be filled by his touch.

The progression of thoughts turned to Jacque as she brought the edge of her coffee cup to her lips. There would be lots of hilarious stories when she arrived, most exaggerated, no doubt, concerning Wind Dancer. But Cleo knew the hard-nosed detective would make sure Wind Dancer didn't get into any trouble while they were separated.

In spite of his whining and complaints, Jacque had taken on the responsibility of educating the Pawnee on the ways of modern man, often with unexpected consequences. Once when he'd given Wind Dancer a soft drink, the caffeine made him drunk. Acetaminophen, an over-the-counter pain medication, worked like a sleeping pill.

The three of them had enjoyed many excursions and trips around the Chicago area. Jacque and Wind Dancer remained a bit too overprotective for her liking, but their intentions were more chivalrous than chauvinistic.

A noise below caught her attention, and her body tensed. Whatever was down there stepped slowly, crunching twigs. A kind of snort or growl carried on the wind so that she expected a monster to appear any second. Should she move out of sight? There was no landline, so she couldn't call Mansi. The big, dark shape moved through the brush. It stopped several times, and Cleo imagined it might be curious about her. Unexpectedly, it stumbled through the trees and checked out the surrounding area before spotting her on the balcony.

There stood the biggest black bear she'd ever seen. Old Moses.

"Hi, big fella," she called, relieved her stalker wasn't a clown with an ax.

The bear startled at her voice and loped into the woods, faster than she thought possible. He emerged on the other side of the stand of trees and fast-tracked across an open parcel of land. When he finally disappeared from sight, she decided her imagination needed a good dose of reality.

"Hello? Mansi? Anyone here?" she called after cleaning up her breakfast dishes and coffeepot. Heading to the inn, she kept a close eye on the woods to make sure Old Moses hadn't doubled back. No one appeared to be manning the lobby desk where she'd signed in the night before. Voices came from the dining room. As she started through the door, Mansi crashed into her, causing her to stumble and drop the basket. He caught her before she sprawled across the shiny wood floors.

"I'm so sorry, Ms. Sommers. I thought I heard someone come in. Are you okay?" He gathered up the basket, and the contents spilled in several directions. Cleo hurried to assist.

"Oh, Mansi, I apologize. The bowl is broken. Please put it on my bill."

"Not a problem. Don't give it another thought. How can I help you?"

Cleo took a breath to pull herself together. "My phone still has only one bar, and I couldn't reach the garage. Were you able to get a call off?"

Mansi wiped his hands on his soiled apron while nodding. "I sure did. Unfortunately, the mechanic is out with a stomach bug and the guy who is helping out didn't know anything about your car. I'm guessing it's still sitting there. He was going to find out for me. If he had to send for the parts, you might be waiting another day."

"That is not the news I expected." She sighed. "Will you let me know when you hear anything? I have work to do anyway." Mansi nodded and turned away. "Oh. I spotted that mystery thing in the woods again."

He jerked around, and his eyes were noticeably wide with surprise.

"That was a bear, and I'm pretty sure by the size, it was Old Moses." Cleo grinned. "He saw me and took off. Didn't want you to go down there in case he decides on another visit."

Mansi's shoulders sagged. "Well, what do you know? I'll call animal control over in Sunset Rock and leave a message."

"I think I'm going to do a little work since I have to wait." She waved goodbye and headed to the door. "I'll check again later."

He returned the wave.

By the time Cleo entered her cabin, she decided a run would be a much better use of her time than sitting down to return emails from attendees of her workshops. The air was crisp and cool up here. Everything smelled clean and fresh. The temptation to take advantage of the opportunity to enjoy Mother Nature won out.

The visitor brochures showed several trails that ran along the rear of the inn in both directions. The one she chose led right into the little town of Kewa Korner where she could check on her rental. It began on the other side of the circle drive, near the entrance to Whispering Pines Inn, giving her time to stretch out and limber up before hitting the trail. In minutes after starting, she could feel the agitation and stress of being stranded melt away.

Most of the trail paralleled the two-lane highway on one side and trees, wildflowers, and large rocks on the other. One section went between two monolithic rocks that towered on both sides of the trail for roughly thirty feet then opened up to a scenic overlook, where she stopped to catch her breath. The altitude here affected her breathing, and she was glad to take a moment to rest. Another couple joined her who came from the direction of Kewa Korner. After pleasantries were exchanged and a little café recommended by the couple, they went on their way.

Cleo took a deep gulp of fresh air and started out again. She hadn't gone far when a rock the size of a clothes basket rolled down the cliff she neared and bounced into a jagged rock formation on the highway side of the trail. She nearly fell trying to get out of the way. As she stared up to determine if any more rocks might fall, something pulled away from the edge. When she shaded her eyes to get a better glimpse of what caused the single rock to fall, Cleo spotted movement among the twisted trees along the edge.

Falling against the bulging outcropping of stone, she wondered if the rock had been forced off to frighten or harm her. Why would anyone do that?

She decided to run again and picked up her pace. When she reached the entrance to the trail next to the picnic area in the middle of town, she decided once more her imagination had gotten the best of her. Several mothers noticed her after emerging from the trail, panting. They called their children to come eat lunch.

The coffee shop was across the street. She jogged in that direction but slowed for an RV to pass. The older couple waved to her and she returned the gesture before hurrying over to an outdoor seating area. Before she could pull out her phone, a petite waitress arrived, wearing a blue checkered apron. Her long dark hair was twisted at the nape of her neck in a messy bun.

"I'll take an iced tea, please," she said, catching her breath.

"Anything else? Momma fixed tuna sandwiches today."

"No. Thanks. Just tea. Oh, and can I have it to go?" The girl nodded and soon returned. Cleo gave her a five-dollar bill and told her to keep the change. Her smile indicated this might be the biggest tip of the day.

After chatting with the high schooler for a few minutes and getting directions to the garage, Cleo decided to make that her next stop. She discovered her cell phone now had two bars. But, to her disappointment, Jacque didn't pick up when she called.

"Can I help you?" a young man asked as he wiped his hands on an oily rag.

She told him her name and indicated her car parked outside on the parking lot. He motioned her inside to sit down while he went to get the boss, who turned out to be the mechanic, Floyd Miller, she'd spoken to the day before.

"There you are?" He motioned to the counter, indicating she should join him. He grabbed the keys off a hook on a pegboard.

"It's finished?" Cleo thought maybe he didn't remember her.

"Yep. Finished last night around eight. You said you needed to get going today. Stayed late since my wife had a baby shower to go to. No need to rush home."

"Mansi said he called this morning and it might be a day or so before you got the part." Cleo took the keys from him.

Floyd scratched his head and shrugged. "Didn't talk to me." He yelled into the garage where the young man had disappeared. "Hey, Tinker. Did Mansi Garcia call this morning about this lady's car?"

At a loud noise, Floyd rolled his eyes. "That kid is an accident waiting to happen. Probably Tinker he talked to, and he doesn't have a full box of crayons, if you know what I mean. Guess I'll get rid of him. Idiot."

"Oh please. Not on my account. Mansi said you were sick."

He shook his head. "I'm sick of unreliable people answering my phone," he yelled into the garage. "Sorry about the miscommunication. Good news is I called the rental company and they're picking up the tab." He handed her a bill stamped paid, with important information to submit when she returned the vehicle. "Probably should call them anyway to make sure they remember our conversation." He raised his chin toward the garage where Cleo could see Tinker walking around one of the cars. "Who knows. They may have stupid people working for them, too."

"But you didn't have a stomach bug?"

"Honestly, if you had my wife's cooking, you'd always have a stomach bug. I come to work anyway when that happens." His mouth twisted in a snarl. "I swear she's trying to poison me." He shrugged. "She'd just put me to work if I stayed home. Gotta love that woman though. We just celebrated another anniversary."

Cleo knew it was time to take her leave. She really wasn't interested in his love life, and it felt like the conversation was headed in that direction. "Thanks again. I appreciate your help."

Before she exited the waiting area, Floyd hurried into the garage, yelling at the young man called Tinker, who had apparently dropped a pan of oil on the floor. Poor kid.

Grateful she didn't have to jog to the inn, Cleo drove carefully to check for more problems then parked in front. In spite of it being nearly noon, she wanted to get on the road. A new person attended to the desk and was happy to help her check out.

Since she didn't have much to pack and carry to the car, she quickly trudged up the path to the parking lot. As she came around the corner, she noticed a tall man moving away from her car and then sprinting around the inn out of sight. Nothing appeared to have been touched on the vehicle though.

Starting the air conditioner, she couldn't help but wonder who had been walking around the area, when Mansi came running out waving a piece of paper. She powered down the window and waited.

"Tuki said she forgot to give you a receipt. I attached a few coupons to it. They can be used in town. A few more are for Sunset Rock. If you like horseback riding, there's a 30 percent off offer for a trail ride in Kewa National Park." His smile was infectious and almost made Cleo forget why she'd wanted to steer clear of him.

She took the receipt and laid it on the seat next to her. "Appreciate it. My car was ready, and Mr. Miller said he felt fine." The tone came across a little more condescending than she intended.

Mansi shook his head. "Probably his wife's cooking. She's a great deal younger than him. He didn't marry her for her recipes." He winked. "Well, you have a safe drive."

"Mansi, there was someone one out here prowling around my car when I came up the cabin path. A really tall guy. Black hair. Dressed in jeans and a long vest with geometric patterns on it."

"Oh, I bet that was Alo. He works here. Does a little of everything. Cooking to maintenance."

"He acted suspicious. Hurried off when I came in sight."

"He's a shy one. Doesn't say much to anybody, not even me. He's a little disfigured and tries to hide from people staring at him." Mansi patted the car door and stepped onto the sidewalk. "Probably checking out your car since it wasn't here last night. Pretty protective."

Cleo put the car in reverse and lifted a hand in goodbye. As she pulled out onto the highway, she glanced up into the rearview mirror and realized Mansi continued to watch her.

CHAPTER 9

The campsite now had more people to show up to help with the search. Other first responders who were off duty came as well, partly because of the missing woman Tonya. She was one of their own. Jacque understood that mentality.

How many times had he gone to the hospital to wait with police department personnel in support of a wounded officer and their family? There had been numerous times he went out in the mean streets of Chicago, hunting the person who took down an officer for doing his job. The rage welled up inside him like an angry volcano. Nothing could calm it until justice was served.

Now here he was, witnessing it again on his no-stress vacation. To top it off, he'd lost Wind Dancer, although he suspected he'd be fine. And now his stomach growled with hunger.

"Chief Perez, I'm going to go over to my camp and make more coffee. I'll bring over a pot and a few cups."

Sun rays spilled across the glassy lake where the patchy fog lifted. Any other time, he'd be admiring how beautiful it was here and admit he rather enjoyed the tranquility of it all.

"Thanks. I sent for some breakfast sandwiches and pastries from the convenience store outside the park. I called in an order about thirty minutes ago."

Perez had dark circles under her pretty brown eyes, and her hair had been knotted at the base of her neck. He noticed for the first time she wore skintight jeans and a light jacket that opened in the front, revealing a black tee shirt with a police motto. Her holster was visible, along with several other things attached to her service belt. The hiking boots gave her a sexier image than he thought possible. He'd found himself admiring her figure when she slapped him on the arm.

"Hey. Wake up. Did you hear me?"

"Donuts and dry biscuits on the way. Got it. I won't be long." Jacque growled without thinking. "Sorry. Need coffee to stabilize my mood."

As he turned to leave, she raised her chin up and eyed him with what he thought was contempt. He gave himself a stinging reprimand on the way to his camp, knowing he wasn't making any good impressions with the attractive police chief.

He'd kept the fire going through the night, and now it was perfect to put on a pot of coffee. While it brewed, he grabbed the bag of disposable cups for the volunteers. Once he returned, he noticed the food had arrived, and those who'd been there all night didn't hesitate to grab breakfast.

Ellie and Ty shared some of their food, but it was mostly fruit and granola. They even offered their energy bars and drinks for them to take along when they hit the trail again.

"How many are out there now?" Jacque bit into a sausage-egg biscuit that tasted like heaven then grabbed his coffee off the hood of a pickup truck.

"Twenty. More coming. ER is standing by in town."

"Didn't think a town the size of Sunset Rock would have a hospital."

"Fifty bed unit with an urgent care attached. Most of the fifty beds stay empty. There's one doctor who comes twice a week from Taos. We do have a retired doctor who fills in when there's an emergency. Several others come and go with different specialties. The others are nurses and nurse practitioners. The big shots make more money in the cities. The people who come and stay here are wanting a different way of life. They feel it a privilege to care for the people."

Jacque eyed the one biscuit left and decided he'd better save it for one of the rescue team members going out on the search. The powdered donut would have to do for now. Of course, it was stale, and the taste resembled chalk.

"These responders are in great shape. Probably don't eat this crap," he said, wiping the powdered sugar from the corner of his mouth.

Perez grinned. "These guys eat like Marines and work it off to stay fit." She gave him an interested once-over. "You look pretty fit yourself. Do you always eat this crap, as you call it?"

He wanted to puff out his chest and flex his muscles but noticed coffee had sloshed on the spanking-new tee shirt he'd bought for the trip, and spots of butter from the biscuit had dripped on his camo hunter vest he'd picked up at an Army surplus store near Fort Leonardwood, Missouri. He set the cup down and tried to dust away the mess.

"Nope. Usually a protein shake for breakfast, a quick run, and lots of coffee." It wasn't a total lie. He did run to the coffee shop across from his apartment building each morning. Diverting the subject to the problem at hand felt like a safer topic. "Any traces of the boy or Tonya?"

She took a slow drink of her coffee. The fact she hadn't loaded it up with milk and sugar said a lot about her resolve as far as he was concerned.

"You make a good cup of coffee. But no, there's nothing so far. Does Wind Dancer have any way to contact you?"

Jacque came close to saying something inappropriate about smoke signals but decided it would be too politically incorrect even for him. "He's not really up on modern communication. He'll find a way." The fact remained he didn't like that they had been out of touch for this long. The Pawnee came across as a badass, but, in truth, he was equal to a five-year-old when it came to the twenty-first century. The guy still couldn't handle riding in a car in downtown Chicago for very long. He preferred to walk. Light switches, microwave ovens, air-conditioning, and flush toilets amused him for hours. Then a litany of why and how questions followed. More times than not, Jacque would make up an answer.

He smiled to himself remembering one such instance.

"How does this work, Jacque?" he asked, turning the lights on and off dozens of times in his office, until the captain came by and told him to tell his friend to knock it off.

"Once a year, we set rocks out in the sun for two or three days. Then we hook these wires up to the rocks and it makes electricity."

"Oh," would be the response. He would then move on to the next oddity.

If Cleo got wind of the deception, she did her own war dance, another term he wasn't allowed to use.

The truth of the matter was that he admired the Pawnee and trusted him more than anyone he'd ever met. Not only was he a good man but brave and trustworthy. Their friendship bonded over a difficult time in his city and without the Pawnee's help, things would be a mess, not only in Chicago but the entire US. The enormity of what he'd done never registered with Wind Dancer.

"I did what was right." He didn't say much else concerning the matter and didn't care to talk about those days.

Because of Wind Dancer's actions, he and Cleo had been separated for a year. Jacque agreed to take on the responsibility of loyal guard dog, thinking he'd never see the Pawnee again. Cleo had never given up hope he'd return.

During that time, he'd come to admire her more than he wanted to admit. She worked hard and was eternally optimistic. The care and attention she gave to her patients inspired him to be a better person. They butted heads constantly over how to be proactive in being safe in a place like Chicago. But their friendship grew in spite of the conflict and, although he was relieved when the Pawnee returned, there was a part of him that missed being the protector of the pretty doctor.

He was jabbed to the present when Perez elbowed him and pointed toward the woods.

"We got company."

Two men dressed more like cowboys than first responders, emerged from the woods. The Kendals moved closer. They held hands, and he couldn't help but feel compassion for their pain and worry.

"Anything?" Perez called.

"Found where your guys stopped last night." Cowboy One took out a kerchief with the Sunset Rock logo then a ballcap. "No sign of the kid, Tonya, or the dog."

"You been out since dawn. Grab some food. Coffee over there."

They nodded and moved toward the table set up for

refreshments.

The walkie-talkie crackled to life, causing Perez to take notice of the Kendals who had turned toward the table to serve the first responders. She moved farther away, and Jacque followed.

"Come back," she said. "Come back."

"Problem?" he asked.

"Not sure."

"Found a little blood on a rock," the voice was a static reply. "Could have been the dog. A few paw prints headed up to higher ground then disappeared. No trace after that. Others are pretty spread out. Those on horseback took another section of the park. They parked up on the ridge on the east side near Culver Pass, almost into Carson National Forest."

"Copy that. Keep me informed." She clicked off.

"I need to find Wind Dancer." Jacque took in the surrounding area and twisted to evaluate the condition of the parents of Liam. "We both know finding the kid unharmed is unlikely the longer this goes. The more people out there, the better the chances."

Perez cocked her head and frowned. "You're not going anywhere. I don't want anyone else getting lost or taken. I figure you couldn't find your way out of a paper bag in this environment. You might be the best thing since sliced bread in a concrete jungle, but out here, Mother Nature has a warped sense of humor when it comes to city slickers."

"Are you always so domineering this early in the morning, because you might have thought I asked your permission to go search for my friend?" Jacque strode away, Perez on his heels.

"I don't have the manpower to come search for you, Detective Marquette. Get over yourself and be a good boy. I would hate to have those two beefy guys chowing down on breakfast to restrain you."

He halted and pivoted so fast, she ran into his chest then jumped sideways.

"You'd hate it worse than that if you tried such a stupid stunt." He surveyed the area across the lake. "I'm starting over there since no one else seemed to think of it. When Wind Dancer returns, he will take a new route. I think I spotted a trail over there when I used my binoculars yesterday. And, if you remember, I told you he said we were being watched from there."

"You said a lot of things that didn't make sense."

"If I head up the trail, he'll be able to find me."

"How?"

Jacque hesitated then thought what the heck. "He'll smell me from a mile off."

Perez threw up her hands. "And you wonder why I say you don't make sense."

"I'm taking that canoe and going to the other side. Come with me or stay. Makes no difference to me. If I get lost, Wind Dancer will find me. That is the one thing I know that makes sense."

She leveled an inspection that would have melted butter. "I'm going with you."

CHAPTER 10

Jacque checked behind him a couple of times to see if Perez still met with the two beefy guys who had returned. Together, they examined the maps spread out before them. From time to time, they smirked his way then shifted their focus on the woods. A lot of head bobbing and pinched expressions passed between them.

"I left those two in charge in case anyone else returns with information." She handed him a radio. "If we get separated, we'll be able to communicate. Let's walk around the end of the lake to see if there are any signs of uninvited guests. I know it adds a little time to the hike, but maybe we'll pick up something."

He'd noticed a mule deer standing there right after they arrived the day before. The lake wasn't very wide at that end, but he realized there wouldn't be any obvious clues if they paddled across.

"Let's go," he said in a gruff voice.

He grabbed his backpack, stuffed with protein snacks, first aid kit, and a couple bottles of water, one of the times when he'd come over to his camp. There was also a whistle, extra ammo, and a flare. Cleo had given him a crash course on being prepared when you camp or go hiking. Now he wished he'd gotten other items on her list.

Perez slipped a small knapsack onto her shoulders and began a brisk walk, leaving Jacque in his statue-like stance. He observed her for a few seconds, enjoying the way she moved. When she pulled on her hat, she tugged her ponytail through the opening. The morning light bounced off it, revealing its silkiness as it moved through the opening.

"Change your mind?" she called without stopping.

Jacque picked up the pace and soon overtook her, seeing the worn trail spread out before them. They were around the edge and directly across from their camp in a matter of minutes. Although it was debatable which method would have gotten them there sooner, the trail didn't hold any clues as to if anyone had been moving through the area.

The trail wound through the wooded area. From time to time, large boulders jutted out far enough that they had to zigzag and climb over a downed tree. He could feel the burn as the trail narrowed and took a steep incline along a rock face. He estimated the drop off to be around thirty feet. A stream tunneled rapidly through outcroppings of smooth rocks leading to the lake where their campsite was located. Along with the periodic loose gravel under foot, several places narrowed enough, the two had to turn sideways and move cautiously.

They were nearing a wider section when Perez, in the lead, stepped on a loose piece of gravel, causing her to lose her balance. She threw her arms up then tried to grab at a tree root sticking out from between two boulders but couldn't stop herself from slipping off the edge of the trail. A scream lifted above the roar of the rushing water.

~ ~ ~ ~

Before leaving the little town of Kewa Korner, Cleo stopped at the café to get an iced tea for the road.

The young waitress smiled when she came in and quickly took the order of a couple she'd met on the trail earlier, before taking her order.

"On the house." She leaned over the counter and whispered, "Thanks for the big tip. I don't get many."

She decided to fill up her car with gas. The map she purchased revealed a lot of open country ahead, and she didn't want to take a chance there would be a place to refuel. If her GPS decided not to cooperate, at least she'd have plenty of gas in the event she took a wrong turn. She folded the map and placed it on the passenger seat.

Before she could pull out, the RV she'd noticed earlier pulled in. The wife walked around the vehicle. "Oh, honey, I'm so sorry. We've blocked you in. I'll have Allen move right now."

Cleo leaned out the window. "No. It's okay. I have to make a call anyway."

Once more, she tried to reach Jacque. His phone rang, but all she got was that his voice mail was full. A wave of anger mixed with concern wafted over her. How could he be so irresponsible? One thing was for sure; when they returned to Chicago, she would get Wind Dancer a phone and insist he learn how to use it. She was well aware of why he still refused to let her buy him one.

"I do not want your little box to talk in, Cleopatra." He'd crossed his arms across his chest and leaned against her breakfast bar. "It is dangerous for me to use it. I might call out evil ones."

"Now that sounds a lot like something Jacque told you." She shook a finger at him. "What nonsense has he been telling you again?"

Wind Dancer stiffened and pulled himself to his full height. "Not nonsense. He says I might call a person to come from other places. They would be angry and could put you in danger. I will always protect you."

"Well, don't you think I might do the same thing?"

"No. Jacque says you have special powers and need it to heal the sick and wounded."

"Jacque is full of it."

"Full of what?" These kinds of comments always led to either laughter on her part or frustration on his. "I think he is never full. He eats all the time. What does that have to do with the talking box?"

Cleo remembered him wrapping his arms around her, followed by a passionate kiss. Things spiraled out of control after that, and the cell phone conversation never came up again. Now she wished there was one more person she could call. Hindsight was always 20/20. Not alerting them that she was on her way was proving to be a big mistake. Other than a couple of friends from the conference, no one knew where she was headed.

The RV couple came over and gave her a gift card for the convenience store.

"What's this? No." She tried to hand it to them through the window.

"I insist," the older gentleman said, waving his hand in rejection at her. "You were too sweet not to make us move and didn't complain when we took too long." His eyes went to the phone she held against the steering wheel. "You'll get better reception a couple of miles out of town. It's a little higher than here."

"That's a relief. I'm trying to reach friends at Kewa National Park." She shoved the gift card into her jeans pocket.

"On the other side of Sunset Rock?"

Cleo pulled out her map and noticed she'd circled the town. "Yes. That's it. How far is it from here? I mean time wise. I know the map says roughly twenty miles. Maybe less."

The wife leaned down to speak. "That sounds right. Of course, with our big clunker, driving around those curves takes a lot longer. But you should make it okay."

The man nodded. "Thirty minutes maybe to the town. Kewa is a ways on the other side though. Parked our RV at the Carson National Forest for a few days then went on to Kewa. Lots of hiking trails."

The woman grimaced. "Unfortunately, I turned my ankle, and we headed to Sunset Rock this morning to their little medical center. That turned out to be a waste. Everyone was on high alert. Said it would be three or four hours before I could get an X-ray. My injury wasn't a big deal, so we left."

"What was going on that they couldn't help you? I'm actually a doctor. Would you like me to examine it?"

The couple smiled at each other.

"What luck!" she laughed. "Allen, can we park in that lot at that little picnic area over there? We're blocking traffic."

"I'll meet you there." Cleo was already getting her medical bag out of the trunk when the RV pulled in. They quickly joined her. The lady climbed up on the top of the picnic table to be able to rest her foot on the seat.

"You're getting around pretty good," Cleo said, wrapping an ace bandage around the ankle. "I'd get it checked out in a bigger town. Or if you're on your way home, give your primary care doctor a call. You never know if there's a fracture. I've seen a sprain be worse than a break."

The lady extended her leg and admired her purple wrap. "Well, that is almost too pretty. Thank you. Sure hope they get things taken care of up at Kewa."

"Yeah. I wanted to ask you about that. You said something was going on?"

The man shook his head. "Terrible. A family lost their little boy during the night. Not sure if it was an animal or a person. Police and first responders everywhere."

A silent alarm went off inside Cleo. "This was in Kewa?"

"Yes," said the lady. "I can only imagine what those parents are going through. The state troopers came by to ask us a few questions as we were leaving. Showed us a picture of the child. Said he had Down syndrome." She laid her hand on her heart. "Prayers lifted for the little fella. I think besides us, there were only a couple of others in the park. Expected to fill up today because of the eclipse activities. We let them check our RV since we were leaving. Didn't want to be labeled suspicious tourists."

Allen assisted his wife when she tried to get off the picnic table. He reached for his wallet. "Let me pay you."

Cleo waved him off and hurried to her car. "Nope. Going to head on up there. Maybe I can help out."

"Great idea," they called as they headed toward their RV.

Pulling out on the road, Cleo wondered if the missing child had anything to do with Jacque not answering his phone. She imagined he was in the thick of it by now and probably didn't consider checking his phone. Besides, she wasn't supposed to be here for another day.

The road curved a great deal but didn't slow her down. As predicted, Sunset Rock appeared closer to twenty minutes than thirty. Since she was on the outskirts of the town, only one stoplight caused her to pause long enough to check the bars on her phone.

"Finally," she mumbled, seeing that her phone had all its bars now.

When the light turned green, she continued down the road. The anticipation of a joyful surprise at her sudden appearance had been replaced with I hope I can make a difference if it's not too late.

The Carson National Forest sign loomed ahead. There was a parking area, and it felt like a good time to pull off and try to call the guys to get an exact location to join them. The phone again went to a full voice mail box. She clicked off and turned the key in the ignition. It was dead.

CHAPTER 11

The police chief, Perez, pitched over the edge of the narrow path like a blow-up tube man outside a tire and lube business. Jacque grabbed the straps on her knapsack with one hand and still managed to catch a wayward branch protruding between rocks, with the other. Her weight and momentum still nearly pulled him in after her.

He steadied his feet and slowly turned loose of the branch.

"Don't move," he yelled as he managed to slip off his backpack that made him feel clumsy.

Glancing over the edge, he clamped onto the straps with the other hand. She'd found a piece of rock with her toes and faced the wall of jagged rock. Her arms reached out to grasp what might have been a grab hole that climbers use.

"Can you move at all when I pull you up?"

When she nodded, he doubled down on his grip and pulled. He caught a glimpse of her using her feet to walk up the jagged wall of rock. The path was slightly wider here. As she came up clawing her way over the edge, Jacque had to let go of the straps or lose his footing. He put a gentle boot on her shoulders to steady her.

With feet still dangling over the edge, Perez took in a deep breath and spread out her arms as if to balance her body.

"I'm going to remove my foot then try and pull you forward.

Most of your body will fit on the path. When you get against the rock wall, there are handholds. I'll help you as you start moving up them. They're embedded. Don't worry they'll fall apart. Ready?"

"Let's do it." Her voice was shaky but strong.

Removing his boot was easier than bending over and grabbing her straps again. His peripheral vision kept taking in the drop-off and the roar of rushing water cascading over boulders the size of his SUV, that messed with his equilibrium, not to mention his confidence.

In slow motion, he wiggled his fingers as they clamped around the straps.

"Pull," he ordered.

She obeyed a lot faster than he expected and with a great deal more agility. Not only did she find the handholds he warned her about, but she managed to get to her knees unassisted. In seconds, she was standing but still facing the rock wall. Jacque placed his hand on her waist in case she wobbled and stepped to close to the edge.

For an instant, she rested her forehead against the rock and sighed, followed by a nod. "Okay. I'm good to go."

He stared at her in disbelief. "Sure you don't need a minute?"

"I said I'm good. Look at those clouds. We need to get in and get out. That cozy river down there will turn into a roaring monster if it rains up in those mountains ahead of us. It might even wash part of this trail out." She felt along her waist. "Great. My radio must have fallen off when I slipped over the ledge."

Jacque took a peek over the edge then cocked his head at her ice-cold lack of fear at what just happened. "Cozy river?" His first thought was it reminded him of a scene out the movie *Deliverance*. "We aren't that far from where we started. If we stay on the trail and don't return, someone will find us."

"Not necessarily." She turned away from him and started down the path.

Relief washed over him as the trail opened up enough for them to walk side by side. She was keeping a good pace. He followed, wanting to make sure he had eyes on the area behind them. The feeling they were being followed nagged at him.

They walked for another thirty minutes, covering a lot of ground since the trail had flattened and was void of loose rocks and debris. For the first time in a year, he was grateful Cleo had put him on a diet and made him join a gym. Although he didn't exercise as much as he told Cleo he did, he had taken to hiking with Wind Dancer around Lake Michigan and trails near the city. He'd also enjoyed those rock-climbing walls at the gym.

"Sorry. I need to sit down a minute." Perez used a downed tree along the path as a bench. She pulled out a bottle of water and drank deep. "Thanks, by the way, for the rescue."

Jacque shrugged and joined her on the log. He would never have asked for a break, but he sure was glad she wanted one.

"I was recently put in charge of the Damsels in Distress Department. Wasn't what I signed up for, but somebody has to do it," he said offhandedly. A smile spread across her lips that drew his attention a little too long. "What did you mean when I said we would be found and you said 'not necessarily?'"

After taking another swig of her water then replacing it in her bag, she fanned her hand out toward the rock formations then the water that now ran along the path where they rested.

"In the past disappearances, there have been common details."

"There have been more than the three disappearances you told me about, haven't there?"

She took a deep breath and let it out slowly as her eyes scanned the thickening forests on the other side of the stream. "Yes. Not right here but within a hundred-mile radius. Even a few outside Santa Fe."

"How many?"

"In the last twenty years there have been fourteen that we know of."

A whistle escaped his lips. "Serial killer? What evidence has been left behind?"

"None."

"Impossible. You said there were commonalities."

"Yes. But no evidence."

"You lost me."

"Okay. Here is what we know. Clustered near bodies of water in national parks and if they are found alive, they often have memory loss. If the person has a mental disability to begin with, we get nothing. I bet the little boy won't be able to tell us a thing because of his Down syndrome. And even if he could, no one would believe him."

"And if they are found dead?"

Perez squinted at the area behind her, as if she expected someone to be there. "The cause of death is hard to determine. The body is often found in a location that has already been thoroughly searched, which was the case of our last victim, Karla. Sometimes there are missing clothes, especially shoes. They'll be found miles from where they should have been and barefoot with no visible marks on their feet."

"Any sexual assault?"

"No. Karla had a lot of scratches, but the coroner determined she'd fallen in gravel. We found where she fell and the gravel matched."

"What items of clothing were missing on her? Serial killers often take souvenirs."

"Nothing that we could tell. There are other similarities in these missing persons. The locations will be near rock walls or rock outcroppings near water. Bad weather moves in within twenty-four to forty-eight hours of the disappearance. And that is every time," she insisted, jabbing a finger into the palm of her hand. "Most of the adults that go missing are experienced hikers and are with friends."

"Like Karla."

She nodded. "They might be camping, like you guys. The children go around a bend or curve in the trail with their parents ten feet behind. The parents round the bend and the child is gone."

"When you find them, is there a particular time of day?"

"I'd have to check. As I said, it has happened over years. But I've been trying to figure this out since Karla died. When Wind Dancer spooked liked he did, I had to wonder if there wasn't something supernatural, we hadn't thought of."

Jacque rubbed both his hands over his face to erase the image of a skinwalker that tried to take his body and had followed him around Chicago for days. He disliked things he couldn't explain. Black and white were his favorite colors when it came to solving crime. The pieces of a puzzle always fit together if you knew where to find them. Supernatural, mumbo-jumbo, voodoo nonsense didn't know how to behave.

Several years ago, he wouldn't have considered it possible there might be things such as skinwalkers or booger animals like owls who carried curses to your enemies. Now, he found he was second guessing himself on all the superstitious crap he'd heard over the years and wondered if parts of it wasn't true—and dangerous.

"What were you thinking? About the time of day, I mean?" Perez stood and stretched which caused Jacque to admire more than he should at a fellow officer, especially one he had considered striking up a friendly relationship.

He blinked away the compromising image he had of them together and forced a squint at nothing in the sky. Those clouds were getting darker. Deciding to observe them innocently offered a chance to hide his discomfort.

"Hmm. Yeah, the time. Maybe a connection between the missing. I mean victims. They were all found right?"

She grabbed up her bag and slipped her arms through the straps then tossed him his backpack. "Most of them."

~ ~ ~ ~

"Could this trip get any more bizarre?" she grumbled and removed the car key and dropped it in the cupholder.

A lopsided sign, with several boards missing off the bottom, appeared to have been involved in an accident. The side with the words had been twisted to face away from the road. Cleo felt she should stretch her legs anyway and exited the car, phone in hand. Since the sign was facing a weedy area, she peeked around the edge to read the words, visitor center ahead, written in white paint that could have been the artwork of a toddler.

No accounting for artistic expression, she thought. Maybe it was meant to resemble lettering from the Old West days. If that were the case, mission accomplished.

The afternoon breeze swept up a few pine needles and moved them across the road as a hawk took flight. A sudden crack drew her attention to a stand of trees across the road where a branch hung precariously, swaying until the next breeze jarred it loose and crashed to the ground. An elk strutted out the entrance to the park, causing Cleo to slowly move to the car. The size of the animal frightened her, while at the same time, it took her breath away. He stopped to inspect her, about as far away as the length of a school bus. He continued across the road and disappeared into the woods.

This was one of the moments she wished Wind Dancer was at her side to admire the beauty of such a magnificent animal. He'd probably want to eat it, but still, it would have been nice to know what the elk might be thinking, since the Pawnee had the gift to figure those kinds of things out.

She activated the speed-dial option for Jacque.

"Hello?" The whiskey voice comforted her. "Cleo? I'm a little busy."

"Jacque, I've been trying to reach you."

"What? I can hardly hear you."

"I'm stuck at the entrance to Carson National Forest. My car broke down."

"Cleo, speak up. There is static. Damn rocks and trees everywhere."

She had to smile as she leaned against the car door. He certainly was out of his element.

"My car broke down. Come get me." The static became too much, and the line went dead. The bars on the phone indicated they were at capacity. She tried dialing again, but got the voice mail is full, message again.

Then she remembered the car came equipped with a roadside assistance device. She paid extra to have it, since she'd be traveling alone. When she pivoted to open the car door, she dropped the phone and accidently toed it under the car.

Kneeling, she reached for it, to no avail. The only thing to do was get down on her stomach and fish it out. As she grabbed the phone, a pair of cowboy boots appeared and remained perfectly still, on the other side of the car.

She tried to scamper up and slipped on a rock, but the second time, she grabbed the door handle of the car.

It was locked.

CHAPTER 12

Jacque frowned at his phone, shook it, as if the action would fix the static, and yelled into the speaker. "Cleo, are you there?" It clicked off. He shoved it in his hunter vest pocket. "That woman will be the death of me."

"Girlfriend?" Perez asked as she started down the trail. He wondered if she was fishing because of a personal interest or just nosey.

"No. Friend. Suppose to meet us here." He explained about the medical conference. "She and Wind Dancer are together."

"Wow. A doctor and Wind Dancer. I thought maybe he was—you know—special."

He chuckled. "He's special all right. There's a lot of unusual things about him that would surprise you. I don't really know you well enough to explain. Besides, I'm not cleared to give out that information. If you want to know more, you'll have to contact that FBI jerk you said you talked to."

"So, you and the FBI jerk, as you called him, are friends after all?"

"Friends would be a stretch." He didn't offer more than that, but she turned around and grinned at him. "When the FBI jerk wants me to help him out, he brings me a five-dollar cup of coffee from one of those ridiculous foo-foo shops on the Million Dollar Mile."

The trail widened enough he could walk beside her. "Beats the hell out of coffee that's been in the pot for hours and most likely made-over coffee grounds from the day before."

She wrinkled her nose. "Sounds disgusting."

"I'm tougher than I look," he said, adjusting his shoulders in a show of strength. She continued to smile then laughed lightly. He decided it was a nice laugh, soft and almost shy.

She stopped and cocked an ear.

Jacque mimicked the gesture, more out of anticipation than having heard anything.

"I thought a voice called out." Perez nodded toward the opposite bank of the stream. "Over there." She pulled out a small pair of binoculars and adjusted the focus. "We can cross a little farther up the trail." Handing them to Jacque, she continued. "Thought I saw movement."

He shook his head. "Nothing."

Thunder rumbled in the distance as they picked up the pace to reach the crossing. Once there, Jacque couldn't believe how calm and shallow the stream was here. Although they were at a higher elevation, he guessed it picked up momentum as it moved downstream. He could see other feeders for the stream trickling in along the way and wondered if maybe there might be a few springs, too.

"Wind Dancer," he called out, feeling it might be a good time to make his presence known. "Where are you?"

"Did you hear him?" she asked as they waded out ankle deep.

"No. Just a feeling." He pulled his gun and shot three times in the air. At least he knew this much about using the distress signal when out in the wild.

The stream narrowed here, maybe twenty feet wide, and came up to Perez's knees as they moved to the middle. The bottom was covered in gravel which made walking across a little easier. Since he was right at six feet tall, he managed to stretch out his steps quicker than the chief and waded onto shore first. There had been a long enough pause for him to try the three shots in the air again.

He noticed a pile of rocks in a triangle. "Isn't that also a cry for help?"

"Yes. Would Wind Dancer know that?"

"No. Where he's from, you didn't want people being able to

follow you. If he doesn't want you to know where he is, then you won't find him."

Perez gave him a bewildered glance until movement in the woods caused several birds to escape the tops of trees. The sound of a dog's bark followed.

"Maybe that's your bloodhound?"

Before she could answer, it came loping toward them then turned and ran into the woods. Both followed easily since the area was wide open. It served as a trail between the trees. Large rocks and downed trees slowed their progress until a bend in the trail narrowed. They had gone only about fifty yards when the dog appeared again and wagged his tail.

Jacque thought of his own dog and how he had filled something missing in his life. Even though he complained about the mutt being a nuisance and taking too much time, he enjoyed watching Sunday afternoon football with his furry buddy. Knowing the handler would be relieved to see the bloodhound, if they could catch him, it would be a job well done.

"Come," Jacque demanded. He'd noticed how the handler interacted with the dog the night before and had even taken note of the canine officers in Chicago, in hopes he could train his mildly trainable pooch a few tricks. Nothing worked.

The dog ran to him and sat immediately. Jacque rubbed his head and pulled out a piece of biscuit he'd been saving for a snack later and fed the dog. He gobbled it out of his hand then stood, looking toward a large outcropping of rocks and started barking. A gust of wind swept through the top of the trees, causing their branches to moan and pop with resistance.

"Storm is moving in." Perez took notice of the sky for a few seconds.

The dog continued to focus on the trail ahead where he'd emerged and whined. A tree had fallen over from above and created a bridge to another large boulder. The branches were still green, so it had happened recently.

When the dog howled and backed up, Jacque tried to see and hear whatever had gotten him spooked. He ran toward, what Jacque felt like, danger and disappeared. He pulled his weapon, as did Perez, before they moved forward. The barking started once more, and just as they stooped to go under the tree bridge, a small figure appeared on the trail.

"Liam!" Jacque called, replacing his weapon. "Liam, it's me, Wind Dancer's friend. We came to take you to your mom and dad."

The little boy cocked his head then turned and ran toward where the trail ascended. Both Perez and Jacque ran after him. They halted when a man stepped out from behind a stand of trees with something in his arms.

Perez pulled up her weapon and aimed only to have it pushed down by the detective.

"Wind Dancer," he called, running to meet him. The little boy stood next to him, one arm around the Pawnee's legs and leaning his little head into the man's body. The Pawnee smiled at him, and Jacque felt relief wash over him like a flash flood. He carried the search and rescue woman in his arms.

"Jacque," he said. "She is hurt. Need doctor. I wish Cleopatra was here to heal her."

"I do, too, buddy." Jacque motioned for the Pawnee to lay her down on the ground so they could check things out. Perez had slipped her weapon in her holster and kneeled down next to Tonya before glancing up at Wind Dancer then the boy. "Check him out, will you?"

Jacque nodded and stepped toward Liam who shied away behind Wind Dancer. The Pawnee put his hand on the child's head and rubbed gently. "He is a friend, Liam. Remember him from last night?" The little boy nodded and peeked out from around the Pawnee. "You must talk to him. Tell him what you told me." This time, he nodded and stepped in front of Wind Dancer who picked him up in his arms.

Perez accepted Jacque's radio sand tried to reach camp. At first, it filled with static but cleared when the wind became still. "We're going to need help." She told them her location and that Tonya was unconscious. Even though the transmission was garbled, it sounded like help would arrive. She slowly stood and eyed Wind Dancer, who didn't appear to be tired, dirty, or frazzled in any way. "Can you carry Tonya a little farther? Others are coming to help."

Wind Dancer set the boy down even though he clung to his neck.

"No. No. The monster get me."

"Little one, I am here. Together we will protect you."

"Hold me," the little one sobbed.

Jacque kneeled next to him. "I can carry you. How will that be?" Liam wiped at his tears. "Wind Dancer needs to carry the lady. We'll take the dog with us, too." By now, the dog had taken a position of obedience next to the Pawnee. Jacque stood and reached down for the boy who eased into his embrace. He patted the child's shoulders and gave him a hug. "Now you be on the lookout for our helpers who are coming. It's going to rain soon, and we have to hurry."

Perez grabbed the extra backpack so Jacque could carry the boy on his shoulders. The little guy smiled and removed Jacque's ballcap to place on his own head. Jacque pretended to protest and was rewarded with a giggle.

"We should get going," she said as the wind gusts picked up again.

Wind Dancer bent down and easily scooped up Tonya, who moaned slightly. He followed the other two. The bloodhound would often lunge ahead for ten feet, freeze as if he thought better of the idea, and return to Wind Dancer's side.

Thunder rumbled across an ever-increasing darkened sky. Trying to cross the stream with a kid on his back took careful maneuvering since the river had risen enough to cause the current to accelerate. Although the water still ran clear, a haze clouded it as they exited on the opposite side. Perez appeared a little concerned as she kept checking the sky and cocking her head, as if listening for the unexpected.

"Are we good? Keep going?" he asked as Wind Dancer waited, poised much like a stoic statue at the Museum of Art in Chicago. The dog had run ahead again, and Jacque couldn't help but wonder if he might be keeping an eye on things for them.

"We have to pick up the pace. The river is rising, and I don't want to get caught in any low areas. Most of the trail is high enough, but you remember where I nearly fell off? The water tunnels through there like a beast when there's a flash flood. Rocks fall, trail gets slippery—well, you get the picture," Perez warned as the first rain moved in, slow at first, followed by quick bursts of downpours.

Jacque strained to walk without hunching. When they got to the narrowed path where Perez had nearly met with an accident, the sky opened up and soaked them in a matter of minutes. They continued to press on carefully, with Wind Dancer taking slower steps than the others. He stopped to check on him, and the Pawnee nodded he was okay. In that moment, he wondered if his friend wasn't part mountain goat considering how sure-footed he walked carrying an injured woman who must be at least one hundred twenty pounds.

The trail widened enough for him not to fear if he slipped, he wouldn't fall to a rocky and watery death below. A rock overhang appeared with Perez motioning for them to join her. Jacque was happy to take a break and stretch when he lowered Liam to the ground. He turned to make sure Wind Dancer made it to the overhang. Deep inside, he'd hoped the Pawnee would appear exhausted and stumble to the protective cover. But he moved in like he'd been carrying a picnic basket and once more adjusted his hold on Tonya. He laid her on a flat rock the size of a table, up under the overhang.

Perez quickly checked on her and tried to move soaked hair away from her face. "Wind Dancer, where did you find her?" Her tone hinted at an accusation.

Wind Dancer appeared to pick up on distrust and shifted his gaze between her and Jacque.

"Back there." He raised his stubborn chin to the area where they had just escaped. "Woods."

"And the boy?" she snapped.

This time the Pawnee forced his lips together so hard, they pooched out as his eyes narrowed. "He was lost."

The little guy moved to stand next to the Pawnee. "I go with Wind Dancer," he beamed. "He said to come with him."

Jacque felt like his hard swallow resembled a clap of thunder. The Pawnee was about to incriminate himself.

"Liam, are you saying Wind Dancer led you into the woods?" Perez bent down to be eye to eye with the child.

He nodded vigorously. "Yep. He said 'let's go'. It was dark. I scared. But he say he would keep the monsters away."

The Pawnee laid a hand on the boy's head, but Perez smacked it away and leveled a menacing expression that could crush stone. "Don't you touch him," she snapped.

The bloodhound let loose a growl from deep inside and bared his teeth at Perez, forcing her to step away. Wind Dancer spoke to the dog, and it withdrew, only to observe another distraction down the trail then his new master. The Pawnee jerked his head up and followed the dog's line of sight down the trail.

"We have trouble," he announced, picking up the boy and placing him up with Tonya. "The dog say we are in danger."

Both Perez and Jacque leaned out to try and comprehend why the dog acted peculiar. A dark shape meandered onto the trail, blocking any means of escape.

CHAPTER 13

Cleo jerked on the door handle, as if by doing so would force it open. At the same time, she peered over the roof of the car to the other side to see who stood watching. There was no one there. In that moment a hand touched her elbow, causing a scream to escape.

The person jumped away and nearly fell.

It was the girl from the coffee shop.

"Lady, I'm sorry," she said, laying a hand on her heart. Apparently, she'd scared the girl half to death. "I saw you slip and fall, so I rushed over to help." Timidly, she reached out and dusted gravel and twigs from her denim shirt. She lifted a finger at Cleo's hair. "You got a dead moth in your bangs." Gently, she reached up and removed it.

"Oh," Cleo said in astonishment. "I thought—" She waved the image of an ax murderer away. The whole weirdness of the inn had haunted her ever since she'd left. "Never mind." She slowly turned around to spot the girl's car. "How did you get here? I'm sorry. What's your name?"

"Abby. And my car ran out of gas down the road. My dad is a ranger here. He's not going to be happy I did this again," she moaned. "He told me two days ago to fill up." She put her hands on her hips and smiled. "Something wrong with your car?"

Relief washed over her. "I'm Cleo by the way. I had it worked on yesterday, but it's still not right. Then I locked my keys in the car. I tried to call a friend who is camped in Kewa, but I'm not sure he understood I was broke down."

"Kewa? It's hit or miss with cell phones there. If a storm came up, it might interfere."

Cleo shaded her eyes from the bright-blue sky. "Clear here."

"Those mountain storms pop up all the time. I hear there's a lot going on over there, too. Little boy got lost and a search and rescue worker is also missing. Why, even one of their dogs disappeared." She shivered. "Spooky stuff always happens in that park."

"Like what?"

"A hiker was found dead. No cause of death, they say." She shrugged. "Probably drugs or something. Of course, that place is full of Indian spooks and legends. Superstition is all. But around here, we try to be respectful of those things." She giggled. "Sure is fun around Halloween though."

"I bet. Don't plan to be here then." Cleo noticed the girl's pink tennis shoes then jerked her head up, wide-eyed, at the girl. "Where's your cowboy boots?"

Abby looked down at her feet in surprise then at her. "Cowboy boots? I don't even own a pair of cowboy boots."

~ ~ ~ ~

Both Jacque and Perez ducked under the overhang but not before the large black bear spotted them. His guttural noise made the hair stand up on Jacque's neck. Perez pulled her weapon.

"Not shoot bear," Wind Dancer warned. "It belongs here. We do not."

"I don't want that bear to decide we are intruders and force us over the edge. See that river? It's rising. And if we don't get moving in the next few minutes, the low areas will be covered and we'll be trapped. I only plan to scare it away."

Wind Dancer turned to Jacque. "Do you want me to talk to the bear, buddy?"

"Yes. Make it snappy." Wind Dancer nodded, paused, then gave a thumbs-up, followed by a grin. He edged out onto the path and was immediately soaked from the pelting rain.

Perez's bewildered expression intensified when the Pawnee approached the bear with an abundance of caution. "Are you nuts?" she whispered to Jacque from the corner of her mouth. "He's going to make me shoot that bear."

The bear tossed its head in irritation before it stood up on its hind legs. Wind Dancer outstretched his arms and bowed his head then took a step closer to the bear as it dropped down to all fours again.

"What the hell is he doing?" she mumbled.

"Watch and be amazed," he said as the bloodhound leaned against him.

The bear came so close to the Pawnee that he reached his hand out for it to sniff then laid it gently on the bear's head. He appeared to be speaking to the bear and turned once to show where they hid. In seconds, the bear bellowed, turned away, and lumbered down the trail then into the woods along the ridge.

When Wind Dancer joined them under the overhang, the rain slacked enough to venture out again. Perez eyeballed him with more respect this time as Jacque slapped him across the chest.

"Thanks."

"That was—amazing." Perez's eyes were wide with admiration, but her forehead pinched in disbelief. "What did you do? Say?"

Wind Dancer lifted Tonya in his arms to start the last leg of their hike and frowned down at the petite police chief. "I told bear about Liam being lost and we were trying to take him to his mother. Her cubs were nearby, and she felt we posed danger. When I explained about the boy, she understood. I said that the woman was injured because she tried to protect him."

Jacque lifted the boy to his shoulders after fishing out a poncho from the backpack to cover him. Perez slipped out and started down the path after he handed her both packs. He helped Wind Dancer place his wet jacket over Tonya. At least it would help a little.

"Did the bear really have cubs nearby?"

Wind Dancer adjusted the woman in his arms and smiled at his friend. "No. It was a hungry male. I asked with respect to let us pass. I tell lie to the angry police woman. The story was good?"

A laugh spilled out before he could stop himself as he stepped out in the rain. "Very good. Let's get these two out of the rain and to camp."

The Pawnee nodded and followed his friend.

By the time they came into view of the lake where their camp was located, a half dozen first responders met them on the trail, carrying medical supplies and basic equipment. Tonya was placed on a stretcher and given a quick once-over before they hustled away. The boy wouldn't turn Jacque loose, but the bloodhound followed his master to the section of the trail that circled the lake.

Liam's parents could be spotted running along the water's edge in front of Jacque and Wind Dancer's camp. Their calls of relief and encouragement echoed across the water as the sun broke through the clouds and sent ribbons of bright light to sparkle against the waves that rippled out from where the boy tossed a stone he'd picked up at the overhang.

When they neared camp, the Kendals were waiting with tears streaming down their faces. The father pulled the boy into his arms and hugged him so tight, Jacque wondered if the boy could breathe. The mother surrounded both of them with her arms and sobbed into the little boy's neck, which, of course, scared him.

"What wrong, Mommy?" He patted her head.

"Nothing, baby. Mommy is so glad to see you."

"I am glad to see you, too." He smiled like a little angel.

The mother turned to Jacque and Wind Dancer and hugged each of them. "Thank you. Thank you for bringing back my baby." She laughed through her tears.

One of the first responders joined them. "We should take Liam to the hospital for doctors to check him out. He can ride up front with the driver. Tonya will be in the rear. There's a helicopter waiting at the entrance of the park for her. Liam can take her place once that is taken care of. That okay with you, little guy?" he said then focused on the mother. "You'll be able to get in there with him."

"Use siren?" Liam's eyes widened in anticipation.

The first responder lifted him from his father's arms. "Sure. I'll let you turn it on until we put Tonya on the helicopter. Okay?"

The child clapped his hands and went to the stranger. "Yay! Let's go."

"You folks follow me up. Tonya is going to Santa Fe. Bigger hospital there. We'll be taking Liam to the one in Sunset Rock. If he needs more attention, then we'll deal with that. Might be staying overnight, so if you need to pack a bag, do it quick."

Ellie leaned in and kissed her son. He snaked out an arm to pull her in for a hug. "Love you, Mommy."

This brought another round of tears. "Love you, too, big guy. Proud of you."

He wiggled free of the first responder and ran to Wind Dancer who caught him up in his arms. "You brave warrior, Liam."

When he placed him on the ground, he reached over and hugged Jacque's legs. Jacque felt a strange emotion well up inside him as he laid a hand on the child's head. "If you want to see that helicopter, you better go, Liam."

In seconds, the little guy was being buckled into the passenger side of the ambulance.

Since the Kendals' car was too damaged to drive, Jacque offered to drive them. While they ran to the tent to pack a few things, Perez turned to him, jamming her finger into his chest like a loaded gun.

"I want you two at headquarters after you drop the parents off." She shifted her attention to Wind Dancer and eyed him top to bottom then snarled. "Don't think because you scared that bear off, I'm impressed with you."

Wind Dancer straightened his shoulders as his one eyebrow arched in a controlled slow burn. "Don't think because you carry a badge and a gun, I am afraid of you." He took a threatening step toward her, causing Jacque to wedge himself between them. Gently, he nudged Wind Dancer to the side. He knew full well the strength the Pawnee possessed since he'd crossed over through a parallel universe, could easily send him flying into the air, without much effort. His senses, strength, and physical abilities had skyrocketed because of it. Jacque reminded himself the Pawnee was like a toddler in charge of the launch codes to World War III.

"Let's take a breath," Jacque said, turning to Perez. "We're all tired. Let me take these folks to the hospital, and we'll swing by to talk. But honestly, I'm beat. I need a shower, hot food, and about ten hours of sleep. I know you gotta feel the same way."

Perez tried to stifle a yawn as she nodded. "Okay. I'm running on fumes." She offered a weak grin on one corner of her mouth. "Tell you what. Let me buy you lunch, and we'll have a friendly conversation."

"Deal," he said extending his hand.

She eyed it a few seconds then gripped it.

When she walked away, Wind Dancer shoved him, causing him to stumble. He jerked around, feeling anger at his friend. "What the hell, Wind Dancer? You nearly knocked me into what's left of the campfire."

"I do nothing wrong. She wants to put me in jail. That would be a mistake," he warned.

Jacque could only imagine what would happen if Wind Dancer was forced to do something he didn't want to do. This would be a slippery slope. Maybe they could talk about what really happened after they got the Kendals to the hospital. Before he had time to run that suggestion by his friend, the anxious parents hustled to join them.

With the passengers tucked in their seats, Jacque carried the bags to toss in the rear of the SUV. When he started to open the hatch, Wind Dancer grabbed his arm.

"Jacque?" He lifted his chin toward the woods then the lake. "The bear say one more in danger."

CHAPTER 14

Cleo second-guessed herself about seeing a pair of cowboy boots on the other side of the car, even as she walked around to inspect the area. Nothing indicated anyone else had been there. There wasn't much room between the car and where the thick brush grew.

"Are you sure you didn't see someone standing next to the car when you walked up?" Cleo retraced her steps carefully, continuing to examine the ground in case she missed something. When Abby didn't answer, she found her scrolling through her phone. Clearing her throat for the teen's attention, Abby casually glanced away from the screen.

"What? Oh no. Didn't see a thing." Her carefree laugh spoke volumes. "Nearly missed you. I guess I was on my phone. This guy from school started texting me and well"—she sighed then rolled her eyes skyward—"he is so dope."

"Dope? He's dumb or on drugs?" Cleo realized an asteroid the size of a school bus could have crashed behind her, and the response would be similar.

Another lighthearted laugh. "No. Oh, I forgot you're older." When Cleo could feel her face contort into a frown, the girl backtracked. "Not that you look old or anything. That means cool or awesome. No offense by the way. I mean you don't look old or anything. Really," she insisted.

"Gee. Thanks." This was one of those times she wanted to reenact a dance she'd learned as a child at the Field Museum of Chicago, from an obscure tribe, and turn the girl into a poison dart frog and make her bite herself. Or maybe a voodoo doll would work. She remembered a few curses and inwardly chanted it over and over until the girl broke her concentration on the phone.

"Let's go find my dad. He should be at the check-in hut. It isn't far."

"Why don't we just call the garage in town? I think I remember seeing a tow truck parked there. I've got AAA. I'll have him bring you a gallon of gas, and your dad will never know." She felt badly about trying to deceive the girl's dad.

"Won't work. I saw it pulling out before I left the coffee shop. Probably a tourist along the road in trouble. Happens all the time. People were pouring in when I left." She moved toward the entrance. "Come on. Not far."

Not far turned into thirty minutes uphill. By the time they reached the check in booth, Cleo was sweating, and the girl had started to complain about the heat.

"Hmm. Wonder where Dad went?" The door was locked, but the screened windows were open.

Cleo touched a note taped to the door. "Says he had to find campers who didn't check out. Is that normal?"

"Yeah. Some decide to stay another night but forget to let the rangers know. Dad has to make sure they're okay. We do have bears and mountain lions." She sighed and put her hands on her hips before surveying the area like it was no big deal. "I've lived here my whole life and never seen either of those. And I live out in the country where my closest neighbor is a half mile away." Cleo took out her own phone. No bars again. "Do you have any bars on your phone?"

"Nope. Never do here. Too many trees and rocks. If we take the trail up to that ridge, we could."

"Let's not." Cleo decided she should go to the gym with Jacque. After the smallpox scare in Chicago, she'd worked a lot of fifteen-hour days. There wasn't any energy left to exercise. The last six months had slowed down, and she'd taken a much-deserved break to recharge.

She spotted a rough-hewn bench nearby. "Let's sit a few minutes." She felt relieved there was a bench at a scenic overlook. Once more, she checked her phone and felt optimistic at seeing two bars. She quickly dialed Jacque.

"Cleo?" The voice of her grumpy detective friend sounded like heaven. "Cleo?"

"Jacque, I'm stranded at Carson National Park. My car quit. I'm parked out at the front entrance. Blue sedan."

"Cleo?"

Static.

"Jacque," she yelled into the phone then repeated the call for help. The line went dead.

"Told ya." Abby shrugged and leaned over the edge of the protective guardrail. "Dad is way over there, I bet. Since his truck isn't here, he probably won't be long. Sit down. I think you're a little wore out."

Cleo hurried over to sit next to the girl before she insinuated again that she might be old. Guess if you're sixteen, everything else feels ancient. Was she ever that way? Growing up in a natural history museum with a father who worked as a cultural anthropologist of Native American culture, age had a whole different meaning to her. Maybe she could make an effort to be more fashionable now, although Wind Dancer had told her many times how beautiful she was and that she was perfect.

The thought of his love gave her confidence. Their time together had been a series of amusing mishaps and discovery. There was no one else she wanted to be with for the rest of her life. He completed her. The thought that the day might come where he might choose to return to his time had never come up. When he had appeared lost in thought, quiet, or distant, Cleo told him she'd understand if he wanted to return home to his people. His response was, "Someday but not today."

She longed to see him. They had not been apart this long since he'd returned from his world a year ago. He gave her peace and created a safe cocoon around her life. For the first time since he'd returned, she felt alone and vulnerable.

Something didn't feel right.

A rumble of thunder drew her eyes upward. Dark clouds rolled across the sky, followed by a breeze that made the pines sound like whispers. The temperature cooled immediately.

"That's weird. I don't remember hearing of a storm coming today," Abby said as she walked to the railing and squinted up at the sky. "Probably one of those pop-up storms." She shoved her phone in her pocket. "My battery is dead."

The first drop of rain fell before a flash of lightning caused the two to flinch.

"Is there a place we can wait for your dad? I don't think we can make it back to your car before the storm hits." Cleo wished she'd stayed with the car. Surely someone would have driven by to flag down for a rescue.

"There's a picnic pavilion down there, just before the road curves. See it?" Even before Cleo agreed, the girl ran in that direction. "Come on," she called as the sky opened up, drenching them immediately. "Run," she laughed.

Oh, to be young again. She took off after her and managed to come alongside as they reached the pavilion. It was large enough to hold six picnic tables and a built-in barbeque area on one end. It, too, had a nice view of the surrounding mountains and valley below. The beat of the rain on the metal roof grew deafening as the two stood between the two rows of picnic tables.

Abby rubbed her arms then felt her pockets. "Oh no! My phone must have fallen out." A bolt of spider-like lightning danced across the sky, causing them to jump.

"We'll find it when this is over. See the sky in the west. Already clear." Cleo spotted a patch of blue in the sky.

The girl frowned then started to pace. "My phone. I had to beg to get that."

"I'm sure your dad will understand." The rain stopped as quickly as it began. Cleo stuck her hand out from under the pavilion to feel only a few reluctant drops of rain before pulling out her own phone. "I now have three bars," Cleo announced as she dialed. She stepped out toward the view where there was more open space and fewer trees. "I'm calling 911 after I try my friends again."

"Whatever. I'm looking for my phone. It's got to be close."

"Sure. I'm right behind you." Cleo turned away when the girl meandered onto the road and scanned their steps carefully.

"I'll be right here trying to pick up the pieces of my boring life without a phone," Abby moaned.

Cleo chuckled as she rang Jacque's phone. "Answer. Answer," she ordered. Once more, she heard his voice mail was full. "Rats. No answer. Calling 911." Abby waved as if she continued her search. The phone rang, but like with Jacque, there was too much static to be understood, even though she tried to make her situation known before it disconnected. "Great."

Shoving her phone into her jeans pocket, Cleo hurried out onto the road to help Abby in the search for the Holy Grail Phone.

"Abby?"

Turning in a complete circle, she now realized the girl had vanished, except for her pink tennis shoes.

Liam jumped up and down outside the ambulance as he held onto the hand of the ambulance driver. The helicopter crew secured Tonya inside with several first responders standing by, in what Jacque guessed, might be support.

The Kendals joined their son and encouraged him to get in the ambulance. Mom got to ride with him this time, and Ty remained with Jacque and Wind Dancer. When the helicopter lifted off, the ambulance pulled out onto the highway with Perez following close behind. There had been a number of cars pull in or slow to watch the emergency vehicles. This kept Jacque from pulling out to join them. By the time he eased out, the others had disappeared from sight.

What was it about tragedy that ignited people's curiosity? He had always thought of it as morbid and twisted.

"Don't worry, Ty. We'll catch up with them." Jacque checked the rearview mirror to make eye contact with the dad. He returned a weak smile and a nod.

"Wind Dancer, where was he?" The troubled father gripped the headrest of the Pawnee's seat and leaned forward.

"He very far away. Lost."

"Why did he wander off? Did he say?"

"Didn't wander. Taken." Wind Dancer sounded matter-of-fact.

"It carry the boy after taking his shoes."

Jacque shot him a look of alarm. "He was wearing his shoes when we met up."

"Yes. Took woman, too. She tried to protect boy. He made her still."

"Wind Dancer, how did he make her still?" asked the father.

"I do not know. He very strong. He leave to go hunt more. I find them. Shoes there. I thought she was dead. Boy sitting next to her, crying and holding her hand. He tell me she fought him. When he see me, I hold him until he stop crying. He put on shoes I found. Then we leave. Said monster not far."

"Did you see it?" Jacque noticed the sign for Kewa Park and wondered why that sounded familiar. There was an abandoned car near the entrance. He slowed when he saw a tow truck hooking up another small sedan a little farther away. Before he could let his thought processes wander, Wind Dancer continued.

"No. But I feel it. Evil. I think it followed us, but I faster than him. But he bigger."

"If you didn't see it, how do you know it was bigger?" asked the father.

Jacque toyed with the mirror again. "Don't ask. He just knows, Ty. He has a sixth sense. It's a gift."

"Oh." Ty's forehead wrinkled in apparent confusion, or maybe it was disbelief. A couple of years ago, Jacque would have called a doctor from the psych ward to come and get anyone who said this kind of stupid stuff. "I didn't get to check him over. Was he hurt?"

Wind Dancer turned in his seat to address the worried father. He touched his head. "He very scared and hurt inside. I know nothing else. I will catch this person and kill him."

"Whoa, there, buddy. Let's not get all John Wayne on us, okay?"

"John Wayne? Is that the name of this man?"

"No. It was a joke. John Wayne is a cowboy or movie soldier." Jacque reached over and patted the Pawnee's arm. "He's a hero to a lot of Americans."

"I remember now. He killed a lot of Indians."

Jacque put both hands on the wheel and sighed. He really didn't want to do this kind of conversation now. "It was pretend. Not real."

"Why is—"

"Wind Dancer," he snapped. "We'll have this conversation later. Got it?"

The Pawnee straightened in his seat and stared out the windshield. "Got it, buddy."

Jacque stole another glimpse at his passenger in the mirror and forced a grin, followed by a nonchalant shrug. Ty nodded and turned his attention out his window.

Breaking the speed limit helped catch the caravan of first responders. It didn't take long to reach the small hospital. The emergency room staff was waiting for Liam and his family. Within minutes, the child was whisked away, his parents following, offering words of encouragement.

Perez gathered with Tonya's friends who arrived, unaware she'd been transported to Santa Fe. She nodded in their direction, as if directing their attention to Wind Dancer in curiosity. They soon filed out in groups of two and three, a few nodding to Wind Dancer and several others who told him thanks for bringing Tonya out to them.

Jacque felt pride in his friend who nodded and said, "Sure," a few times. The man was an imposing figure with his chiseled face and rock-hard stature. When he shifted his eyes to take in the room, Jacque couldn't help but compare him to one of those science-fiction cyborg types. It continued to be intimidating to anyone he met.

Perez joined them, lifting her chin in a kind of show of being in charge. "Let's go get lunch. We can make this easy, if that's okay with you." She was speaking to Wind Dancer mostly, but all he did was give her the cyborg stare when his bottom lip stuck out a little farther.

"Sounds good to me. Huh, Joseph?" He finally used the first name he and Cleo had given him when he'd first crossed over to this universe. When the Pawnee shifted the icy gaze to him, he remembered the call from Cleo. "Nearly forgot. Cleo called earlier." He pulled out his phone and checked for a voice mail and realized he needed to empty the inbox.

"She coming soon?" Wind Dancer asked as he grabbed the phone from him and held it up to his ear. "Cleopatra?"

"She's not there. Called earlier. I couldn't understand what she said. Something about…" he paused and pieced together what he thought she said as a fear bomb hit his stomach. He was so caught up in getting to the little boy and Wind Dancer that he'd brushed her off. "I'll just try and call her." The Pawnee returned the phone to him. "We're going to get you one of these when we get home."

"You don't have a cell phone?" Perez asked incredulously.

"No. He doesn't. Don't make any smoke signal jokes, either. He doesn't like it." The phone rang until it went to voice mail. "Sorry, Cleo. Couldn't talk earlier. You aren't going to believe how much fun we're having. Not. Joseph is missing you. Call me."

"I am not having fun," Wind Dancer declared as a frown distorted his usual handsome face.

"I was making a joke."

The three moved toward the automatic sliding doors.

"A John Wayne joke?"

The doors swooshed open.

Jacque took a long, deep breath and shoved his phone in his pocket. "Oh, brother. Let's get something to eat and then we'll head to our camp."

Perez reached her patrol car and motioned for them to get inside. "We'll see about that."

The catlike smile unnerved Jacque. His friend might be in trouble if Tonya didn't wake up, and Liam couldn't give a decent account of what happened.

CHAPTER 16

Even though the sun burst through the clouds, sending ribbons of light through the trees, Cleopatra Sommers felt a darkness spring up all around her as she lifted the pink tennis shoes and held them close.

A limb cracked and fell behind her, causing her to whirl around and cry out for Abby, yet again, but she knew the girl was gone. A dark figure moved from behind a boulder half covered in brush. It hunkered down and moved farther into the protection of the trees. She felt transfixed with what she saw, paralyzed with a blend of curiosity and terror. Then it disappeared into a misty, vapor cloud, caused by the streams of sunlight and mist that dripped onto the warm earth.

Panic gripped her as she ran to the ranger shack and jerked on the doorknob, over and over, to pull it open with no success. There was still no sign of Abby. She screamed her name before deciding to run toward the park entrance. Even though she covered a lot of ground because it gently sloped downward, the gravel caused her to slip and fall to one knee several times, ripping her jeans.

When she tried to get up, a blur caught in her peripheral vision. She scampered to her feet and fought against the exhaustion plaguing her body, along with the pain in the bloody knee.

The entrance of the park came into focus as she heard footsteps behind her. They sounded distant but steady. Barreling through the entrance, she tried to steal a look over her shoulder for mere seconds. That's when she spotted a familiar SUV speed by.

"Jacque," she tried to scream, but the words came out like the croak of a frog. Waving frantically, she tried to call out. "Jacque." This time her words were filled with disappointment and muffled as she dragged her sleeve across her face to wipe away the cascade of tears. Hope evaporated, until she noticed a white tow truck down the road a ways, where Abby had abandoned her car. Cleo found herself backing toward the tow truck in order to see if whatever followed her had stopped. When no one appeared, she pivoted and ran to the truck parked in front of Abby's car.

"Hello?" Cleo ran to where Abby's car had run out of gas. "Hello?" she called once more, now turning in circles in hopes of finding a knight in shining armor to get her to a safe place. "My phone."

She reached in her pocket only to discover it was gone. It must have fallen out when she fell. There was no way she wanted to search for it, considering something lurked in the park.

Where was the driver? Maybe the truck had a CB radio or at least a phone.

"Hello?" She reached up and grabbed the door handle and turned. It felt stuck as she tugged hard. When it came open, she fell onto the ground, catching herself with her hands. Instantly she became aware she'd broken her left wrist. A bone twisted outward in a hideous warning of possible surgery.

Sitting upright, she lifted her eyes to the cab of the truck. Slumped across the seat lay the driver. Cleo scrambled up without giving another thought to herself and rushed to the cab. With awkward momentum, using only one hand, she managed to pull herself up onto the step-up outside the door.

Reaching in, she shook him, then did her best to pull him up. He was slight of build, and she managed to tilt him up enough to see that it was the young man, Tinker, who had so irritated the garage owner. It took awkward effort, but she managed to grab his wrist. There was no pulse, and his eyes were wide open. The expression reminded her of her patients who had come into the ER with gunshot wounds, knowing full well they weren't going to survive. Pure terror.

Luckily there was a radio, but the microphone was missing. When she turned it on, there was no static or chatter from other radio operators. It, too, was dead. Quickly, she did a search for something to be used as a weapon. Under the seat was a lug wrench. She pulled it through a combination of discarded coffee cups, hamburger wrappers, and various sticky candy papers stuck to what appeared to be a sex toy.

"Eww. Gross." There was hand sanitizer in her purse but locked in her car.

Funny, the things you think of in a stressful situation.

She stole a glance out the window and relief washed over her when no one appeared. Gingerly, she eased out onto the cab ledge and tried to navigate her way down onto the step-up. Balancing the lug wrench with her good hand and grabbing the steering wheel with the other with the broken wrist proved a bad idea. A pain shot up her arm as instinct forced her to release her grip and plummet toward the ground.

The lug wrench swung up and hit her in the face just before the end smacked into her chest. In that split second, before she sprawled into the dirt, a pair of hands wrapped around her lower body but couldn't stop her momentum. The wind was knocked out of her when she hit the gravel. She grabbed her chest when a man's face shrouded in a shadow, hovered above her. With the sun shining behind him, it was impossible to distinguish any features. With a quick intake of air, she tried to use her legs for traction to escape but hands reached down to stop her.

~ ~ ~ ~

Jacque watched Perez nibble on the last French fry out of her veggie burger basket, suck on the last of her lemonade from the bottom of her cup, then lean back in her chair. She leveled a hard observation at Wind Dancer and tried to smile, but it came across as a tight, narrowed appraisal.

"Why don't you start from the beginning, Joseph." She tilted her head and appeared to be calm.

Jacque didn't like it. He'd used the same technique many times when he tried to subliminally get inside the suspect's head and get them to trust him. Wind Dancer didn't pick up on such tactics and was suspicious by nature. The Pawnee had learned a lot about the white man in the short time he'd lived among them in Chicago. One of those important lessons was to be careful. He once asked Jacque about why the white man spoke out of both sides of his mouth.

"I don't know, buddy. I don't think all of us are that way. The people you've met have a hidden agenda, most likely."

"Agenda? I do not know this word."

"A plan. Like a menu at a restaurant. You know what I mean? There are things to choose from that you might want. With the people we meet in the police department, there are times it's criminals and other times it's politicians. But they all want something. They have a plan or agenda which will help them get it."

"If politicians and criminals want the same thing, why do you not arrest them?"

The conversation had lasted into the night after he took a pizza to Cleo's condo, just like every Wednesday night. She'd worked late and fallen asleep on the couch while the men talked. Jacque had to admit, he enjoyed the talks. Those nights, he and Cleo shared American history and life in general with their unusual friend. These moments made him feel like a teacher, given Wind Dancer's lack of twenty-first-century knowledge.

Jacque jerked his mental wanderings to the here and now. The Pawnee folded his arms across his chest before shifting those cyborg eyes to him for direction, he guessed.

"Why don't you just ask him what you want to know, Chief? That way we don't waste a lot of unnecessary time."

Perez never wavered from her steely-eyed connection with Wind Dancer. "Okay. Where did you find the boy and Tonya?"

"Where the flat rocks stack up. I hear water. Maybe a waterfall." Wind Dancer became laser focused on the chief. "Boy was cold. No shoes."

"Yet, he had shoes on when we found you." He didn't respond. She switched her attention to Jacque with a bewildered gaze.

"That wasn't a question, Chief. You are going to have to be more specific." Jacque rubbed his jaw in irritation before addressing his friend. "And you need to stop being hardheaded. You know the drill."

"Hardheaded? I do not—"

"Yes, you do," he snapped. "Answer the damn questions so we can get out of here. If you know something more, then tell her. I know you did nothing wrong. But you sure as hell act guilty." Jacque thought for a split second a grin toyed with the corner of Wind Dancer's mouth. He realized in that moment, the Pawnee had expanded his understanding of modern-day lingo, along with the art of "the stall."

Wind Dancer shifted his gaze to Perez. "The shoes were nearby. I helped him put them on. The woman hurt. I needed to get her to camp. I held the boy until he felt safe. He say the monster disappeared for a while then go get Tonya. Boy on a high rock. All alone. He could have fell if not for woman. She hurt but stopped boy from moving around so much. Told him help would come. That was me."

"That is at least five miles away from the camp, from what you're describing."

"Yes. Long way."

"How did you get them down?"

"I first bring boy then go get the woman. I worried monster come before I can get them to safe place. She heavy and rocks were…" He turned to Jacque and skidded his hand across the palm of his other hand. "How do you say it?"

"Slick?"

He nodded. "Slick. The rocks were slick. I almost fall two times. I think we should go different way so monster not find us."

"Did you smell him?" Jacque asked. For some reason, Wind Dancer's senses and strength had increased immensely when he crossed over to this universe. Several times the Pawnee had helped him in his police work by using his sense of smell.

"No. But I hear it. Slow."

"You can smell people? That's preposterous."

Jacque groaned knowing that was a big word for his friend to know, but then he surprised him. He leaned in to explain when the Pawnee held up his hand.

"I can tell by the sound of your voice, the squint eyes on your face, you do not understand the ways of holes in the universe." He unfolded his arms and leaned on the table. "I smell the same blood in you as in me, and you know what I say is truth. There are things in our world, the world of our ancestors, you have forgotten to believe. I come from another time and place. This monster may be from a hole."

"A sipapu."

"Is this a hole?" Wind Dancer asked with interest.

She nodded and waved her empty glass at the waiter to refill. When another drink arrived, Perez continued. "The hole is called a sipapu and found in the north corner of an underground chamber called a kiva. Native people say it represents the Ancestral Puebloan's emergence from the underworld."

A shiver tingled its way up Jacque's back. "Great. More spooky crap I have to get used to."

"A kiva was also used by Puebloans for rites and political meetings. It was connected to the kachina belief system."

"Field Museum have kachinas in gift shop," Wind Dancer informed Jacque and slapped him on the shoulder, as if saying he should know this already. "Remember?"

He shoved the Pawnee's hand away. "Hell no. You know I don't like all that creepy stuff in the Field Museum. Mummies. Voodoo. Shrunken heads. Pawnee earth lodge. Skinwalkers. I'll do my shopping at a good old Army surplus store or a gas station like normal people."

This made Wind Dancer chuckle. Something he didn't do often. "Out here, you are not normal people."

"Anyway, kachinas are benevolent spirits for the most part. But there are evil ones, the most noteworthy one being Chaveyo." Perez took a long drink of her lemonade and motioned for the check. "He is portrayed as a giant ogre who trots around on the hunt for victims. He wears a skin mask with bits of cedar bark fixed to the top. Oh, and he carries a war ax and a saber which he uses as a staff more times than not."

"Sounds like a heck of a guy," Jacque said as he snatched the check from the waiter. "It's on me. Thanks for creeping me out. It's not like I didn't have enough to give me nightmares around here. So much for a relaxing vacation. If I wanted drama, I would have stayed home." He stood.

"Where are you going? I'm just getting started." Perez jabbed a finger toward the chair. "Sit down."

CHAPTER 17

"I don't take orders from you, Chief Perez. Keep that in mind." Jacque straightened to his six-foot height and squared his shoulders. "Unless you're going to charge us with something, then I suggest you change your tone."

The chief let a dangerous smile spread across her generous lips that he really didn't want to admire.

"You're absolutely right. I apologize. Let's head to your car and we can finish this up like civilized adults."

Wind Dancer opened his mouth to make a comment, but Jacque held up his hand to stop him. "Not a word from you. Let's go get our car then we can head out."

Once in the car, Perez casually asked a few more questions of Wind Dancer. This of course was a bad idea, since being in a car caused all kinds of sensations in him, one being fear. Fortunately, they didn't have to go far before they exited the car and stood in the shade.

"Okay. Wind Dancer, you started to walk out of the park. How did you know where to go?" Perez didn't waste any time returning to the interrogation of the Pawnee.

"I find trail and a sign had a map. Tonya had a flashlight so I could use it to see the sign. The boy hold it for me. Tonya heavy."

"Yes. I'll be sure to tell her that when she wakes up."

"Good. She smell like those sweet round things."

"Donuts," Jacque explained.

"Yes," Wind Dancer continued. "I think maybe she eat many of those. Jacque says they make you heavy."

Perez arched an eyebrow in his direction. "I bet he has a lot to say about women."

"He say better to lie than tell the truth to a woman so she doesn't go postal."

Her jaw appeared to flex as her eyes narrowed at the detective. "Really?" She dragged the word out like a child pulling Silly Putty.

"Well, I'm sure this is all taken out of context on your part," Jacque interjected as he leaned against the car door and rubbed his face in a nervous act of trying to maintain control. "I was merely telling my friend here that sometimes it was better not to answer a question directly."

Wind Dancer nodded. "Like 'does this dress make me look fat?' I say yes and Cleo not happy."

"Does Jacque ever tell you to lie to the police?"

Wind Dancer folded his arms across his chest again. "He tell me I have the right to remain silent."

"I think we're getting off track here, Chief." He nodded to Wind Dancer who mimicked an intimidating opponent. "You need to tell the chief what you did next, after finding the trail."

Wind Dancer shifted his eyes from Jacque to the police chief. If the narrowed expression had been a laser, her head would have been seared off and rolling across the parking lot. He clearly didn't like her, and the feeling appeared to be mutual.

"I follow. Hard for boy to keep up. Stop many times until I let him climb onto my back. He very tired."

Perez shifted her attention between the two men with bewilderment etched in her slow-to-blink eyes. "You carried both of them?"

"I am very strong. It was"—he stopped and searched for a word— "awkward. But soon I knew the monster was not close. He go other way. We rested. I follow sound of water. I hoped it would lead to camp. Rested again until I hear you."

Now her attention turned to Jacque. "How is it this guy can do that and not break a sweat or be just a tiny bit frazzled? Is he some kind of freak of nature? And what's with the way he talks? Are you guys messing with me?"

Wind Dancer straightened and dropped his arms to his side. "I do not mess with woman called Tonya. That is against the law and evil. Jacque not mess with you for same reason. You think bad of us and not know we are good. I don't like your words."

"It's okay, buddy. She isn't talking about messing with women to hurt them. She means she is confused and thinks we are tricking her, maybe teasing her about the information."

"I always tell the truth." He paused. "Except when Cleo asked about that dress."

This, apparently, she found amusing because she grinned. "I apologize, Joseph Wind Dancer. You are such a throwback to another time that I just can't wrap my head around what you're saying."

Jacque knew that mental picture to his friend would generate a lot more questions, so he held up his hand, a signal to the Pawnee, not to speak or ask any questions until later.

"Did Tonya ever regain consciousness. I mean wake up?"

"Moan but no words. Open eyes once. Scared of me, I think. I tell her taking to get help. Then she sleeps more but can't wake up after that."

Both Jacque's and Perez's phone started buzzing at the same time. Checking the caller ID, he realized it was Cleo again.

"Hey, Cleo. Sorry, I'm just returning your call. It's been…" He heard crying. "Cleo?" More sobbing. "Cleo," he yelled. All he could hear was a distortion of his name. "Tell me where you are?"

"Kewa—" The line went dead.

"Cleo's in trouble," he said to Wind Dancer whose face had morphed into an angry, dark picture of rage. "We need to find her."

Perez clicked off and jumped in her car. "Better follow me. There's been another murder, along with a missing and injured female."

"Cleo," growled the Pawnee. "I will kill this monster if he has hurt her." The man must have been a formidable warrior in his time because his taut posture and rage forming in those narrowed eyes, gave him an idea of what would happen if Cleo had been hurt.

When they pulled out onto the highway, an ambulance was

already driving up behind them. With lights flashing and the siren going full blast, for the first time in his life, Jacque felt a wave of panic for his friend whom he'd left in danger. He would never forgive himself if something had happened to her. Even as his speed increased, it felt like they were going in slow motion.

Wind Dancer remained rigid and mute until he swerved in behind Perez and slammed on his brakes. Before he could put the vehicle in park, the Pawnee had removed the seat belt by jerking it from the connection. He threw open the door and jumped out. Jacque fumbled with his own restraints for a second then rushed after the Pawnee.

The ambulance arrived, blocking their path, allowing Jacque to catch up with the Pawnee. Perez stood on the other side of the ambulance talking to the driver. Coming around the vehicle, Wind Dancer rushed forward as a woman lunged into his arms.

"Cleopatra," Wind Dancer breathed as he picked her up in a bear hug and buried his face into her red hair. He sat her feet on the ground, but she didn't release him. "Are you hurt?"

The paramedics swarmed in and touched her gently, only to have Wind Dancer shove them away.

Jacque tugged her gently away from the Pawnee and felt sick at seeing the bruise on her face and clearly a broken wrist. He wrapped his arms around her and stared at his friend, feeling the same kind of rage well up inside him as he'd seen in Wind Dancer.

"I'm so sorry, Cleo." He rubbed the back of her head then kissed her cheek. "I didn't know you were here."

"I was so scared," she choked. She reached out to Wind Dancer and pulled him in for a group hug.

"Okay. Enough of this kumbaya moment. Wind Dancer, the paramedic wants to treat her injuries. This isn't up for discussion. Don't make me shoot you." Perez started talking to a ranger and motioned for Jacque. "Stay with her, buddy. She's hurt. Okay?"

"I kill this thing." His voice sounded primal.

"We'll talk about this later. Don't be making threats that could come back to haunt you."

The dark rage remained in his eyes in spite of nodding compliance as he moved to join the ranger and Perez.

The ranger had a cut over his eye and panic filled his voice.

"She's a baby, Chief. We gotta find her. She's my only child."

Perez touched his arm in a show of support. "We're going to find her, Marty." She turned to Jacque. "The girl vanished when Ms. Sommers turned away to make a call. To you, I'm assuming. You kept getting calls from her as I remember."

"Yeah. Wouldn't go through."

"She got stranded here, and Abby, Marty's daughter, ran out of gas. That's her car down a ways. I remember seeing the driver getting it ready to tow. Anyway, the driver is dead and the girl is missing. I've called in search and rescue, along with the highway patrol. I'm sure locals will come in for the search, too. Still early afternoon. Plenty of time to find her."

"Ms. Sommers says my Abby was looking for her phone, but I found it near the pavilion in the middle of the road. Your friend found her shoes, but she was gone. Gone." His voice cracked. Tears rolled down his cheek.

"Marty, we're going to send an officer after your wife, okay? Anyone else I should contact, a priest, friend, or other family members?" He shrugged and turned watery eyes to the sky. "Well I'm going to have Officer McClure wait with you a few minutes in case you think of anyone. In the meantime, I'll send for Betty. I'll be back in a few minutes to ask you a few questions. Coffee is on the way and some food. I want you to keep up your strength."

"I have to go find Abby."

"Yes. But right now, you need to calm down and think clearly before you do that. It will make things easier. Now you go with Officer McClure." She waved toward another officer with a bulging belly and red cheeks. A few quick instructions for the officer then she tilted her head toward Jacque to follow her.

He shoved his hands on his hips impatiently as he caught a glimpse of the paramedics treating Cleo. The Pawnee turned slightly and met his gaze. They still held a controlled rage. Besides piecing together what had happened to the girl, he wanted to keep an eye on Wind Dancer. Dropping his hands to his side, he joined Perez at the ambulance.

"Cleo. Right?" Perez had turned on the charm. She'd never spoken to him in such a personable tone. Maybe it was to keep his friend calm and clearheaded. "I have to ask you a few questions. Are you okay with that?" Cleo nodded as the paramedic wrapped her wrist. "Can you tell me anything about what you saw?"

Wind Dancer frowned at the chief then nodded to Cleo and answered for her.

"It was Chaveyo, the evil one."

CHAPTER 18

The chief's face contorted in disgust as her lips pooched out at the mere mention of Chaveyo. Jacque imagined if that kind of threat got out, it could affect the tourist trade around these parts. Considering how far apart these towns were and lack of industry, he guessed tourism to be the main bread and butter for the locals.

"Chaveyo? Seriously?" Perez twisted her mouth where her speech spilled from the corner. It gave her the appearance of a bully, which he was coming to realize, she was exactly that. "That's a folktale. Nothing to it. I should never have mentioned it at the restaurant." She glowered at Wind Dancer for a few seconds before shifting her attention to Cleo. "Cleo." The pit bull growl offered a warning when Jacque stepped up to defuse the moment.

"Why don't you let me ask the questions, Chief? Cleo knows me, and, clearly, she's upset."

Cleo smiled weakly at him and nodded a thank-you to the paramedic. "I'm okay, Jacque. You two are so protective." She leaned against Wind Dancer who slipped an arm around her shoulders to hold her tight. "I saw you drive by. I tried to wave you down, but you kept going."

"If you were prettier, I might have noticed. I keep telling you to get a makeover," he said offhandedly as he cocked his head. Even though she pursed her lips in attitude, a smile still teased the corners of her mouth. Perez on the other hand appeared to want to jump in to her defense. "You're a mess," he added.

"The medicine man thinks she broke her wrist." Wind Dancer raised his chin toward the paramedic, who also appeared to be Native American. The corner of his mouth turned up at the reference.

Cleo sucked up as much air as she could and stepped away from Wind Dancer in a flimsy show of bravery and calm. "Okay. Ask away. I know the drill. I didn't really see anything. One minute, Abby was there. I tried to call you—oh, and by the way, clean up your voice mail box, will you? Anyway, it really was all of ten seconds I looked away. Turned around and she was gone. I called, and called," she whimpered, "and all I found were her pink tennis shoes."

Jacque didn't usually get upset with this part of investigation because he never knew the victim or the story behind it. It was but one piece of the puzzle. But Cleopatra Sommers was his friend. He could feel his blood pressure spike at not being able to make her fear go away. She was a good person and could fix a gunshot wound while telling a gang banger to chill out or she'd kick his butt. Other than nearly losing Wind Dancer to another world, he'd never seen her this shaken.

"Did you see anyone?"

"Yes. No. I'm not sure. There was something moving in the brush. Big or maybe tall. It blended in with the surroundings so much, it could have been an animal. I thought I heard a guttural sound. There was a smell."

"A smell?" It was Perez.

"Yes. Like spoiled meat. Or maybe the smell a dog gives off when it's scared. Know what I mean?"

Perez nodded.

"Cleo, you managed to get out this far. Was something still following you?"

Marty, Abby's father joined them. "It was me. I found Abby's phone near the pavilion. Her initials are on that cover, so I knew it was hers. I left my truck at the pavilion because I thought Abby was nearby and might be in trouble. I hurried to the welcome center shack and thought I could see a person running then disappear around the curve. The shack was jarred open and ransacked. The extra set of keys to my truck were gone so I ran after this lady, thinking she'd broken in and stolen them."

Cleo rested her sympathetic gaze on the distraught father. "That's the weird part. I couldn't get into the shack. I thought something was moving in the brush. So, I ran. I hoped I could get to my car." She pointed to her knee where a portion of her jeans had been cut away from her knee. A large bandage now covered the area where she'd ripped it open. "I covered a lot of ground because the road went downhill. Once when I fell, I thought I noticed movement again." Shaking her head, Cleo ran her hand through her hair to shove it away from her face.

"The same as you saw earlier near the pavilion?" It was Perez, who held up a hand for Jacque not to interrupt her.

"I don't know. Maybe. I just wanted to run. It ran alongside me in the woods. I could feel it."

"But it didn't come out?" Jacque interjected.

"No. Then it stopped. I could see the entrance and I ran and ran and ran…" her voice trailed off as Wind Dancer took her hand and tugged her into his arms.

"I will find him." Wind Dancer's face showed a murderous rage that concerned Jacque.

"And what do you think you'll do if you find him?" Perez snapped impatiently.

"Kill him," he said without hesitation.

Perez shifted her attention from Wind Dancer to Jacque. Her frown spoke volumes.

"What he means, Chief Perez, is that he will make sure whoever this is will be brought to justice."

Wind Dancer stiffened and squared his shoulders. "No, Jacque. That is not what I meant. He has taken a young girl, and a little boy, hurt the woman friend of the chief, and tried to do harm to Cleopatra. He is also responsible for the dead woman in the building where you study dead people. I mean to kill him."

Marty came to stand next to the Pawnee. "I'll help you do it."

"Now let's all calm down. You can't go around without a plan. Marty, whoever broke in your ranger shack did so quickly, considering the amount of time between when Cleo was there and you arrived. How do you think the intruder got in?"

"Brute strength."

"What does that mean?" the chief asked.

"The door was ripped off the hinges. The desk attached to the wall was also jerked out of the studs."

"How is that even possible?" Jacque felt skeptical. He'd seen Wind Dancer do such things due to his unnatural strength which came from crossing over from his time, but for a human to do this? Not likely. "Didn't you see anything?"

"No. All I saw was this lady here, running like a scared rabbit. Since I couldn't use my truck, I went after her." Jacque tilted his head and squinted his eyes at the ranger. Before he could ask another question, Marty continued. "And no, nothing followed her in the woods, but I wasn't paying much attention to that, either. Anyone in these parts know we carry a weapon. My holster"—he laid a hand on it—"is clearly visible, as you can see. Whoever it was didn't want to get their head shot off, I'm guessing."

"If whoever it was took Abby, probably needed to get back to her, too," Perez added offhandedly, then appeared to realize she sounded cold. She patted the man's arm. "We'll find her, Marty. Rescue is ready to go in. We got ten people. More are on their way."

"I'm going, too," he insisted, shaking off her hand.

"Wind Dancer and I'll join in after we get Cleo checked out at the hospital. Or you can have one of your people take her," Jacque informed the chief. "We can help."

"Thanks. But no thanks. You're not from around here and we don't want two more tourists getting lost being a do-gooder."

"Do-gooder?" Jacque barked. "We are probably worth more than ten of your best guys. You don't know what my friend here is capable of," he said, stretching an arm toward the still-disgruntled Pawnee.

"Careful you don't break your arm patting yourself on the back, Detective Marquette," Perez said flippantly.

"Excuse me, Chief Perez, but Jacque is right. Wind Dancer can find her. Please." Cleo laid a hand on Jacque's chest, which forced him to focus on her. "Besides, I'm a doctor. I can help out here. I'm fine."

"No," the chief fumed. She motioned for another officer. "Make sure these three get to the ER in town. The officer handed the chief a smashed phone. She motioned for him to show Cleo. "Guess one of our vehicles ran over your phone. Worthless now, I'm afraid."

Wind Dancer bristled and pivoted toward the forests. "Chaveyo is near."

Jacque pulled his weapon in anticipation, as did Perez, except hers was aimed at him.

CHAPTER 19

The girl opened her eyes and tried to understand what had happened. She felt soft, sandy soil squeeze between her toes as she pulled her knees toward her chest to hug them. A circle of sunlight poured through an opening in the ceiling. It was enough for her to realize she was in an underground kiva. How did she get here? She rubbed her temples frantically to recollect the events that brought her here.

Jumbled thoughts flooded her brain at first, until she began to piece them together.

Talking to the nice lady, Cleo.
Search for phone on ground.
Notice some dust on new shoes.
Bend down wipe away dust.
Stand and turn to tell Cleo she'd meet her at the ranger shack.
Someone or something standing two inches in front of her.
Open mouth to scream at what she sees.
It lunges forward and covers her nose and mouth.
Smelly hands make her sick and feel limp.
Lifts her over shoulder and pulls off shoes.
Maybe moves toward woods but not sure because her eyes are heavy.

Abby stared up at the circle of light above her head. She

couldn't remember anything else. Had she been assaulted? Her clothes were intact, and there was no indication whoever took her had taken advantage of her while unconscious. But her midriff felt sore. Must be from being carried over its shoulder.

With an awkward wobble to stand, Abby moved under the light. She screamed for help, over and over while tears cascaded down her face, until her body shook with sobs. Then she remembered kivas always had a ladder to climb out. She moved around the circular wall and found nothing, except a hole near the backside, farthest away from the light. The stories told around a campfire in her childhood talked a lot about these holes.

Hopi Indians called them sipapu. They symbolized the portal where their ancient ancestors emerged to enter the present world. Modern-day Puebloans still used them for ceremonial purposes, although she'd never been to one. The campfire stories usually involved a wicked creature or other terrifying ideas coming out of the hole. One story was about Chaveyo.

What if the stories were true?

The chill of the kiva seeped into her arms and bare legs. The temperature down here was cool; probably why the Pueblo people had them. It protected them from the harsh summer sun. But where was this kiva located? How far was she from her car, her dad, and the park? Where was Cleo? Did she see this happen? Maybe she was looking for her or had found her dad to help. Unfortunately, it occurred to her, Cleo might have been taken, too. If so, no one would find her.

Sobs once again led her to cry out for help, to be heard, to give her hope of rescue.

But there was only silence.

Could she climb out?

She wiped the tears and snot away with her short sleeve. No one was coming for her. She had to try and escape. Hadn't her dad taught her a lot of survival tricks in her sixteen and a half years? Between hiking, camping trips, and his boring nature lectures to tourists, surely something would get her out of this mess. Taking a deep breath, she stood beside the light pooling on the floor to observe the kiva.

The kiva appeared to be constructed of wooden logs, adobe, and stone. According to her dad, adobe used by Ancient Pueblo builders was made from water, dirt, and straw. The builders used stones to make the walls of each room that were covered with a layer of smooth adobe. This one must be old because the adobe had begun to flake off and no restoration had repaired it. Abby wondered if this kiva might be hidden or undiscovered. It seemed like every couple of years her dad got excited about a new discovery in one of the parks. Obviously, someone knew about this one.

With a momentary peek toward the sipapu hole, another disturbing thought occurred; maybe something else knew about this kiva. What just moved near it? Dust shifted up and down with a breeze that came down the light hole, followed by a moan. Terror blinded her as she grabbed at stones and pieces of wood that jutted out from the brittle adobe. She rushed to climb toward the light. Then she felt a light touch on the back of her leg.

~ ~ ~ ~

Jacque held up one hand in surrender and raised his chin in caution. "Hold on, Chief Perez. I'm not the problem here. Let's just take a breath."

"Then put your weapon away, Detective Marquette."

He noticed movement in his peripheral vision. The situation now was a powder keg. Lowering his weapon, he felt someone from behind him reach for his weapon. At that same instant, Wind Dancer jerked up his arm under the young officer's chin, sending him sprawling into a slide that a normal person shouldn't be able to do. Before Perez could react, the Pawnee had also relieved her of the threat leveled at him.

"What the hell?" she stuttered, jumping away in bewilderment.

While Cleo rushed to the downed officer, Jacque grabbed the weapon out of Wind Dancer's hand and returned it to Perez.

"Never try something like that against us again," Jacque warned through clenched teeth. "He's faster, smarter, and stronger than all of you put together. Just call the FBI friend you say I have and get him up to speed when you have time. In the meantime, I'd call those Feds in to handle this."

"We don't need the Feds for a missing kid," she snapped.

Wind Dancer folded his arms across his chest. "She was taken.

Not just missing." He shifted his focus to the girl's dad. "I can find her. Let me try before it too late."

"Chief Perez, what could it hurt? It's already three o'clock. We need to get out there." He pivoted and ran to join the last two search and rescue volunteers entering the park.

Jacque turned to his friend. "Do you still smell him?"

"No. He run away. Big steps. Gone now."

Perez slipped her weapon into her holster and waited for him to do the same. "Wind Dancer, if you ever try a trick like that again, I'll shoot you."

"If I try a trick like that again, you will not have time to shoot me." Her eyes narrowed at him, but he only narrowed his eyes backs, unconcerned at the threat. "You are lucky this time."

Perez opened her mouth to speak, but Jacque took her by the elbow and led her away from the confrontation she would not win. After about ten feet, she dug her heels in and shook him off.

"Is he for real? How did he do that? What are you not telling me?"

"You wouldn't believe me if I told you. Now if I were you, I'd get those FBI guys who handle abductions here ASAP and have them take charge. I figure this is a serial killer…"

Perez's phone lit up in her pants pocket. Before she retrieved it, he received a disgruntled frown that caused her lips to snarl. She listened and occasionally nodded with the comment, "interesting" or "you're sure about this?" When she turned toward Wind Dancer, who now helped the downed officer to his feet for Cleo to check out, Jacque felt a sick feeling well up inside him.

"Tonya is awake," Perez said matter-of-factly.

"That's good. Was she able to give information about what happened?"

She put her hand on the holster and started tapping with her index finger before making eye contact with Jacque. "Yeah. She said an Indian with incredible strength and speed attacked her. Remind you of anyone?"

CHAPTER 20

Abby screamed at the feathery touch and grabbed at a handhold to pull herself up, but her foot slipped. The weight affected her grip on the log jutting out from the adobe. Her legs dangled only a second before she readjusted her footing and fought to reach the top. Hot breath moved against the bend of her knees as she cried out in horror. Once more, a gentle touch but sharp like a long fingernail or claw, traced her leg from the one knee to her ankle.

Reaching into the light with every ounce of strength she had left, Abby used her elbows to help give her leverage and her feet to push against the inside of the kiva wall.

Once she'd crawled out onto her stomach, she wasted no time in staggering to her feet. Without looking back, she ran like a lopsided dog with three legs. The rocks, sticks, and holes tore at her feet, but she didn't stop. Once, she fell forward, but a tree stopped her from hitting the ground. It was hard to breathe in afternoon heat and fear. Now, she dared search the area behind her, but no one was there.

A crow cawed and flew from the branches of a tree, startling her. It was a warning. She knew she had to keep moving in spite of not having a clue to where she'd been taken. Nothing appeared familiar. With a reluctant shove away from the tree, she turned to head into the woods when something loomed up in front of her.

A scream tried to escape her mouth, but a hand silenced her.

~ ~ ~ ~

Jacque knew Wind Dancer was aware of the conversation. Early on, when he'd crossed over through a hole in a parallel universe, he soon realized the man had very sensitive hearing. This was true of most of his senses. Along with an increase of strength and agility, Wind Dancer moved faster than seemed humanly possible. It wasn't like one of those superhero kinds of fast. Just really fast.

He'd once asked the Pawnee if this gift was also true in his world and he admitted he was ordinary. However, compared to modern man, he would have been considered exceptional. In the 1800s, men of all colors were tougher. Cleo said it had to do with no processed foods and more physical exercise. Although they may not have lived longer due to health care and incurable disease, overall, people appeared to survive things today's world might find difficult.

Wind Dancer lowered his chin and gazed at him through hooded eyes that sent a chill up his spine. There were many things the Pawnee didn't understand about the twenty-first century, but placing the blame on a tribal man, he understood very well. Jacque wanted to end this line of reasoning as quickly as possible before Wind Dancer put his foot in his mouth.

"Maybe the man who attacked Tonya and took the little boy was from a local tribe. Ever think about that? And keep in mind, it was dark."

"She had a flashlight on before he knocked it out of her hand," Perez reminded him.

"Doesn't mean it was Wind Dancer. Besides, he found them and brought them back. If she got a bump on the head, her recollection could be fuzzy. And remember, we were all together when this local girl disappeared. Then there's the dead driver over there." The young man, covered in a white sheet, was being loaded into an ambulance. "And you've got another body of a girl in the morgue."

Chief Perez continued to evaluate Wind Dancer and took a step in his direction when Jacque cut her off. "Get out of my way," she growled through gritted teeth.

"No way. You don't have any evidence Wind Dancer was involved in this."

"Really? From what the kid's parents told me, the little boy took to him right off. Then your friend is walking about camp and tells you the kid is gone, and, oh yeah, he finds him. A little convenient, don't you think? Especially since trained professionals were out there trying to find him."

Jacque leaned in to invade her personal space, causing her to step to the side. "Seems to me your search and rescue squad could use a little refresher training. Didn't take much to have them scurry into camp. And they left one behind. Good thing my friend over there didn't give up, or we might be planning a funeral. Wait. Make that two funerals."

"I don't like your tone or your insinuation, Marquette," she snapped.

"It's Detective Marquette, in case you forgot," he said, pulling out his cell phone. He punched in some numbers and let a sarcastic, thin smile spread across his mouth as he walked away toward his friends. The chief followed him with quick stomps of irritation. "Agent Farrentino, please. Tell him it's Detective Marquette from Chicago P.D."

"What the hell do you think you're doing?" demanded Perez.

Wind Dancer's bottom lip jutted out before he spoke. "He is using his phone machine to call Agent Farrentino. You should get one of those since you have trouble keeping track of the people who work with you. It comes in handy for Jacque." His tone was so matter-of-fact that she leveled a bewildered gaze at each of the strange friends before her.

"Agent Farrentino." Jacque didn't realize how cheerful his voice sounded as he moved away from the chief and his two friends. He kept a watchful eye on the other three and tried to listen and talk at the same time.

"Unbelievable," the chief moaned throwing up her hands. "He's calling the FBI over my head."

"No. He calls the phone. FBI man would not hear Jacque if he talks over your head."

Cleo gave a muffled laugh and laid a hand on his forearm before rising on tiptoe to kiss him on the cheek.

"I say things wrong again." He smiled down at her.

"Yes. But it is okay. The chief here means Jacque is doing things without asking her permission."

"And this makes her angry," he decided. He chuckled then nodded at Cleo.

"I'm right here, ya know," Perez spat out like venom as her hands went to her hips.

"I am not blind, Chief Perez. I can see you," Wind Dancer added.

"I don't appreciate being made fun of, Mr. Wind Dancer."

"I don't blame you," he said. "Who does this to you? I will talk to them."

This time Cleo couldn't help but laugh out loud and then covered her mouth to hide too much of a jovial attitude in such a trying time.

"It is good to hear you laugh, Cleopatra. I have missed you. I will keep you safe now." He nodded at Perez. "And you, too, Chief Perez. In my village we always protect the women and children."

"Oh brother." She rolled her eyes.

Wind Dancer opened his mouth to comment, but Cleo rubbed his arm and shook her head no before turning her attention to the chief.

"Wind Dancer can help in the search for Abby. I really think if you'd stop being so suspicious of him and let him do what he does best, then we could bring this to a speedy conclusion. He told me you suspect him of being involved with the boy's disappearance. Did the child show any fear of Joseph when you found him?"

"No. But that doesn't mean—"

"What it means is that the boy trusted Joseph and wasn't afraid. I'm a doctor. I've seen a lot of traumatized kids in the ER. It's pretty easy to spot when an adult is the abuser. Was the child injured?"

"No," she sighed. "Exactly the opposite. It was obvious the two of them had a good relationship. We got the report that Tonya said an Indian attacked her."

"In a terrifying situation, it's easy to get the facts and information mixed up. From what I understand, the woman, Tonya, was badly hurt. The slightest suggestion can become her reality. Let's wait and see what happens. Right now, all I care about is that Abby is returned to her family."

"I don't understand how Wind Dancer can help or you as far as that goes. You need to be checked out at the hospital in town."

"I probably have a broken wrist. Hurts, but the paramedic gave me some over-the-counter pain meds. I'm already feeling better. The rest is just scrapes, and I'll probably be sore in the morning from taking a few falls. Besides, the ambulance is taking that poor kid who died in the truck. You'll not have anyone here until they finish up. I know how these things work, Chief Perez. If the girl, or anyone else, needs medical attention, I'm your best bet."

"No. You're going to the hospital to get yourself squared away or at least make sure you're all right."

"Then let me ride along with the ambulance so Jacque and Wind Dancer can help out."

Jacque joined them as he shoved his phone in his pocket. Wind Dancer followed close behind. "The FBI is waiting for your call, Chief Perez, but honestly they're probably going to come anyway."

"Why is that?"

"They have several other missing persons with this same MO. Lucky for us, Special Agent Farrentino is in Pueblo, Colorado on a similar missing person's case. He'll be here later tonight."

Perez bristled. "You shouldn't have done that. We don't want outsiders coming in and running the show with their big-city ways and their high-and-mighty attitude."

"Afraid you'll learn something, Chief Perez?" he snapped. "Because right now, there are too many unanswered questions. If there is a connection, then Farrentino will find it."

"I find it odd that not long ago, you didn't seem to have anything but contempt for the FBI."

He offered a contemptuous smile with gritted teeth showing before speaking. "Well, you know how those pretty boys at the FBI are—like to hog the show and the recognition."

"Then why did you call them?" she hissed.

"Because he knows what he's doing, and I can trust him."

Cleo chimed in. "Jacque is right. He gets things done. His work on the terrorism attack in Chicago got him a promotion." She nudged Jacque who frowned down at her praise. "Of course, my superhero here did all the hard work. Right, Wind Dancer?" She encouraged the Pawnee with one of her smiles.

"What she said." he nodded. "Special Agent good man."

"Whatever," she sighed and walked toward the ambulance driver waving her over.

"Jacque, we need to take Cleo to hospital. She is hurt." Wind Dancer gently lifted the hurt arm, careful not to touch the wrist, but she winced anyway.

"No, I'm—"

"Let's go. Doesn't appear the chief is going to give on this. But, Cleo, we are dropping you off and coming back. I'll see that your car is towed to town and that the rental company comes to get it."

"That dead kid came from Kewa Korner where I spent last night. Not sure how he ended up here unless my 911 call actually went through. I think the number is on the side of the truck. Maybe someone spotted the vehicles and called the garage?"

"No idea. I'll find out, but right now you're going to the ER. You're white as a ghost. I'll come back, but I really need Wind Dancer with me. If that kid isn't found soon, we're going in without their permission."

When the ambulance pulled out onto the road, Perez joined them. Jacque informed her of their plans, and she didn't object to them returning after getting Cleo checked out.

"By then, we should have this wrapped up. The girl can't be far."

Wind Dancer focused on the park entrance. "Girl is crying. You should hurry."

CHAPTER 21

She fought, scratched, and kicked whoever held her from behind. With so much twisting, he removed the hand from her mouth. In that split second, Abby tried to scream, but because she was so winded, it sounded more like a croak as she whirled around to face her attacker. The sight of the giant of a man with a disfigured face frightened her enough that she stumbled backward, tripping over forest debris. She fell, hitting her head against something hard. The last thing she remembered was a large shadowy figure bending over her then slipping hands beneath her body.

~ ~ ~ ~

"I don't want to leave you here alone," Wind Dancer said, eyeing the ER waiting room. "You might need me."

Jacque rolled his eyes and pretended to gag into his empty coffee cup. "You two make me sick. I swear I'm going to get tooth decay with all this sweet, syrupy, lovey-dovey crap. Let's go. She'll be fine. Can't you see the place is full of people who take care of the sick people. Besides, Cleo is a doctor. She'll probably be telling them what to do before they figure it out for themselves."

"Jacque, you are such a softy," Cleo cooed sarcastically before patting Wind Dancer on the cheek. "I'll be fine. That girl needs you. Hopefully, they've found her. It's getting late. It'll be dark soon. Please. Go. Maybe since Agent Farrentino has to come through here, you can have him stop by to get me." The desk attendant called Cleo's name. "See. Safer than safe. Go."

Wind Dancer hugged her tenderly, as if she'd break, and walked her to the doors swinging open to receive her. "I love you." He kissed her on the mouth, making her smile.

Jacque joined them and made unflattering kissing noises. "I'd say get a room, but then I'd have to explain it to this guy."

Wind Dancer grinned. "That I understand, buddy."

"Figures."

Cleo watched them pass into the fading light of day before she followed the male nurse into the examining area.

As with all things in an emergency room, it takes longer than you think. The sun had begun to set by the time she'd been released. The wrist had a clean break and should heal nicely with a few restrictions for a while. With a promise of a follow-up with her own doctor in Chicago, Cleo decided to go outside for fresh air. After taking Tylenol for pain, she shoved a prescription into her jeans pocket. Since her purse was still in her rental car, there was no use trying to fill the pain medication that most likely would put her to sleep.

The hospital café had closed late afternoon, but she spotted the same convenience store chain less than a block away, she'd used earlier in the day. Remembering the gift card in her pocket, she dug it out and smiled. At least there was one good thing that happened today. With no phone, wallet, or money, other than the gift card, she left a message inside the ER in case Agent Farrentino appeared.

The few stores that lined the street had closed and, other than cars coming and going at the convenience store, the town appeared to have gone to sleep for the day. A number of people stood in line to pay for their gas, an older couple licked ice cream on the outdoor patio, and the smell of pizza lured Cleo to buy the largest piece of pepperoni they served. She grabbed a bottle of water and plenty of napkins before paying and moving outside to the patio surrounded by blooming yucca plants. A cool breeze almost made her ignore the rising soreness in her leg, and especially her knee where she'd taken a hard fall. The broken wrist throbbed by the time she'd gobbled down her pizza. When the streetlights flickered, she realized that half a block to walk back to the hospital might as well have been a mile.

By the time she made it to the sliding doors, the pain nearly brought tears to her eyes. The realization of what had happened to her and even how lucky she was came crashing in like a tsunami. With head down, she staggered in, anxious to find a seat in a now-crowded waiting room. She collided with another visitor.

Cleo sidestepped away and realized it was Mansi Garcia from the Whispering Pines Inn. Confusion took over at seeing him.

"Mr. Garcia. I'm. I'm." She rubbed her head then laid a hand on her wrist. "Sorry. Guess I'm a little addled.

He took her elbow. "Please. Sit down. You don't look so good. Let me help you."

"Thank you. I guess I'm a mess." Letting him usher her to a chair with all the comfort of stadium seating, Cleo lowered herself to sit awkwardly. Now her hip ached. "Been one of those days." She tried her best to smile as he pulled another chair up in front of her. "Why are you here?"

"My cook—"

"The tall guy who was poking around my car?"

"Yes. He never came back. I had to have my desk clerk help out, since so many were coming in the next couple of days due to the solar eclipse. Then she got word her daughter was in labor and having problems. She needed a ride, so here I am."

"What about the inn? Don't you need to be there?"

"Fortunately, I'd hired extra people and called them in early. They were happy to get the work. And as luck would have it, my new cook was ready to get busy. There's a hospitality intern that assured me he was ready to take over. I had no choice."

"Oh," she sighed. "I hope everything will be okay with the daughter." The doctor part of her kicked in, and she wanted to know if she could help, make a difference, or learn from the experience.

"But why are you here? I thought you were meeting friends today."

She kept the story short and sweet but realized when he paled that Mansi probably knew both of the victims today. The community was small and most likely consisted largely of generations of people who seldom ventured far beyond the mountains and parks that surrounded this part of New Mexico.

"My car broke down is why I ran into Abby and Tinker. I should go help out if I can."

"You could use a little rest. There's a motel down the street and a B&B on the edge of town. Always a good option. Let me take you there."

"Mansi, do you think Alo, I think that is your cook's name, did something to my car?"

He shook his head. "Alo, is weird and hardheaded, but not a mean bone in his body. I've known him his whole life. I wouldn't think so."

"Does he live close by?"

"He used to live with me. Took him in as a foster child when he was ten. My wife had died, and we both needed each other. I homeschooled him because before he came to me, he'd been bullied. He loves the outdoors and disappears there sometimes for days."

Cleo wondered if he knew Abby and Tinker. Maybe they bullied or made fun of him in the past. "How did he become disfigured, if I might ask?"

"In a fire. Playing with his grandpa's lighter. Just four years old. Lost everything. The grandpa was outside doing chores when the house went up in flames. The parents and sister made it out, but Alo was in bad shape by the time the firemen reached him. The medical bills and an already unstable home drove them apart. The sister went into foster care just like Alo. She eventually was adopted by another family. But nobody wanted Alo. Too ugly. Got the reputation for being spooky."

"How amazing you took him in and gave him a home."

"It wasn't easy. We've been good company for each other. I lose my temper at times and fuss, but I'm only trying to keep him out of trouble. He's almost thirty now." He smiled. "Doesn't like for me to be telling him what to do. That Abby girl took up for him once when that worthless Tinker kid harassed him so many times. Called him a stupid giant. I told him to just walk away. But one time Tinker threw a rock at him. Clobbered him good. Fell. If Abby hadn't been there, I'm not sure what Alo would have done.

She fussed at Tinker and said she'd call the police."

"Then what happened?"

"He just laughed and shoved her out of the way." He sighed. "Alo told me later she helped him up and walked a little way with him. Not ashamed at all to be seen with him. She's a good girl. He didn't go in public places after that. Even at the inn, Alo didn't want people to see him."

"You said Tinker called him a giant. Is he?"

Mansi shrugged. "Guess so. Not sure. He has Marfan Syndrome. Just adds another layer of being different and easy targets for bullies."

A soft bed and clean sheets sounded pretty good right now. Maybe she should go to that B&B for the night. Surely, Agent Farrentino would arrive soon.

"So, what do you say? Call it a day?"

"Very tempting, but I'm supposed to wait for an FBI agent to pick me up and take me out to the park. I promised my friends I'd stay put."

Mansi gave her a smile revealing several crooked teeth before he laid a cold hand on her good arm.

"I could take you."

CHAPTER 22

Chief Perez hadn't been able to reach the repair shop where Tinker worked to notify the owner of the untimely death of his tow truck driver. She finally reached his home, only to get his answering machine.

As a last try, she called the Kewa Korner convenience store in the middle of town. They agreed to go down and let Floyd know. It was common for them to be working and not hear the phone considering how loud they played their country music.

Tinker lived with an alcoholic dad who worked for the highway department. No telling where he might be. She'd sent an officer to find him. Strange no one tried to figure out where the kid had disappeared to. Don't they have to call in their location when they stop for a job? But then again, the owner, Floyd Miller, probably hadn't even noticed. His employees were notorious for being late or unreliable.

When she spotted the Chicago detective and his unusual sidekick parking their car, uncertainty welled up inside her. Things had gone from bad to worse ever since those two arrived in the area. Although she implied Wind Dancer was a suspect, the evidence said otherwise.

She wanted the mess to be his fault, but that didn't explain the death of the first girl lying in the morgue. Didn't explain how

Abby went missing, either, considering both of the men were with her at the time.

The doctor certainly wasn't big enough to drag off a teenager without help. After all, the woman was a victim, too. That kid Tinker, dumb as a rock, had a reputation for being a bully, so maybe he received a little payback. He was a long way from his little wide place in the road.

The father had given him free rein years ago, and other than Floyd Miller, and the garage and repair shop job, it was the only stability he'd ever had. If anyone would be upset, it would be Floyd. Everyone knew he threatened to fire the kid but never had. Guess he felt sorry for him.

Both communities shared services: hospital clinic, repair shops, towing, fire and rescue, and other services. They even shared the school district which was about four hundred square miles. The population of the entire school system was no more than fifteen hundred kids, K-12. Sports teams brought both communities closer in more ways than one. People were used to driving a long distance for almost everything. It was nothing for Perez to make a trip to Santa Fe once a month to restock her pantry, shop the bigger stores, and eat at a restaurant that had something besides a hamburger and greasy fries.

Then there was the FBI agent on his way. Chances were good he'd breeze in and disrupt her people and keep them from getting the job done. It would be that, or he'd take the credit for finding the girl. Pueblo, Colorado wasn't far, maybe four, five hours at most, provided traffic and weather behaved.

She took note of Jacque and Wind Dancer as they exited their car. The detective wasn't a bad-looking guy, and why that even crossed her mind disturbed her. Being a cop, she didn't meet many men who didn't feel threatened by her position or personality. The last date she'd had was eight months ago with a high school math teacher from Santa Fe. There were no sparks or talk of another encounter, making her not eager to put forth the effort again.

The Chicago detective was certainly not a yes guy and pretty quick to bomb her with his advice and smart-ass remarks. Any other time, she might find him interesting enough to begin a flirtatious move. Clearly, he wasn't a slave to fashion with his five-year-old mismatched clothes and the attempt at camper cool, with the khaki-colored vest and safari hat. The fact his nearly six-foot frame appeared toned and his hard jawline hinted of a five-o'clock shadow, made her wonder how it might feel to slide her finger from his ear down to his firm lips that frowned more than smiled. Those attentive eyes had appraised her when they first met, and felt surprise when she experienced a slight warmth move up her body. She guessed the unfamiliarity of that sensation caught her off guard, forcing her to keep him on a short leash laced with threats and accusations.

That didn't appear to be working.

As to the Pawnee, she wasn't sure what to make of him. Other than being taller than most of the local tribes around here, he wasn't remarkable, except for his uncommon quickness, strength, and lack of understanding for the English language. When she had time, she planned to investigate further to discover exactly what he did in Chicago. Why did the FBI have a gag order on how much anyone close to him could say? The way he leveled a sinister observation of her, and the surroundings, gave him a dangerous vibe. With the long black hair, pouty mouth, and eyes too dark to read, Perez wondered if he was even human. Maybe he was an escaped experiment from one of those science labs at Los Alamos. Who knew what really went on there anyway? However, Dr. Cleo Sommers had taken his comfort eagerly with an obvious romantic involvement from the way they embraced.

No accounting for taste, she guessed.

~ ~ ~ ~

"She is eyeballing us like she might serve us up for dinner on a barbeque spit, Wind Dancer." Jacque slowed his pace and spoke out of the corner of his mouth. "Let me do the talking."

"You always talking. And she is eyeballing you, not me."

Jacque halted and gave his friend a bewildered, "Say what?"

"She is giving you what Cleo calls bedroom eyes." Wind Dancer's eyebrows lifted slightly as he shifted his gaze between Jacque and Perez.

He couldn't help but roll his neck to pop then pulled his shoulders back to hide his tired body. It'd been a long time since a woman showed any interest in him, and this one reminded more of a hungry piranha than a woman with a romantic interest. But hell, what did he know about women. She was feisty and a looker, both admirable attributes in his book. It wasn't like he had a long checklist for the women he wanted to date.

"Keep that observation to yourself, huh, buddy. She's probably on women's lib overload and wouldn't appreciate that kind of talk."

The Pawnee nodded then gave him a thumbs-up as they closed the distance between them.

"How's your friend? You weren't gone long?"

"We left her in capable hands. Agent Farrentino will stop by and pick her up on his way here." Jacque surveyed the area when an ambulance pulled in to an already crowded entrance and parking lot. Two guys exited the vehicle and joined them. They were the same ones from last night. They nodded recognition and addressed the chief.

"Any word yet?"

"No. Not a trace. Nothing."

"Let us help. Where can we be the most help?" Jacque asked.

"I don't know. Chicago, maybe?" she snapped, making the two ambulance drivers chuckle.

"Funny," Jacque moaned.

Wind Dancer's forehead furrowed. "Then why aren't you laughing, Jacque? Is it another double meaning?"

"Yes. Double meaning."

"You should not talk to Jacque in this way if you want him to return your interest. Is the women's lib overload making you rude?" Wind Dancer folded his arms across his chest.

"Excuse me?" she growled. "Where did you get that idea?"

He pointed to her eyes, but before he could explain, Jacque weighed in and moved his friend toward the entrance. "You wait over here. Keep your mouth shut," he warned then turned to Perez. "Sorry about that. He leaves a lot to be desired in the subtle department." He turned to make sure the Pawnee wasn't going to weigh in again. But he appeared to be searching the ground for something. "For some reason, he thinks you and I would make a good match."

"So, is he mentally challenged or an escapee from the mental ward?"

"You don't have to get testy, Perez. I'm well aware you and me would be like gas on a fire." She arched an eyebrow at his comparison. "Then again—"

"Oh, shut up." She grinned even though her voice came out irritated. "Do you have a map? I don't want to have to come search for you, too."

~ ~ ~ ~

For whatever reason, Mansi turned on the car air-conditioning, rolled down his window about three inches, and lit up a cigarette. It had been a long time since she'd ridden in a car that didn't have power windows. The ashtray was overflowing and left a putrid smell clinging to the air. It reminded her of body odor. The little flat Christmas tree swinging from the mirror probably gave up the pine smell days ago or maybe just refused to keep trying. Cleo aimed the air vent toward her face even though she was cold.

Darkness felt thick enough to cut with a knife. She guessed if the inside of the windshield were cleaner, she would be able to spot stars. The number of curves in the road required Mansi to slow down, although he was already using an abundance of caution. When he jabbed out the cigarette, he took his eyes off the road long enough to make her nervous.

Then something huge loped across the road.

"What was that?" she cried, placing her hands on her chest at the same time he slammed on the brakes.

With wide eyes, he stared ahead for a few seconds, gulped, then turned his head toward her. "I didn't see anything."

CHAPTER 23

"What do you think you're doing?" Cleo asked when Mansi carefully put the car in park. The car continued its quiet hum when he turned off the air conditioner. The immediate waft of cigarettes butts choked her. The wounded left wrist rested on the console. She tried rolling down the window but only managed halfway down before a pain shot up her knee from the applied pressure.

Mansi exited the car and closed the creaky door, tipping Cleo to the fact she'd stepped into a horror movie which screamed, "Don't leave the car!" Bad things always happen about this time in a horror movie. His window was still cracked enough for him to lean down and speak through the opening.

"Lock the doors. I'll only be a minute."

"No. Wait."

A long, slow exhale escaped his lungs as he looked over his shoulder then to her. "If I'm not back in ten minutes, take the car to Sunset Rock."

"Aren't we almost to the park entrance? Let's go get help. Lots of police there. My friend is a detective. We can come back if you think that, whatever it was, might be what we're looking for."

"Probably an animal."

"It ran on two legs. What animal does that?"

"Ten minutes. Then go."

Before she could continue to protest, he disappeared across the road and into the abyss of darkness that swallowed up her surroundings. Having a window rolled down more than halfway now felt like a bad idea. Once more, she reached her good hand over and started the round and round movement to close it when something reached in and touched her hair.

The scream came from deep inside her gut as she jerked away from the window in time to see a bony hand with extra-long fingers retract. As she finished closing the window, a wide shadow moved around the rear of the car, trying each door handle for entrance. She popped the seat belt and tried to find the magic spot to activate the horn. When the first blast exploded the quiet night, the figure stopped moving. She twisted around to try and see whomever or whatever it was when it lumbered off.

Cleo realized she was panting with terror. Tears rolled down her cheeks, but her resolve kicked in, much like it had in those days when a Chicago gang had taken her as a hostage and forced her to steal drugs. Up until that moment, she had never experienced such fear. Now, again the unknown lurked in the darkness draining her of courage.

Was this another one of those things that could cross over from a parallel universe? Could there be a Pueblo myth which was activated by the impending solar eclipse tomorrow? Growing up in the Field Museum of Natural History in Chicago had led her to believe a great many things about culture, science, and the impossible. Wind Dancer was proof of that.

She fumbled in the dark to try and find the headlights Mansi extinguished when he put the car in park. The switch was almost out of reach. Fortunately, she knew where it should be since it was a Chevy. All her cars had been a General Motors car, so the switch would be in a similar location.

Reaching across the console, Cleo felt she'd transformed into a contortionist but managed to switch on the lights. The darkness ripped open the night as the light burst across the road. At least if a car came along, they wouldn't run over her. But her attention caught sight of Mansi standing on the edge of the road, shaking his finger at something then throwing his hands upward, as if in frustration. He extended his hand toward the car then to whomever he was talking to.

Who was he talking to? Why didn't Mansi look concerned?

He waved off with an irritated hand gesture and stormed toward the car. When he grabbed the locked doorhandle, Cleo considered not opening it. He leaned down and glowered at her, his face contorted with rage.

"Open. The. Door."

~ ~ ~ ~

Jacque and Wind Dancer followed a trail already covered by the rescue team. However, since other missing people had later showed up in places already covered, it seemed logical for them to retrace those same trails. Both men carried flashlights, but Jacque knew that his partner's built-in night vision would make a Navy SEAL envious. Since this whole mess creeped the hell out of him, Jacque knew his partner had the light on to reassure him, just like he had with the little boy.

"This is the way Abby went."

"How do you know?" They had stopped to let their heartbeat slow down after a strenuous climb. "Do you smell her?" It was yet another gift the Pawnee acquired when he crossed over to this time.

"Yes." He picked up a bracelet and sniffed. "I think this is hers. There are words on it."

Jacque shined his light on the leather and silver bracelet with Abby in cursive script, from Mom and Dad. "Yep. Hers all right." He removed his backpack and took out two bottles of water then shoved the bracelet inside. "I'm beat. I'm not sure how much longer I can go on. We've been up almost twenty-four hours."

"We should sleep here. Safe for now." He sat down on a fallen log and surveyed the ground.

"I'm not sleeping in pine needles or anything else you think is normal because, buddy, it ain't normal." Jacque waved his flashlight to create light patterns dancing across the ground. "For all I know, there is one of those rattlesnakes waiting to get his daily quota."

"There are many snakes in this park."

"How do you know that?" He finished his water. "Let me guess. You hear them plotting to come after us."

Wind Dancer gave a thin smile and tossed a rock in the brush near the trail's edge near Jacque's feet. The Pawnee's laughter burst through the stillness as Jacque yelped and jumped toward the Pawnee.

"Not funny, Wind Dancer," he snapped. "I probably need a change of clothes now."

Caution set in as Wind Dancer slowly stood up and stared into the abyss of darkness. He held a finger to his lips and motioned for Jacque to extinguish the light. Both men hunkered down and waited. A breeze stirred the treetops for a few seconds then a deathly quiet and stillness wrapped around them.

Jacque laid a hand on his weapon, and a sense of security eased his rapid pulse. Whatever was out there, he didn't require Pawnee sensitivity to experience a chill coming up his spine. He hunkered down, shoulder to shoulder with his partner, and thought he felt a shiver in the man. That couldn't be a good sign. Usually, Wind Dancer didn't appear to be afraid of anything. He placed a hand on Jacque's shoulder.

"Chaveyo?" Jacque whispered.

"No. Something just as bad." He pulled his knife from the sheath he wore on his belt. "Get ready. Coming for us."

A thunderous movement of snapping twigs and brush approached. The growling and breathing reminded Jacque of an air compressor about to give up the ghost. A dark shape the size of a bear lunged through the trees with the scream resembling a wounded animal.

~ ~ ~ ~

Mansi leaned down closer to the cracked window and cast a leery eye over his shoulder. "Hurry, Ms. Sommers."

Whether it was his tight voice or the glazed expression on his face, Cleo, with a trembling hand, managed to unlock the doors. As soon as it opened, she punched the lock again to seal them in safely. He put the car in drive and eased forward with no sign of trepidation.

"Who were you talking to?" she demanded. Reaching up to her hair with her good hand, she attempted to touch the spot she'd felt a feathery touch.

"No one. I was—"

"Then why all the hand gestures and the angry voice?"

"Just trying to scare the evil spirits away."

"You can't be serious. Do you really think I would believe…?" When Mansi turned cold eyes on her, she hushed.

"There are things in these mountains and parks you know nothing of. Tomorrow will be a solar eclipse. You should stay inside."

"Inside? Why?"

"You would not understand. But the Pueblo people say to stay inside and keep babies away from the windows, to be mindful. We have to wear something sharp."

"I believe more than you think about the ways of Native people. I will be careful."

The car slowed again. "Good."

"Something reached in the window and touched me when you left the car."

"If no harm came to you, then you have nothing to fear now."

Lights flashed ahead and Cleo could only guess that they were at the entrance to Kewa National Park. Mansi drove into a small space on the edge of what was left of the parking area. He jumped out and ran around the car to help her out since she struggled to open the door. The touch of his rough hand felt clammy when he assisted her out of the car.

"Thank you, Mansi. Come meet my friends."

He walked around the front of the car and shook his head. "I have to find my son."

"Was that him you were talking to?"

"Good luck, Ms. Sommers. And remember to stay away from windows tomorrow."

In seconds, he got inside the car and pulled onto the road. She watched him disappear into the darkness.

She spotted Chief Perez listening to her walkie-talkie. The pinched brow and downturned mouth hardened her face. One of the paramedics joined her and listened in.

"What's going on, Chief?" Cleo sensed she wasn't going to like the answer.

"It's your friends. They're in trouble."

CHAPTER 24

Gunshots came across the radio, mixed with growling and what sounded like a scuffle.

"Anyone there?"

Chief Perez's voice, now tight and loud, spoke into the radio as the paramedics rushed to the ambulance and returned with, what appeared to be, rifles. After they checked to see if they were loaded, they stood stiff-legged, cradling their weapons.

"Officers in trouble. I repeat. Officers in trouble. Last check-in on Carson Trail near Moonlight Overlook. Anyone. Need response."

The radio crackled to life. "On our way, Chief. Almost there," came an out-of-breath voice. "What the—"

Silence.

"Are you there? Over."

"Chief, you aren't going to believe this."

Cleo tried to grab the radio away from Perez, but she jerked it away and shoved a hand in her chest. "Back off, Doc." She raised the radio to speak again. "Status?"

The radio crackled with static and the chief had to repeat the instructions.

"We're on our way in. That detective friend of yours is hurt, but his partner is okay—I think. He's carrying…well, you won't believe it. Too big for us to carry."

"What are you talking about?" Perez snapped.

"Two of us trying to come in. The rest are still searching for the girl."

"Roger that."

Cleo wanted to run into the night in search for her friends. Knowing Wind Dancer remained unharmed helped, but Jacque didn't have super strength or the ability to bounce back like a time-traveling Pawnee.

"Ask them how badly he's hurt, Chief Perez. I need to know how to treat him when he gets here."

"You're not treating anybody, Doc, until my guys check him out first." She opened up the radio again. "How bad is the detective? Over."

There was a pause then, "Hard to say with just a flashlight. Got some cuts and he's limping, but he's waved off any assistance. Said Dr. Sommers will know what to do."

"Let me talk to him," Cleo insisted.

"Can you put him on? The doc is here and needs reassurance."

"Hello?" came a familiar voice.

Cleo snatched the phone out of the chief's hand. "Jacque," she said with a sigh. "Are you guys okay?"

"A little banged up. Wind Dancer is his usual Superman self. Might need a stitch or two. Got any of that pain medication you give those worthless gangbangers in Chicago?"

Cleo chuckled. "I'll see what I can do. Take care of the big guy for me."

"Oh sure. Nothing like once again making me feel like a bridesmaid instead of a bride."

Taking a deep breath, she handed the radio to Perez, who observed her with interest. "So, you and Detective Marquette an item?"

"Absolutely not," Cleo smiled. "But if you're interested, I wouldn't let that hunk of steel and muscle get away. He's smart as a whip and a straight-up guy. He's more like a big brother to me. A very annoying one at times."

Perez's eyes narrowed when she smiled suspiciously at her. "I'm a little busy with the job."

"That's what he always says. Probably why both of you are

single."

"I see light. Here they come," called one of the paramedics who placed his rifle in the cab of the ambulance while the other man rested his weapon against the side before jerking open the rear doors of the vehicle.

Perez and Cleo ran to the entrance to watch as a distant orb of light moved back and forth across, what must have been, a trail. They were still a ways out, maybe two hundred yards when the light vanished only to reappear once they emerged from the cover of a dense stand of trees. Both women leveled their beam of light toward the men then lowered it to the road so not to blind them.

One rescuer appeared to be helping a man; Jacque, she imagined. The other shone a light on their progress toward safety. It was Wind Dancer she wanted to find and run to, although it was wiser to wait for him to come to her. At first, she didn't see him until they were closer. He followed behind, carrying a large bundle in his arms. They hollered to bring a gurney. In seconds, the two paramedics were headed at full throttle, with the gurney.

"Jacque must be really hurt," Cleo choked as her hand laid on her heart.

"I don't think so," Perez replied, shining a light in their direction.

The entire party halted as Wind Dancer laid whatever he carried on the gurney. The paramedics jumped and nearly fell then eased closer to take a better look. Cleo thought she heard one of them swear. Jacque moved away from the group, and everyone started toward the entrance. It took all four of the men to push the gurney.

Wind Dancer came around and lifted Jacque's arm around his neck to help him. Even though she didn't witness it, Cleo imagined the stubborn detective tried to refuse help from his partner to give the appearance of toughness. The temptation was just too great for her to wait and bolted toward the two men who had become such a part of her life over the last few years. She didn't know until she reached them that Perez had followed.

Both women relieved Wind Dancer of the detective. The Pawnee staggered a few steps and stopped long enough to take a deep breath. She had never witnessed him become exhausted.

"Wind Dancer?" she asked and reached her bad hand toward him.

He waved her off. "I am okay. Jacque is hurt. I can walk on my own. The beast was heavy."

Beast? A quick observation of the moving gurney revealed a creature the size of a bear.

Jacque smiled over at Perez with a lopsided grin. "I'm touched, Perez. Didn't know you cared."

"I don't," she snapped but couldn't resist ending with a smile.

"Really, Jacque?" Cleo groaned. "Is this the only way you can get a date?"

He leaned over and kissed her on the temple. "Pretty much. I'm not proud of it."

"Shut up and walk," Perez ordered, "or I'll make you ride on the gurney with that thing."

Once at the entrance, the paramedics helped the women with Jacque and led him to the ambulance where he refused to do anything but sit on the rear edge of the vehicle.

The attention now turned to the beast lying wide-eyed on the gurney.

"What the hell is that?" Jacque asked, pointing a shaking finger toward the gurney.

Everyone gathered around staring at the beast the size of a bear with spikes on its spine. The eyes, wide open, glowed red.

One of the paramedics who was an Indian explained. "I heard tales from the old ones about these. It is a Chupacabra. Some say it is a rabid beast and can fly." He nodded to Cleo. "He'll need to get checked out and may have to have shots if it has rabies."

"Great. Some camping trip this turned out to be," Jacque fumed.

"It is said they can fly. Do you see wings?" the paramedic asked, shining the flashlight on the hideous beast. He picked up a stick from the ground and pried open the lips. "Look at those teeth," he mumbled. "It is also said that it's known to suck the blood out of your pets and family."

Perez shook her head in disbelief. "I've heard about these things my whole life but never believed in them, although a lot of people do, which is, in a way, scarier, since I didn't pay it any attention."

Cleo put her arm around Wind Dancer, finding him soaked to the skin with sweat.

"Are you hurt? Did it scratch you, too?"

"Not sure. I fight it. Attacked Jacque."

"Thank goodness he is quicker than lightning or I'd be dead," Jacque admitted as they joined him at the ambulance. "Got my leg with those claws. Reminds me of a monster from a Spielberg movie."

Wind Dancer sat down next to his partner, exhausted. "Should we call this Spielberg to tell us what to do?"

Both Cleo and Jacque smiled and laid hands on the Pawnee's leg in appreciation of his strength and innocence.

"No, buddy. I think we'll let the chief take it from here. We need a good night's sleep."

Cleo called for more supplies to get to work on Jacque, knowing he was going to give her a hard time when she started to cut the leg of his jeans. He slapped at her hand, knocking the scissors free.

"These are my favorite jeans. You're not going to dissect them."

"Maybe if Wind Dancer holds him down, we can take them off," Perez said, joining them as she slipped her phone into her pocket.

Jacque twisted his mouth in a pout. "And who says dreams don't come true."

Both women burst out laughing. Wind Dancer folded his arms across his chest and chuckled at the joke before adding his own take on the situation.

"Jacque, you need to remember both women are armed and dangerous."

"Even better," he said sarcastically.

The radio crackled alive in Perez's hand as she lifted it to her mouth.

"Go ahead.".

"Chief, we found Abby," came a winded declaration.

CHAPTER 25

"Alive?" she said, waving her hands at the ambulance crew.

"Yes. Unconscious though. Will mark the area for investigation tomorrow," came an excited response.

"Sending you help. Give me your location."

A loud round of cheers lifted the gloom of first responders as Perez sent two officers and the ambulance team in with a stretcher.

"I don't understand it." Perez shook her head. "That is no more than twenty yards from the ranger shack. We searched there first. Nothing."

Wind Dancer started to follow the men toward the entrance, but Perez grabbed his arm.

"You've done enough." Perez stepped in front of him and quickly moved two steps back when he towered over her and leveled a dangerous frown. The good mood had left his dark face that now resembled storm clouds.

"They are not safe. I can help if there is trouble."

"Detective Marquette, you better rein your partner in before I do."

Cleo moved in front of him and touched his side with her good hand. "Jacque and I need you now. Chief Perez is doing her job. She can use us here. Please," she spoke in a whisper. He smiled down at her and ran his hand down her cheekbone.

"Okay, Cleopatra."

"I'm calling another ambulance," Perez announced as she activated her phone. "Just called a zoologist friend. Will be here in the morning. Talked to him about the beast an hour ago." She turned to Jacque. "You should go to ER. That beast is going to be in the cabin section of the ambulance, and I don't want the paramedic to be in there with it. He'll ride up front with the driver."

"Did anyone try and open my car?" asked Cleo. "My purse is in there."

Perez dug in her pocket and tossed her the keys. "We got it open after you left. I have your key and locked it up since your purse was still there. Now." She nodded in the direction of town. "I've got to stay here or I'd take Detective Marquette to the ER, but you will have to do it unless Wind Dancer can drive."

"No," shouted both Cleo and Jacque.

"There's no reason I can't drive." Jacque spoke through gritted teeth as he eased off the step of the ambulance.

"I'll drive. It's my left wrist that's broke. It won't be a problem. We could all use some rest. Chief, I just want to wait until they bring Abby out so I can check her out, if that's okay with you."

"Here they come. I'll have an officer swing by and take her mother to the hospital."

Abby's dad ran alongside the gurney as the men carried her in. He held her hand and kept saying, "Daddy is here. You're going to be okay."

The ambulance pulled in and they swung into action immediately. Cleo gave a quick exam to make sure she wasn't bleeding, surprised at how clean she was, in spite of having a few deep scrapes, and bruises, nothing appeared to require stitches. One of the paramedics retrieved a stethoscope for Cleo to check her other vitals. She suggested an IV of fluids as soon as possible and noted her blood pressure was low. A dark bruise around her ankle the size of a hand and another one on her upper arm already was evident, but in the poor lighting, it was hard to tell much.

"Hopefully, your doc on duty will take charge quickly. I want her seen ASAP. Understand?" The paramedics nodded and wheeled her to the ambulance. She reached out and touched the arm of her father. "I don't see any big problems right now. Be sure they check everything." He nodded and had started to walk away when she grabbed his arm. "I mean everything." His bewildered expression forced her to continue. "To make sure she wasn't sexually assaulted." The realization his child may be changed for life dawned in his watery eyes as he hurried to the ambulance.

Perez sighed as she joined Cleo. "Poor guy. At least we found her."

"Can you radio in and make sure they check under her fingernails. They were dirty and I thought I spotted traces of blood."

Perez called the hospital and asked for the ER doctor, giving him instructions from Cleo. He remembered her from earlier in the day and assured the chief he'd make it a priority. When she clicked off, the chief tilted her head at Cleo before speaking.

"Dr. Berman said you had no business driving and should rest. Said the meds he gave you would knock out a horse."

"I didn't take any. I took an over the counter they gave me at the hospital. Saving it for tonight."

"I would like some of that, too," Jacque called from the open car window of his SUV.

"I'm having one of my officers drive you in." Perez motioned for an older man to come forward. "George will take you."

"Happy to, young lady. The chief never gives me enough to do. Thinks I'm too old." The smoker's voice explained the yellow smile.

"Not true, George. Don't want anything to happen to you before you retire next month is all."

He chuckled, making his over-the-belt belly bounce. Cleo wondered how long he actually had left with being overweight and a smoker. Chances were good, he had high blood pressure. Those brown spots on his neck and under his ear showed signs of skin cancer, too.

"Thank you, George. We appreciate it." Cleo moved toward the car backward as she directed her voice toward Perez. "Should we wait for you at the hospital?"

"No. Making sure everything is secure here then I'll drop by to see what you found out about the girl and the detective. They're waiting for you and Abby at the hospital. Get a room at the Mountain View Inn. Across the street from the hospital. I'll make sure they keep a room for you. On us. I'll swing by when I can."

Cleo gave two thumbs-up. "Glad this day is finally over."

The darkness swallowed them up as they headed toward Sunset Rock. Except for the beam of light ahead of them, it appeared they had fallen into a black abyss, swerving this way and that. Exhaustion lay heavy on Cleo and her two friends.

Jacque rode in the front seat with George, only because Wind Dancer could be a handful at times when the car moved and he couldn't get his bearings. Since their driver remained unaware of how special the Pawnee was, she thought it best she sit next to him in the back seat. Holding onto her usually redirected his train of thought. Most of the time, this could turn into a pleasant experience, but tonight she ached and felt like she had drowned in a sea of still-unanswered questions.

"How ya doing, Jacque?" She reached up and touched his shoulder, which caused him to flinch.

"Nothing a good night's sleep won't fix. You?"

"Same. But wanted to run this by you. Abby's hands were clean and so were other parts of her exposed body. Wouldn't running through brush or over a trail leave you a little more banged up or at least dirty?"

"I'd think so. I noticed that, too. Even her face looked like it had been scrubbed. Couldn't hide those bruises though. Bottoms of her feet were slick as a baby's. That was rough terrain, too. We're missing something."

"The monster carried her," Wind Dancer said offhandedly. "Not want to hurt."

Cleo agreed and continued. She quickly brought them up to speed on Mansi and his son.

"I'm telling you, something isn't right there. They are involved. I just know it. He has a history with both Abby and Tinker, the boy found dead in the truck."

"Did you tell Perez this?" Jacque winced as he adjusted his seat.

"Everything happened so fast with you guys being hurt, that creature, then finding Abby, I didn't have a chance. Anyway, according to Mansi, his son has Marfan syndrome."

"What the hell is that?" Jacque grumbled as he tried to get comfortable. "Give me one of those knockout pills, Cleo."

"No. Not until you are checked out."

"I can knock you out, buddy." Wind Dancer leaned in and gave him a pat on the shoulder.

"Stop being a cry baby, Jacque," Cleo ordered. "Marfan is a genetic condition that affects the connective tissues in the body. Lots of things can go wrong like heart valve problems, scoliosis for starters. People with Marfan syndrome are usually very tall and thin. Their arms, legs, fingers, and toes are also disproportionately long. Some symptoms can be severe. I saw Alo, Mansi's son, at a distance and he fit this description. He is also disfigured. Tinker tormented him from time to time. Abby took up for him."

"Maybe that's our guy." Jacque tried to roll his shoulder. "Come on, Cleo. I'm in pain."

"No pills. Anyway, from what I understand, whoever took little Liam moved fast and was strong."

"Yes. He strong, too. Liam say woman tried to protect him and fought hard." Wind Dancer spoke quietly and stared out the window as if remembering.

"That's where it gets tricky. People with Marfan aren't usually all that strong. Depending on how severe Alo's condition is, he may not have had the energy or ability to run fast or take a beating from Tonya."

Jacque sighed. "For heaven's sake. This is just a freak thing you're talking about. Probably more weirdness you found out in the museum growing up."

"Okay. How about this. Did you know Abraham Lincoln had Marfan syndrome?" Jacque gave her a bewildered frown. "And so did Julius Caesar and Tutankhamen. There are a few basketball players and Olympic swimmers with mild cases. In more recent times, authorities believe that al-Qaeda leader Osama bin Laden had Marfan syndrome."

George put his two cents in. "I know Alo. Strange guy. Sneaks around like a ghoul. Always with his head down. Likes to spend a lot of time in the woods, too. Several campers have been scared by him and filed complaints."

"There was blood and dirt under her fingernails. That needs to be analyzed. DNA doesn't lie," Cleo said as she rested against the seat.

"Who is DNA?" Wind Dancer asked in his most serious voice. "Is this a friend?"

Jacque twisted in his seat to focus on the Pawnee and smiled. "You better believe it. Hey what's that?"

Barreling out of a side road with large spotlights aimed at them, all Cleo heard was Jacque yell, "Look out!" then the unmistakable sound of shattering glass, followed by the roll of their SUV as Wind Dancer crushed her beneath him.

CHAPTER 26

How long had she been unconscious? Seconds? Minutes? Hours?

Wind Dancer lay half on and half off of her body. She managed to wiggle out by shoving on his chest. A bright light flooded the SUV, exposing the blood on the Pawnee's jaw and hairline. It was hard to move in such a confined space. Through her fog, Cleo realized they rested in a tilted position.

The revved-up noise of an engine then the movement of the SUV being released from the pressure of another vehicle made the light pull away. She hoped help would come. The quiet movement of footsteps on gravel followed. The door opened and a figure appeared. Rough hands reached in and grabbed her by the front of her shirt, jerking her forward.

"Please. Help my friends." It was difficult to keep the hysteria out of her voice as the slamming of the car door exploded in her senses. What was happening?

When her body had cleared the car, she was tossed on the ground like a rag doll. She rolled over to see the figure peering into the car. The lights from the vehicle that hit them still blinded her. Identifying who had pulled her free remained impossible. Whoever rammed them, turned to glower down at her. Fear mixed with helplessness engulfed her even as she tried to use her one good arm and feet to thrust her away from the figure who moved closer. When he grabbed her foot and jerked, a snicker escaped as one shoe came off in his hands.

Cleo could see the outline of his face and tried to kick him. "You," she gasped. Was she hallucinating?

A rustle in the brush behind the SUV caught his attention. He dropped her foot and gaped at something she couldn't see then ran to his vehicle. In seconds, he was squealing tires and on the road.

Cleo collapsed and tried to catch her breath. What had scared him? Did he see the strobe lights from an approaching police car? An animal? Whatever it was, he didn't want to get involved with more trouble.

She touched her forehead and felt a trickle of blood. Her head hurt, along with most of her body. Tomorrow would be a bad day.

The noise in the bushes became louder. Closer.

"Wind Dancer?" She tried to roll to a standing position. The vehicle was hard to see in such thick darkness. Once on her feet, she staggered to the car and tried to see in. The three men weren't moving. Just as she wrapped her fingers around the door handle, a large hand covered hers.

A scream escaped her mouth in surprise as she twirled around to stare up into the hideous eyes of a monster. It kicked the door hard enough the door handle fell to the ground. With little effort, he lifted Cleo into his arms and stomped toward the woods as she cried for help from her friends.

~ ~ ~ ~

Jacque experienced confusion at sitting lopsided in his SUV. Why wasn't he behind the wheel instead of the chubby guy with thinning hair and wide-open eyes. Blood covered part of the driver's face, and he gasped for air. A moan from the back seat reached him at the same moment he managed to unsnap the seat belt, dropping him against the blob dressed in a police uniform. While he pushed away to right himself, the memory of the driver, why he wasn't driving, and his friends in the back seat, swam up to give him clarity.

"Wind Dancer?" he coughed, inhaling smoke. "Wind Dancer," he demanded.

Moans of confusion and pain lifted as did the Pawnee. He reached over the seat to steady Jacque by grasping his shoulder. A dark streak trailed from his temple, and, like himself, there appeared to be momentary confusion with the creases around his eyes.

Smoke clouded over them as he heard a pop under the hood, followed by an explosion of sparks.

"Buddy, can you get us out of here? This car is about to blow." Wind Dancer blinked several times and nodded.

It took Wind Dancer twice to slam his shoulder into the passenger side door to make it open. The car had landed on a dinner-table-sized boulder at an angle, but the fall hadn't blocked the doors. Once Wind Dancer managed to free himself, and, in spite of being exhausted and injured, he went to work on Jacque's door with a great deal more ease. The door kept wanting to shut, preventing him from dragging the detective outside. The Pawnee grabbed a rock and wedged it underneath the door to prop it open long enough for him to drag Jacque, who struggled to climb out.

"I will get the man called George now," the Pawnee said after getting Jacque away from the car that now was engulfed in flames.

Jacque grabbed his arm as an explosion lit up the night. "He died before you got the car door open." He jumped to his feet. "Cleo," he screamed. He staggered forward. "She must have been thrown out. I didn't see her in the car when I came to."

Wind Dancer caught him as he lost his footing.

"Jacque. She is gone. I heard her cry out but could not move." He jerked the detective around. "The Chaveyo took her."

"Chaveyo? Are you sure?"

"Yes. She has stopped crying. I hear nothing now. I don't know where they are." His tight voice held a nervousness Jacque had never heard before. That couldn't be good.

The flashing-red strobe of the police car came around the curve, followed by a second car. They pulled up and jumped out. The night was ablaze with the fire as Perez ran up to them.

"George?" she cried as she tried to run forward.

Jacque caught her arm and prevented her from running toward the fire. "He died shortly after impact. When Wind Dancer got us out, the car exploded. I'm sorry, Perez."

He expected her to cry, scream, or maybe let loose enough

colorful words to make a sailor blush, but she appeared mesmerized at the blaze as it popped with the kind of noises that haunts the toughest of hearts. Her face was void of expression, except when her nostrils flared with a kind of seething anger he'd seen on many a cop when they were trying to hold it together.

The other cops who had followed now tried to put out the fire with little extinguishers. But it was of no use. With a slow pivot, Perez surveyed the area before focusing on Jacque.

"Where is the doctor?"

Wind Dancer pointed to the woods. "Gone. Chaveyo did this." He squatted down and lifted a handful of dirt then sniffed it. "I can smell him."

"Yeah?" Perez snorted sarcastically. "What does Chaveyo smell like?"

"Death."

~ ~ ~ ~

Cleo awoke when the jostling of her body felt like it was being carried down, maybe a ladder. When she opened her eyes, she was cloaked in darkness. A pain across her midriff helped her understand she was hanging over a boney shoulder. Each step jabbed it into her rib cage, sending a jarring pain throughout her body. Once her captor touched the floor of wherever they were, he took a few seconds to inspect the area. She knew this only because, what felt like feathers touched her neck several times as he twisted his head back and forth.

What did he see? Her eyes couldn't adjust. When he lumbered forward then stopped, he pulled her down off his shoulder before pressing her body against a wall. She was too terrified to fight and besides, her body was exhausted. The stiffness of the accident had already set in, along with the fall earlier in the day. In spite of the thick darkness, Cleo could make out the large head covered in dark paint or animal skin. The eyes bulged white and clear. His breath was rancid as he leaned his face closer, causing her to turn away. Slowly he turned and disappeared into the darkness.

Whatever was happening, he made little noise. The sound of dragging things over and over made Cleo force herself to try and calm down. With her hands flat against the wall, she realized she was in an underground room. The walls felt cold and clay-like. She slid two steps along the perimeter, not knowing if it was toward the ladder. When she took one more step, the dragging stopped. Was he keeping track of her movements?

A flame appeared deeper into the room, tiny at first, as the creature fed it small sticks and leaves. It was enough light to let her know she'd moved farther away from the ladder. A curl of smoke drifted up and disappeared into what Cleo thought would be a ventilation shaft.

Having spent many a summer camping in the Southwest with her father while he studied the tribes of the region, she sensed her location might be an underground kiva. The strong pungent smell of smoke made her cough and eyes water, drawing the creature's attention.

Without warning, he whirled around and rushed at her when she took one more step into nothing. He caught her by the collar with such force, her feet dangled over a large hole, a sapapu. A chill ran up her spine as he jerked her away and into the wall. Had he risen out of the sapapu? Was it another hole into a parallel universe? He moved to squat by the fire.

Was this thing real? Had she been given a concoction of peyote to make her have hallucinations? He shifted attention to her then motioned vigorously for her to sit down across from him at the fire. What choice did she have? Cautiously, she did as he demanded.

She realized in that moment one of her shoes was missing. A pain surged through her forehead, causing her to rock back and forth. When it passed, Cleo lifted her eyes to find him staring at her, probably curious, by the way he tilted his giant head at her.

Standing at least seven feet tall, he was huge, an ogre-like being who seemed to be both man and beast. The head appeared to be a wooden mask or covering. However, the bulbous eyes moved constantly. The mouth opened and closed, revealing large canine teeth that could have ripped open a wild boar with no problem. Long feathers protruded from the mask or head.

The clothing was a mix of pieced blanket and skin materials. The arms were uncovered from the elbow, down to his hands covered in leather, leaving the fingers uncovered. Loose-fitting pants reminded her of something the Sioux wore on the plains. In one hand, he held an ax then lifted a saber from the kiva floor. It could have easily been used as a staff.

It dawned on her who he was as she staggered to her feet.

"You are Chaveyo."

The reaction was swift as he circled the fire and rushed her, waving the saber.

CHAPTER 27

"I have no money," Wind Dancer admitted to the nurse who prepared to give him a tetanus shot. She smiled at him, adding a seductive tilt of her head, Jacque noticed.

Wasn't that always the way? Wind Dancer acted clueless when it came to women. He wondered if that were true. Wherever they went, you could bet some babe or cougar would flirt with him. Maybe it was his aloof attitude toward the strange world around him that kept him a little off-balance to notice the obvious. Did the women in his world play the same kind of mental games with men that drove them crazy? Jacque understood he wasn't tall, dark, and handsome like his Pawnee partner, but he certainly wasn't invisible.

"We got it covered for now, Wind Dancer," Perez said, walking in the examining cubicle. "Are you about finished?" she asked the nurse. After sticking the arm of the Pawnee, who never even flinched, she took a little longer than necessary placing the Band-Aid over the spot and whispered encouragement. He jerked his head up and blinked at the nurse, who fluttered her eyelashes and grinned.

"Thank you."

When she exited, Jacque swung his legs off the bed. "Thank you? For what?"

"She said if I needed anything at all to be sure to ask for her. Helen, I think."

Jacque rolled his eyes upward then over at Perez, who pooched out her lips as if withholding a grin. "And this is why I can't get a date."

"You cannot date because you are a chauvinist pig. Cleo told me."

"Really?" he growled. "Do you even know what that means?"

"I think it means tough."

"Oh." Jacque smiled and straightened up at the praise. "You could be right. Women just think of me as a handful."

"A handful of BS, I'm thinking," Perez added.

"I will remember this." Wind Dancer frowned and wrinkled his forehead in the way he pondered new information.

Perez sobered then jabbed a slender finger toward the bed for Jacque to get back in. "We have people combing the woods where the accident occurred." She held up a hand to stop Jacque from speaking. "Nothing yet. We'll find her."

"Chaveyo take her," Wind Dancer insisted. "You cannot catch him. I can. You should have let me go for her."

"I'm not going to argue with you, Wind Dancer, so shut the hell up."

The Pawnee straightened at her orders and frowned at Jacque, waiting for instructions as to how to proceed. "She must be chauvinist pig, too, Jacque."

"My partner is right."

"Excuse me," she huffed.

He fanned a hand in the air, as if erasing the last comment. "I mean, we need to get back out there."

Perez arched an eyebrow and shifted her weight to one hip, a move Jacque found a little bit sexy.

"You two could pass for the walking dead right now. You'll get some sleep before I agree to that."

Jacque noticed Wind Dancer's wide eyes of alarm at the mention of the walking dead. "Easy, buddy. It's an expression. No skinwalkers here."

Perez formed an evil smile. "You don't know that. You're a white man. What do you even know about skinwalkers?"

"He was a skinwalker once." Wind Dancer yawned through his

words. "FBI say I cannot talk about it."

Jacque noticed the heaviness in his partner's eyes. "What the hell did they give him besides a shot?"

Perez picked up a chart at the foot of the bed. "Just Tylenol. Probably for pain. No big deal. I'm sure they asked if he was allergic to anything."

The Pawnee shut his eyes and swayed until Jacque scooted off the edge of the bed and went to help his friend lie down. "Sleep, buddy. We'll go as soon as you rest." He then refocused on Perez. "He's not allergic. It just knocks him out. Not sure why. Doesn't work on him like it does us. But I'm thinking I need a couple hours shut-eye, too."

The now-familiar, bewildered expression the chief wore appeared again, and Jacque knew she was still trying to figure the two of them out. "I'll come get you in a few hours. I'm going to get some rest, too. Then we'll all go back to the scene. Okay?"

Jacque could only nod as he yawned and climbed into the bed.

His body rocked gently, driving the cobwebs of sleep from his head. Long strands of black touched his face that tickled an irritating slap at the disturbance. The rocking persisted until Jacque pried open his eyes to see a face looming over his.

"Ahhh," he shouted as he took a swing at Wind Dancer who caught his fist before it impacted his nose. "Get away from me, damn it. What do you think you're doing?"

"You sleep like a fat bear. Time to get up. Sun rises. This is the day of darkness. We must find Cleo before the moon crosses the sun. Hurry."

"He's right." The sound of Perez's voice made him sit on the edge of the bed. She handed him a cup of brew from some place called Psycho Deceiver Coffee. "Brought you a mood stabilizer."

"What, no donuts?" He took a sip.

"Cleo says no more donuts, Jacque. Cholesterol is high." The Pawnee directed the information to the chief. "Do you have oatmeal? He can have that."

Perez laughed when Jacque narrowed his eyes over the lip of the Styrofoam cup.

"If I want a donut, I'll eat a donut. Cleo wants to make my life miserable." The cobwebs of a deep sleep slipped away. "Any word on her?"

"Nothing. We did find tire tracks, however, from the vehicle that hit you. Similar to truck tires. Little bald in places. Had an oil leak. Not sure if that was from the accident though. A truck driver reported a car on fire in an abandoned quarry on the other side of Kewa Corner this morning. Still waiting to see if it might be our vehicle. The volunteer fire department made it there in time before it burned completely up or spread to the surrounding forests. That could have delayed the entire investigation."

"Strange place to find a burning car."

"There's a dangerous curve there. Been several accidents over the years. No guardrails. State keeps saying they will do it, but you know how slow the wheels of progress turns." Perez handed Jacque his shirt then helped him slip into it since every bone in his body screamed stop. She passed him a pair of jeans that probably came from a secondhand store. Cleo had pretty much destroyed his pair when she cut them off completely to suture the rip in his leg. "Want me to help with that, too?"

The coy expression on her face irritated him. "I got it. Thanks."

"Anyway"—she moved to the end of the bed—"it appears the vehicle went over the edge and burst into flames when it hit the bottom. We should have an ID soon."

"Any info on DNA or the stuff found under Abby's fingernails?"

"No matches. They're running it again for me since it was such a rush job. The dirt is consistent with the entire area."

Her phone buzzed, and she stepped outside the room to answer.

Wind Dancer helped Jacque with the jeans and hiking boots while he grumbled about not needing help the whole time. His protests were ignored. "Stand up," Wind Dancer ordered, removing the cup of coffee from his partner's hands.

Determined to not show pain turned out to be more of a job than he imagined. His leg still hurt from the stitches. His ribs felt as if they'd been used as a therapy tool for someone with anger management issues. Extending his arms in frustration, he rolled his shoulders and grumbled. "See? Right as rain." He caught himself using the expression and braced himself to explain. Fortunately, Perez joined them and lifted her chin toward the door.

"Let's go. We may have someone in custody that is our guy."

~ ~ ~ ~

The glowing embers of the fire remained in the kiva, along with the sweet smell of pine. Enough warmth remained from last night's fire that Cleo managed to stretch her legs out from the fetal position she'd taken for most of the night. Her face felt grimy and hot, having faced the small flames. The Chaveyo stared into the fire or at her until she couldn't resist closing her eyes to the horror of the ogre before her.

There had been one horrifying moment when Chaveyo came storming around the fire, waving his saber like a crazed ninja before swinging it within a few inches of her throat. Now she wondered if he missed on purpose, but at that second, all she could do was shout out the Hopi word Tuuhikya, which meant true healer. She had no idea if she pronounced it correctly or if it would be the same for Pueblo people from this area. The Chaveyo stopped his advance as she fell against the hard clay wall.

Every muscle appeared to tightened and release as he stood spraddle-legged with his saber still held toward her.

"Tuuhikya," she choked out and patted her chest. "Tuuhikya," she repeated softly and clumsily tried to stand tall.

The Chaveyo, if she remembered her father's teachings correctly, respected healers as did most tribal people. There were times the Chaveyo was summoned to find the person who didn't walk the Hopi way and would confront him. Now that she'd been confronted with that sharp saber, she could only imagine how ancient people might have responded.

Lowering his saber, the Chaveyo moved to the opposite side of the fire and sat down cross-legged. The struggle to refrain from crying and begging to be set free overwhelmed her. Instead, she sat down, cross-legged and waited patiently, maybe to die. But nothing happened.

Now here she was, unsure of her location or how long she'd been asleep. A glow of pink covered the entrance hole in the ceiling, indicating the sun was rising. A piece of wood sat near her with a pile of pinon nuts. She gobbled them down, knowing they were healthy and provided the energy she needed. A turtle shell held water. She gulped, realizing the fire had parched her. The throbbing in her wrist made her feel drunk from pain.

Since there were pinon nuts, she had to be at an altitude of 4000 feet. She remembered one year her father had taken her up in the mountains, along with several graduate students. When they reached 6000 feet, one of the students became ill. He kept saying it was the pinon nuts they ate, but after getting him to the hospital, he suffered from altitude sickness, not the pinon nuts. The experience gave her an interest in native plants and medicines.

She rubbed her wrist and cradled it in her good hand.

A sound came from the dark side of the kiva, revealing Chaveyo had been there all along. This time, instead of a saber in his hand, he carried part of a yucca plant with exposed roots and dropped it next to her. Was this a test to see if she were indeed a healer?

Carefully she examined the roots even though it had been years since she'd used plants for healing. She knew how important herbal remedies had been to the Hopi and Pueblo. It had been said these tribes now suffered health problems because they no longer depended on the old ways.

Cleo met the monster's wide eyes and shivered. "Thank you, Chaveyo. I can mash the roots to make a poultice, but I need more water." She lifted the turtle shell. "I will use it for my wrist." She lifted it to show him the bandaged area. "I will make enough for us both."

There was no way she could be sure if he was suffering from pain, arthritis, or a blood disorder. But if he was, this might help. It certainly would ease her pain. Maybe he would begin to trust her and remove the hideous mask.

With the grace of a ninety-year-old using a walker, Cleo grunted as she rose to her feet and was amazed at how gigantic the ogre stood. Then she realized, after staring up into his face—it wasn't a mask.

CHAPTER 28

After Jacque had a chance to stretch out his legs and downed a second cup of coffee, he managed to rid himself of the hobble he displayed from his injuries. Even the slight swagger returned to give the appearance of confidence. Much to his relief, the rabies test on the Chupacabra proved negative. At least now he could focus on finding Cleo.

Once at the quarry, with Perez driving, the three of them joined the last of the firefighters checking to make sure no sparks still existed. Since the quarry was near Kewa Corner, one of their local cops had arrived on scene.

He was a stout fellow with dark skin and close-set eyes. Even though he wore a hat, the obvious short haircut gave him a military vibe. Standing to the side with an out-of-gear stance, hands on hips, and chewing gum, he reminded Jacque of one of those stereotypical cops from movies that no one liked. All this guy needed was a pair of sunglasses which he, no surprise, pulled from the front pocket of his shirt and placed on his long, hawk-like nose.

"Perez." He nodded then raised his chin as if examining Jacque and Wind Dancer.

"Jimmy," she chuckled. "I see you got some of those fancy glasses they advertise on TV. Isn't that what the SEALS wear?

You know they make you look ridiculous, right?"

Way to put him in his place right off the bat, Perez, Jacque thought.

His bottom lip contorted at the insult, and he tried to change the subject. "Who are they?"

Perez smiled like a Cheshire cat. "Chicago PD. Have some experience with the nonsense going on around here. I asked them to put their two cents worth in since you seem to have your hands full directing traffic for the solar eclipse today." It was yet another jab at his usefulness.

"Detective Jacque Marquette," he said extending his hand. Jimmy hesitated but did finally reach out and clasp his hand with a firm squeeze. "My partner, Joseph Wind Dancer."

Wind Dancer did not extend his hand but arched a menacing eyebrow at the local cop.

"Anyone inside the car, Jimmy?" Perez took a step toward the truck before turning back as an afterthought to the younger officer.

"Nope. But I recognize the truck. Belongs to that stupid kid who works at the garage. Everyone calls him Tinker. Pulled him over just a week ago for speeding. Doesn't have enough sense to wad a shotgun. Took my car in for an oil change not long ago, and he dropped the oil pan, spilling it everywhere, including on the boss." He laughed at this. "You never heard such language."

By the condition of the vehicle, there wouldn't be anything left inside. Jacque noticed, when he went to take a closer inspection, that even the tires had melted.

"Chief Perez, we're going to check out where the truck came off the road, if that's okay with you?" Jacque wanted Jimmy to understand he didn't mind working with a woman cop.

"Sure," she said. "I'll pick you up in a couple of minutes after I check all this out."

Jacque nodded to Jimmy and saluted the couple of firefighters who took note of them as they walked out of the quarry.

"See here?" Wind Dancer said as they walked the road at the top. It wasn't difficult to figure out where the truck went off since tracks led there. "Tire slipped off the road then went over."

Jacque backtracked about ten feet and took out his phone to take a picture. "Stopped here. Then got out. See? Slight footprint. Maybe the toe of a boot." Jacque followed the path to the drop-off to the quarry below. "I think the car was pushed over. My money is on this being the one that hit us."

"Front of truck smashed."

"Yeah. Whoever drove it thought going over the edge would bang it up enough to look like it happened here on impact." He turned and walked to the tracks. "Wasn't much left of those tires, but from what remained appeared to be bald, just like the ones where our accident happened."

Wind Dancer studied the ground. "Tracks look like bald tires."

Perez joined them in the car, careful to park a ways from the spot of interest. She had on her strobe in case another car came along. "We have this blocked off about a half mile down the road in each direction. This road is used mostly by locals. All those tourists and Syfy geeks won't come this way, but in case anyone gets off track, that should turn them away. Find anything?"

Jacque pointed at the tracks and the toe print. "I think someone got out here."

"Figured as much," she said. "The gear shift, although melted, was in the neutral position. Besides, there was no body inside the vehicle. Maybe we can talk to our guy in custody. Ready to go? We'll let Jimmy manage this." She chuckled. "Thanks for back there."

Jacque knew she referred to giving her respect in front of Jimmy. "I don't know what you're talking about."

"I think she means—" Wind Dancer started, until Jacque leveled a shut-up frown. "I should not speak."

"Right," he said in a slow drawn-out tone.

~ ~ ~ ~

Little activity at the police station meant either the available police and staff were at the designated locations for optimal eclipse viewing or hadn't checked in yet. Perez voiced concern that their small town, along with Kewa Corner, would not be big enough for the crazies expected to pour in. The number of people had swelled overnight, and the RVs had created a small city in the Walmart parking lot.

The night before had taken on the appearance of a college tailgate party with the grills full of brats, burgers, and steaks, country music playing at full volume, and a great deal of flag waving. Although the most trouble expected was fender benders, food poisoning, and a lost dog, Perez canceled anyone's time off or vacation for the next few days. Besides, with the missing little boy and now Abby, their rescue services might be running on fumes.

It worried Jacque that Cleo would not get 100 percent of what was needed to find her. Although the sun was barely up and only a few locals could be seen leaving the café where they'd had lunch the day before, he considered one of those RVs might be something more than an eclipse fan. These kinds of events were perfect opportunities to snatch people off the street and, next thing you knew, your loved one was in some hellhole in a third world country with a needle in their arm and being abused until they gave up hope or died.

"Let's do this. We want to get out there and find Cleo. We're wasting time."

The lady at the reception desk wore her gray hair in a bun on her neck. She reminded Jacque of a character from reruns of The Andy Griffith Show. He wondered if the tough old girl carried a gun on her thick waist. However, the smile she greeted them with put him at ease.

"Mansi is waiting for you. He's in the conference room. Not happy to be dragged away from the inn. Busy time. Don't expect him to be all warm and fuzzy." She rolled her eyes toward, what Jacque imagined, was where they'd be headed. "Made fresh coffee about ten minutes ago. Already gave him a cup. Help yourself, boys." She again leveled a wide, toothy smile at them.

"Mansi? What about Alo? I thought that's who was brought in?" Perez's voice took on that what-the-hell tone.

"Don't know anything about that. I think they're out searching for him now."

"Alo? What's going on?" Jacque butted in.

"Mansi's son. Abby has been in and out of consciousness, what with the sedative she was given. She kept saying Alo over and over. Tonya roused for a few seconds and said giant. That's Alo."

Jacque remembered what Cleo had told him about Marfan syndrome and how it affects the body. He couldn't imagine in this day and age of NBA players that anyone would think an overly tall man would be unusual or a monster, for that matter.

The conference door was ajar. A man sat staring out the window. Hunched shoulders, a shirt that needed pressing, and a crooked tie gave Mansi Garcia a humble appearance. He hadn't touched his coffee. When they entered, he jumped to his feet and paced.

"Do you know how many people I have at the inn today? Or how shorthanded I am?"

"I'm very sorry, Mansi. We have a problem. Where is your son?"

"I don't know. He took off yesterday, and I haven't seen him. I looked for him last night."

Jacque extended his hand and introduced himself then Wind Dancer. "I'm a friend of Cleo Sommers. She stayed at your inn. You were kind enough to bring her out to us last night."

Mansi nodded and smashed his lips together so tightly, it made his brow crease.

Jacque continued. "She thought maybe you saw him last night. You were talking to someone in the dark. Remember?"

"She was mistaken. Where is she? And what does my son have to do with anything?"

Wind Dancer stepped forward in his usual menacing way and growled a reply. "A tall man took her from me. If harm comes to Cleo, I will kill him."

Jacque shoved Mansi aside, the innkeeper's face whitened in shock. His eyelids fluttered as if the fear could be covered. "My partner and Cleo are close." Jacque smiled at Mansi. "He isn't as understanding as I am. I just want to be sure you and your son get a fair shake."

Before Jacque could stop him, Wind Dancer grabbed Mansi by the front of the shirt and shook him violently. It took both him and Perez to pull him off. The Pawnee's face had gone red. With flaring nostrils and bulging eyes, he'd put the fear of God in the man.

Jacque put his palms on Wind Dancer's chest and shoved him up against the wall. "What the hell, Wind Dancer?"

"I give him a fair shake," he yelled.

Jacque sighed and pinched the top of his nose as his eyes closed. When would he learn not to say things that could be misconstrued by an angry Pawnee from the 1800s. "You! Stay put.

I mean it. This is no way to find Cleo. Got it?" The heavy breathing continued as the Pawnee leveled a steely glare at Mansi, warning more trouble brewed. "Wind Dancer? Got it?"

The Pawnee finally nodded and crossed his arms across his chest, a clear sign that he would wait for further directions. "I wait short time. No more. He should talk now."

Perez turned her attention to Mansi. "Sorry about that, Mansi."

"Sorry? I'm going to file a complaint," he snapped, raising a fist at Wind Dancer.

Perez tilted her head and tried to straighten Mansi's shirt then patted his chest. "Now, Mansi, it was a misunderstanding. We're in a tight spot here. We need to talk to your son. That girl, Abby, kept saying Alo's name over and over. Seems to me he might know something about what happened to her. Simple as that. Come on. You and I have always been friends."

He slapped her hand away and leveled a finger near her nose. "No," he growled.

Before Jacque could bat an eye, Perez grabbed his finger and brought him to his knees with a bang. "Don't touch me, Mansi. I might get the wrong idea." She applied pressure until he whimpered.

Wind Dancer stepped forward and cocked his head at Jacque. "Is this fair shake?"

Jacque grinned. "Maybe better."

CHAPTER 29

How long had Chaveyo been gone? Time would stand still if it weren't for the light growing brighter in the exit hole. After saying she needed more water, he'd disappeared by climbing a ladder he'd stored in the dark area of the kiva. When he reached the top, Cleo held her breath, hoping he might leave it and go on his way. That hope was dashed when he pulled it up so slowly, it appeared to float.

To pass the time, she crushed the yucca roots with the ax he'd left next to the piece of wood where she'd found the pinon nuts. The next activity, while there was still enough light from the fire, was to search the kiva. The sipapu, or hole in the floor, was the portal where the ancient ancestors first emerged to this world.

As a little girl, these stories her father had shared with her had both terrified and thrilled Cleo. This hole measured larger in diameter than the ones she'd seen over the years. Could Chaveyo have emerged from that hole? What would have happened if she'd fallen all the way inside? Why did he prevent her from doing that?

The ancient Pueblo builders used stones to make the walls of each kiva and then were covered with a layer of smooth adobe. This one had a lot of the adobe missing. She wasn't sure what it meant. Could she climb out without killing herself? It didn't appear to be all that deep. The Chaveyo had to stoop over to walk unless he stood in the middle of the kiva. Then again, Cleo realized she had only one hand that worked well enough to haul her body upward. It would take all four limbs to escape.

A wave of helplessness washed over her. Fear, mixed with the pain in her wrist, clouded any thought of survival. Tears flowed down her cheeks. Then she remembered how Wind Dancer's sense of hearing intensified when he crossed over from his universe.

"Wind Dancer," she screamed. "Wind Dancer. Wind Dancer. Help me! I need you. Wind Dancer!" Over and over until her voice grew gravelly and raw. "Wind Dancer," she whispered. "I know you're there. I love you. I don't want to die here. Wind Dancer, please."

The light from the exit hole disappeared, except for a halo effect. Cleo took a step back and squinted up at the dark shadow blocking out the dappled sunlight. A large hand reached down and wiggled its fingers.

She sniffed before dragging her nose across her upper arm and gawked at the hand. Where were the Chaveyo's leather gloves? Curiosity got the best of her until she moved closer and used her two fingers to touch the rough palm, now spread open, as if waiting. The flesh felt warm. Once more, her attention went upward. At the same time, she began to withdraw her fingers, the hand snapped shut, like a vise, around her good hand. Her screams and struggle did nothing to release the upward momentum of her body.

~ ~ ~ ~

The door opened to the conference room just enough for the woman at the front desk to stick her head in. Her attention went to Mansi struggling to get in the chair as Perez gently assisted and smiled at the intruder.

"Yes, Barb?" Her voice, sweet and calm, left no room for suspicion of rough play.

"Some city slicker out here says he's from the FBI. Asked for those two." She tilted her head at Jacque and Wind Dancer.

"Send him to my office. We'll be right there. Could you bring Mansi one of those Danish rolls I spotted in the break room?"

Mansi snarled, "I don't want any..." His voice faded when

Perez leveled a steely-eyed glare of contempt. "I mean, thanks. That would be nice."

The corner of Perez's mouth turned up as one eyebrow arched. "I'll be back in a minute, Mansi. Be ready to tell me what I want to hear." Before he could respond, she guided them to her office.

"Remind me not to piss you off, Perez." Jacque opened the door to her office for them.

Wind Dancer slapped him on the back, causing him to stagger at the strength. "I will remember for you. I wouldn't want her to hurt you, too. You aren't very strong."

Perez smirked at him then focused on Jacque. "I suspected as much. Is that why you always take muscle with you?" She cocked her head toward Wind Dancer.

"No. Wind Dancer goes along for comic relief," came a familiar sound in the office. Agent Farrentino stood at the window, coffee cup in hand, grinning at the banter. He stepped forward and extended his hand to Perez who couldn't stop smiling all of a sudden.

Those blue eyes and olive skin must be physical traits women are into these days, Jacque surmised. The giddy laugh she emitted at the agent irritated him just a little.

"Farrentino. Chief Perez," he introduced with a wave of his hand.

"It is Special Agent Farrentino, Jacque," Wind Dancer corrected and extended his hand. "It is good to see you again, my friend."

Jacque felt his frown deepen. Even Wind Dancer appeared smitten. There was no denying, the man was a charmer. He'd give him that. Could be a qualification to join the FBI.

"Wind Dancer, I brought you those chocolate-covered macadamia nuts you like." He reached inside his coat pocket for a small bag and handed them over.

"Thank you. I will save them to share with Cleo when we find her."

Agent Farrentino appeared bewildered. "Find her?"

The three of them caught him up to speed, at times all talking at once.

By the end, his hands were on his hips and his forehead creased. "I got a message from Cleo last night she wasn't going to wait on me to pick her up. Said she caught a ride. Sorry I'm just now getting here. There was a terrible accident, and I got trapped."

"So, you talked to her?" Perez asked.

"No. Message on my phone. Didn't find it until later. Since it was about 3 a.m. by that time, I parked at a rest stop and got a few hours' sleep. Came the rest of the way when an eighteen-wheeler thought it would be amusing to pull in front of my car and use that blasted airhorn. Needless to say, I had to change clothes." Jacque grinned. "Stopped at the hospital to see if that girl had been found, and one of the paramedics informed me you guys had been in an accident. Nothing about Cleo. He directed me here."

A young officer appeared and gave his boss more information. "Had to ticket a few guys who took it upon themselves to search for Dr. Sommers when they heard about George getting killed. Then a tractor trailer overturned between Kewa Corner and here. Traffic is a mess both ways. Everybody in a hurry for the eclipse. Not watching what they're doing. Search and rescue are still out there."

Jacque checked his watch. "She's been missing a long time, Chief. We need to find her." He turned to Farrentino. "You thought this sounded like other missing people you've been studying?"

"Yes. One minute, they're there, and next, they're gone."

Perez took a deep breath and let it out slowly. "Same here. Has happened several times over the last ten years or so."

"But you have three that survived. Very unusual. Can we talk to them?" Farrentino asked in his no-nonsense FBI tone.

"Not Tonya. She's in Santa Fe. Let's head over to the hospital."

Farrentino retrieved his phone from the inside pocket of his suit coat. "I'll get an agent from Albuquerque up there. I sent a guy there two days ago to check a few records. He can head up there to see her."

"Let's go." Perez moved to the door. "Let's go out to where we last saw Dr. Sommers." They stopped back by the conference room to see Mansi shoving a cheese Danish in his mouth. "If you know anything, Mansi, now is the time to tell me. I can't promise I can protect Alo without your help."

"I did see him last night like Ms. Sommers said. He heard about Abby. He just wanted to find her. I told him he should go home. He wouldn't listen. I swear, Chief Perez. Now, can I go take care of my inn?"

"Barb?" Perez stopped the front-desk lady who waddled by. "Keep Mansi here until I get back. Agent Farrentino may want to talk to him." She stuck her head in the conference room. "Thanks, Mansi. I'll do my best to find and protect him. Okay?"

He nodded and sat down with his cold cup of coffee in hand.

The parents of the little boy were checking out as they arrived. Liam spotted Wind Dancer and ran as fast as his short chubby legs would carry him. The Pawnee gathered him up in his arms.

The child slipped an arm around his new friend's neck and got comfortable while his parents joined them. They were happy to follow them into an unoccupied waiting room to have a chat.

Liam hadn't been injured but was given fluids and a tetanus shot since he had a few scratches on his hands and face. From what they could find out, he'd fallen in brush when he tried to get away from his captor.

"Did he say who or give a description?" Jacque realized in all the chaos they'd not been given a chance to question the boy before he'd been taken to the hospital. "They kept him a little longer than usual."

"I left orders to keep him here in case the…" Perez's gaze went to Liam to gauge how much to say in front of him. "In case his friend returned."

"He couldn't remember, Chief Perez. We tried to get a little information, but he was so tired, we let him sleep. When he did wake up, he didn't want to talk about it. All he said was 'scary.' A counselor dropped by yesterday, but, like us, didn't get anywhere."

"Little one, can you tell us more about the one who took you?" Wind Dancer stroked the boy's head. The child buried his face in Wind Dancer's neck for a few seconds then whispered in his ear. When he finished, he buried his face in the Pawnee's shoulder once more.

Everyone waited and seemed to hold their breath as Wind Dancer tightened his embrace and spoke soothing words in his native tongue before addressing the group.

"We must hurry. There is more than one Chaveyo out there. Cleo is in much danger."

CHAPTER 30

The boney hand lifted Cleo by the good wrist, but the weight of her body made her shoulder feel like it would dislocate. The suspension caused her to involuntarily kick the air beneath her twisting body. She tried to use her broken wrist and hand to strengthen her hold. The weakness did little to remove the pressure from the other arm. With the upward motion, her body slammed into the rocky wall, now void of the slick adobe. The scratches opened enough to draw blood. By the time her head cleared the entrance hole, she could feel the slow trickles of blood moving down her arm.

Once the cool morning air touched her face, a hope of escape magically strengthened her.

~ ~ ~ ~

Once back at the scene where Cleo had vanished, Agent Farrentino and Jacque took a look around. Crime scene tape gave the area a haunting, if not helpless vibe. Many times, Jacque had examined these scenes, but now his friend was involved. Cleo was one special lady, and he didn't want to lose her to a killer. The thought of such a thing happening blurred his reasoning power. His first inclination was to kill whoever did this.

The feeling of rage surprised him, since he had always been able to step outside himself to solve a case. Wind Dancer and Cleo had changed all that. They were family. The realization he loved them almost overwhelmed him as he imagined Cleo being terrorized by a monster serial killer.

Where was she? Was she hurt? Heaven forbid, was she dead? How would he handle the worst-case scenario? Not well, he imagined. Then there was Wind Dancer. If the love of his life could not be found alive, would he also leave, crossing to his time? To think of losing both of them brought a lump to his throat.

He pivoted to observe his partner amid the question-and-answer session between Perez and Farrentino. Wind Dancer stood like a statue, staring into the woods, chin up, ear cocked. His fingers opened and closed. The Pawnee listened, but to what?

All Jacque heard were the annoying morning chirps of birds and the wind rustling the tops of trees. This was another indication how much of a city boy he was. Give him the sound of blaring car horns, belligerent street workers, and the smell of garbage and exhaust fumes any old day. At least he understood that kind of crazy.

Wind Dancer turned his head to lock into Jacque's psyche. How did he do that?

"She is alive," the Pawnee announced to his friend as Jacque approached. "She calls my name. I am going to go get her."

Jacque knew it would be pointless to argue. "How far away?"

"Not sure. Her voice carries on the wind."

"Is she hurt?"

Wind Dancer blinked and refocused on the woods. "She is in deep hole. I smell campfire. Not sure how far I can, what is the word?"

"Detect?"

"Yes. I am not sure how far my hearing and smell can detect. In the past, it has been several miles if I already know what to sense. In Chicago, very dirty, and I have to think and separate. Out here, it is clean. The smell and sound travel long way, I think. May bounce off rocks and trees."

There was a time when Jacque would have dropped down laughing his head off at such talk. Those days were long gone. Now he knew parallel universes, skinwalkers, Native Americans, and that communication between man and beast was possible. Whatever was out there taking innocent people had to be stopped. So the question now was sthat even possible? His own experience with a skinwalker had nearly ended his life in Chicago. Whatever creeped around in these woods had to be just as bad, if not worse.

"Let me go with you," Jacque stated in a low voice as he cocked his head toward Perez and Farrentino. "Cleo is my friend, too. It might take two of us."

"Your leg is injured, my friend," he said, resting his large brown hand on Jacque's shoulder. "You cannot keep up with me. We both know that when I am on the hunt, even when your leg is good, you struggle to follow. It is not because you are weak. It is because you have not crossed into this world or any world, to change your body. I was like you in my world."

"Maybe I should cross over into your world and show you what this feels like. I mean, having a friend with super strength," he huffed out the words. He winced and removed the Pawnee's hand. "You deserve a little payback." Jacque watched his friend's eyebrows lift, like they often did when he didn't understand. "Payback means—"

Wind Dancer patted him on the back of the head and smiled, which managed to make Jacque stretch his mouth into a frown. "I know what it means." He tilted his head toward the other two. "Will you take care of them for me?"

"I'll try. Don't you need supplies?"

"No. The land will provide what I need."

Jacque slipped out the walkie-talkie from his backpack and handed it to the Pawnee who hid it inside his denim jacket. "Remember how to use this?"

He nodded.

"It's already on the right channel so don't mess with it."

"Roger that," he said then jutted out his bottom lip.

"And don't use crazy words like 'roger that' when you don't even know what they mean." He nudged the Pawnee toward the woods. "Go. Bring Cleo home. I need her to keep me on the straight and narrow." A bewildered frown creased Wind Dancer's forehead at the reference. Jacque rolled his eyes and waved for him to go. "Ask Cleo when you find her. It will give you something to talk about."

He arched an eyebrow. "We don't talk much after we've been apart."

Jacque pinched the top of his nose and shook his head in frustration. "That is way more information than I needed. Now, go."

Jacque knew by not alerting Perez and Farrentino that Wind Dancer had gone rogue, his chances of getting to first base with the pretty police chief had evaporated. Besides, the way she was listening so intently to the FBI agent and the tilt of her head, making her appear sultry, helped him decide the flirting would be the much-needed distraction his friend needed to put distance between them. The Pawnee was like a bloodhound at times, as long as people, normal people, didn't get in his way.

"Where's Wind Dancer?" Farrentino asked, casting a suspicious gaze around Jacque as he approached.

"Taking a leak. Told him to go before we left, but you know he never listens to me."

Farrentino continued to level a narrow gaze at him. The man was a different kind of bloodhound. He didn't get to be the FBI darling who could request any job he wanted by being a pushover. You certainly couldn't trip him up with a lame story about taking a leak. The surprising thing about this situation was Farrentino let it slide. While Perez read over her notes and continued to talk, both men locked gazes, causing Jacque to lift his chin in a signal to not ask too many questions.

"Excuse me. I need to take this call." Perez lifted her phone and walked out of earshot.

"Where is he? Really," Farrentino mumbled as his mouth took a definite downward turn.

"Did you think he was going to wait for her permission? We're burning daylight."

The corner of Farrentino's mouth tilted up as he tried to suppress his cocky grin. "You've been out here less than a week, and you're already talking like a cowboy on a cattle drive." When Jacque didn't respond, he removed his jacket and draped it over his arm, revealing a shoulder holster. "I've got boots in my bag and a few more things to hike. You look prepared." He eyed Jacque. "I've called a helicopter in to scout ahead since we can't smell, hear, or run like a damn superhero. I'm not about to go traipsing around in miles of terrain others have already searched."

"I thought the quirk in this series of disappearances was that the body shows up in the area already searched? Maybe they missed something."

"True. But I'm thinking there's a place out there where this thing hides. It's only a matter of time until we find it."

"Thing? What do you mean thing?" Jacque tried to control his voice so as not to show surprise or fear.

"These incidents are happening all over the country. Even in Canada. Generally, in heavily wooded areas but not always. But it consistently involves a large park and hikers. They disappear and about half are never found. The other half are either found dead or…"

"What?"

"They're so confused about the incident or traumatized, they can't remember, or they report crazy things that would make a great Twilight Zone episode." He moved toward the car and pulled out his phone and made a call to the helicopter to let them know they were headed out in a few minutes. He turned to Jacque to continue. "Then there are the survivors who are not particularly injured, like Liam."

"You mean kids?"

"Yes and no. A few kids can't tell you anything. They're found almost naked but no injuries. Then there are kids with disabilities like Liam, although he appears to be very high functioning. We may actually be able to break a few things down after he recovers a bit longer, although I don't like to wait. Kids tend to forget or bury their fears. The parents may put the brakes on if Liam acts distressed or fearful. Parents feel guilty they couldn't protect their child and just want to move on."

"Can you blame them?" Jacque noticed Perez talking to a few members of the other search and rescue team. They were staring at the ground, shaking their heads. She gripped one man's arm and appeared to be offering some kind of bad news. "Well, that can't be good."

Perez hurried over to join them and sighed. "Tonya died an hour ago."

"Let me guess. The cause of death is hard to determine," Jacque blurted in frustration.

She nodded. "The medical examiner will take a closer look, but the doctors could find nothing overtly wrong." Taking a deep breath, she hurried on to say, "I put security on Abby at the hospital and told them not to discharge her. Her parents have been alerted."

Farrentino finished tying his lace-up boots. "I'm telling you right now. Whatever took the girl isn't going to be coming into a hospital. But if I were you"—he spread his hands out toward the crew preparing to go into the woods—"I'd keep a buddy close."

CHAPTER 31

Once Cleo sucked in the fresh air, it was knocked from her when the creature dropped her face-first onto the ground. A painful moan escaped from deep inside as she landed on her injured wrist. She rolled over onto her back and stared upward to what appeared to be a giant tree, but as the fog of pain cleared, she realized it was something more menacing.

Scrambling to her knees then feet, she stumbled backward like a clumsy turtle who had landed on its shell and tried to right itself. If her body had not stopped against the drooping boughs of a lopsided pine tree, she might have once more found herself on the ground. The penetrating gaze and statue-still stance of the over-seven-foot creature, paralyzed her with fear. This was not the same one from inside the kiva.

Although just as tall, this Chaveyo wore things that reminded her of a costume she'd seen in Native American museums her entire life. It may have even been more accurate than those she'd studied. This one reminded her of the stories she'd heard about the Chaveyo ritual of trotting through the plaza, searching for victims. Resembling those stories, this one wore a skin mask with bits of cedar bark strung over the top. A war ax and a saber, much like the other Chaveyo, appeared as if it were handmade of wood. How could they be so different yet the same?

Strangely enough, he held her shoe she'd lost the night before and tossed it to her. Slipping it on quickly, Cleo followed his movements as he lifted the saber from the ground and extended it at her then toward an opening in the woods.

"Run. Chaveyo returns. Run. Now."

Cleo realized this creature was a man, not a Chaveyo from the sapapu hole in the kiva. Although just as terrifying, this one could speak. She eased to a standing position and prepared to run, but he blocked the path to the way he'd pointed. With a few side steps, she tried to edge closer to what appeared to be an overgrown trail. His chest moved in and out at a rapid pace as he began to twirl the ax like a baton. The irritated grunts he uttered caused her to freeze in place. Without warning, he charged her, yelling words she couldn't understand. Her foot slipped as she tried to outmaneuver him, but it was too late. Swinging the ax up over his head with one hand, he dropped the saber from his other hand, and grabbed the front of her shirt, yanking her forward.

~ ~ ~ ~

Jacque grudgingly agreed to let Farrentino take the lead down a trail. After all, his leg wound still ached in spite of the pain meds. With the FBI in the lead, he wouldn't have to be so mindful of every step he took as closely or determine which way to go. The guy was such a Boy Scout when it came to this stuff. Probably why he and Wind Dancer had hit it off several years ago after the whole Chicago attack occurred.

A helicopter reported they'd seen a man running down a little-traveled trail. From the pilot's description and amazement at how fast he was moving, it had to be Wind Dancer. Agent Farrentino took the same offshoot trail after getting directions and told the helicopter to keep searching.

"Think we can catch up with your partner?" Farrentino quizzed. "Sounds like he's a couple of miles ahead of us."

"He was pretty determined on going his own way. I think that 1800 Pawnee stuff kicked in. If there is a trace of her or anyone moving about, he'll find it. We should be on the lookout for signs of where he's headed. The guy is part bloodhound. I'm pretty sure he heard her earlier, which prompted him to take off without us."

"And you had no idea he was going to do that." It was more of a statement than a question.

"Of course I knew. Two other things I knew: one, Perez would have said no, and two, you would have said go for it. Telling her anything about the remarkable talents Wind Dancer possesses could land him in jail. It nearly did when Liam went missing."

Perez, had indeed, fumed when she discovered Wind Dancer had left without them. She reiterated how dangerous it could be for one person to head out alone. Next came the speech about being shorthanded, and didn't they understand this was the exact kind of scenario that got the others taken? The eclipse would make things dark soon, causing yet another problem. Both men had twisted their mouths in disgust and nodded in hopes of appearing chastised. Then she'd made a mistake.

"Agent Farrentino, I thought you would have known enough about this case to warn both these men not to do anything stupid. Guess I was wrong."

"Well, fortunately, I don't work for you. And if you worked for me, I'd have your badge for dragging your feet. I'm sure you read the email sent to you from FBI headquarters stating I was to be given whatever resources and assistance I required. At that moment, these two men began working for me, not you. Whatever they want to try, I support them 100 percent. And just to catch you up to speed, I know a lot more about this case than you. Now, if you have a problem with that, I do have the authority to call in a replacement."

They trudged on, discovering this part of the trail was rougher. Jacque managed well enough since it was slow going. After mulling over the earlier conversation, he couldn't resist a chuckle. Farrentino paused to take a deep breath and give him the once-over.

"What's so funny?"

"You. The way Perez was batting those pretty brown eyes of hers at you, I thought you might get lucky. No chance of that now." He took the opportunity to sit on the edge of a small boulder.

"And the way you were frowning at me, I figured out you probably had already ticked her off, keeping yourself out of the running. You need to take a few romance lessons from your partner. He certainly helped me," he offered matter-of-factly.

"You? Mr. Playboy of the FBI?" This drew a laugh. "I can't wait to hear this." He held up a hand. "No. Wait. I don't think I can stand to hear it. And besides, I don't need any help in the romance department, thank you very much."

The last comment got him a snicker and a nod to get moving.

Light turned to an odd yellow glow as they moved down the trail. Birds grew deathly quiet, and breezes ceased. The air felt dryer up here. Every pungent fragrance of the forest seemed to weigh heavier each time Jacque inhaled, until his eyes watered from possible allergies. A twig snapped. Both men stopped, their bodies stiffened to high alert.

"Hear that?" Jacque whispered.

Farrentino nodded and motioned for them to take cover under a ledge that overhung part of the trail. A trickle of water gurgled down the side of slick rocks. An armadillo hurried across the trail away from them. Both men sighed at the same time and smiled at their overactive imaginations. Then three more armadillos crossed the road at what must have been top speed for those small legs, followed by five or six deer and more jack rabbits than Jacque had ever seen. The strangest part was that a number of coyotes with tails tucked between their legs ran onto the trail, and not because they were hunting. They were escaping.

"One thing Wind Dancer told me was that coyotes don't run in packs. They hunt alone for the most part." Jacque felt he was holding his breath. "I think they're trying to get ahead of something."

A puma followed with her cubs and stopped for only a second when she noticed them. She stole a quick glance over her shoulder and then disappeared into the rocks above them.

"There is something out there, and I'm not sure it's human," Farrentino admitted.

Both men pulled their weapons and readied themselves.

CHAPTER 32

Before Cleo could get a steady footing, this new Chaveyo swung the ax, landing it in the bark at the base of the tree she'd leaned against. He reached around her and withdrew the weapon with a rattlesnake still attached, held it up for her to see then slung it off with the force of snapping a whip.

This new threat dragged Cleo by holding onto the front of her shirt. A couple of buttons lost their grip and flew into the air. No amount of pleading or digging in her heels stopped his forward motion. For a few seconds, when he approached, she'd thought he was going to chop off her head. She tried to say the same thing to him as the other Chaveyo, about being a healer, but this one didn't appear to understand. Maybe he didn't care.

"Move," he demanded.

"Let me go," she screamed as she struggled to free herself.

He halted and released her so fast, she fell into him then quickly shoved herself away.

"I won't hurt you. The Chaveyo will return soon and then you will disappear forever. I tried to save the woman with the little boy, but it was too late."

"You didn't take her?"

He didn't answer, only held her with an angry stare through the horrific mask. His gaze darted all around, surveying the surrounding area.

"Did you take Abby?"

"Yes. To protect her, but Chaveyo took her from me. I then went to help you."

"I ran."

He nodded and reached for her again.

This time, she jumped out of his reach. "And the boy in the truck. Did you kill him?"

"I didn't have to."

"Chaveyo?"

He shook his head.

"Then who?"

"We must hurry now." This time, his reach caught her by her broken wrist, and there was nothing to do but submit or scream with pain.

Even with this new creature knocking aside brush that got in their way, a few branches managed to snag her hair or brush against her face. Perspiration beaded up at her hairline and trickled down her face, mixing with the blood from the scratches. There was hope now that Wind Dancer could smell where she was in time to mount a rescue. In her heart, she knew he hunted for her.

This creature's long strides forced her to take more steps than normal for her much-shorter legs. Exhaustion threatened to collapse her body. If she fell, would he continue by dragging her after him. Why was he doing this? Was there a reason he had pulled her out of the kiva?

The forest grew thicker, but the brush grew sparse, making it easier to follow. The ominous darkness of the eclipse began to block out the sun. A yellowish haze turned the blue sky into a freakish omen of danger. She remembered Mansi's warning. Stay inside and keep babies away from the windows, and wear something sharp.

She once sat in on one of her father's seminars concerning other pueblos in New Mexico and how the people had been astronomers. There were always elders who believed in taboos with eclipses. Some thought it was a time of transformation and should not fear them. Could this be why Chaveyo had chosen now to reveal himself? Others in the tribe may have committed a wrong and felt fear. Cleo remembered one of the elders present said to pray with cornmeal, respect the silence, and accept the transformation coming.

Could this be what was happening? Transformation? Taking revenge on a person who had done wrong? Even though this new creature had not been moving all that fast, to her it was a sprint. He stopped and let Cleo lean against a tree. She wished desperately for the air to stir so she could cool off before he decided to start again.

She wondered if whatever this ogre wanted, it might be transformation, to be something it could never be: normal. In that moment, she remembered seeing a person at the edge of the property at the inn where she stayed in Kewa Corner. Later, Mansi had told her about his adopted son who had Marfan syndrome. Could this be him?

"You went back for Abby, didn't you?" She leaned forward and put her hands on her thighs to try and suck up more oxygen. He remained silent and continued to study the trail that opened up ahead. "Why did you take her in the first place? Did you want to keep her for yourself because she protected you from Tinker. Stood up for you?"

He slowly turned his head, the edge of the mask catching on his collar. The movement made it uneven on his face enough so the openings no longer lined up with his eyes, giving it a hollow appearance. "I did not want her to disappear into the underworld with the Chaveyo."

"You're Alo." The declaration made him jerk his head around then his whole body.

"I am Chaveyo," he growled.

"No. You are good. Chaveyo takes people, hurts them."

"He does not mean to hurt anyone. I have tried to help him. Stop him. But he comes from the sapapu in the kiva to right wrongs."

"The little boy hurt no one. He is innocent."

"And he lived."

"And the woman, Tonya, from the rescue team. What wrong did she do?"

"Who knows the heart of anyone?" When Cleo didn't answer, he continued. "Chaveyo knows. When people do not guard the little ones, they are punished. When people wander into spirit-filled mountains without permission, they are taken."

"Many of those hikers, hunters, children are enjoying nature. They mean no harm to anyone. The land is for everyone. Why did the Chaveyo take me? I'm a doctor. I heal people who are sick and injured."

"You were with the girl. You saw him. He does not like to be seen. He touched you through the window when Mansi stopped on the road. He chose you because you are a healer."

"What does he want?"

"Peace. To be left alone. Yet, more and more people come to this land, taking pictures and taking plants that are protected."

Cleo realized more than ever that this was not an ogre. "Alo, why do you protect him?"

"We are alike. Ugly. Big. He does not judge me."

"You don't have to live like this, Alo."

"How would you know how I have to live? I am not Alo. Here, I am Chaveyo and should be feared."

"Then why are you taking me away from the kiva? Won't your friend—"

"My brother!" he snapped angrily as he stepped toward her.

Cleo tried to edge away and held up her hands. "Okay. Brother. Won't he be angry with you?"

"I have done it before. He lets me save a few. The little ones. The old ones." He checked the darkening sky. "But it doesn't always work out. They die, or he decides to keep them. Then they are gone for good. It is pointless to keep searching. Many have disappeared."

"Is that why you brought Abby back? She was your friend?"

"I do not know her."

"She stood up for you with Tinker."

"I do not know her," he insisted.

The sound of frustration came through his tone of voice as he began to twirl the ax.

"Okay. Okay. Do you know what happened to Tinker?"

The giant twisted his body around several times and cocked his head. A few pieces of bark fell from the covering on his head. "You must walk down the trail. It is up ahead." He pointed with the ax. "The faster you go, the closer to safety you will be. My brother comes. He will be angry you are gone. If he catches you before the moon crosses the sun and turns the day to night, then you will be gone forever. Run." Cleo straightened and wondered if it was a trick to hunt her down. Then he shouted, "Run!"

Two steps backward, before she pivoted and ran until she found the trail. Although the trail was crisscrossed with crooked roots and small rocks, she managed not to trip and fall. It didn't take long to regain enough speed to feel confident she would escape. When her lungs felt like they would burst, she stopped to check behind her then up at the darkening sky.

She took a deep breath and spun around to slam into a hard body that loomed in front of her. The scream that escaped from deep inside was smothered by a hand pressed across her mouth.

<h1 style="text-align:center">CHAPTER 33</h1>

Birds took flight, and the screech of a hawk added to the chaos around the two men. They took steps farther under the overhang and aimed their weapons at the unknown threat. The slow crack of tree limbs breaking then hitting the ground forced Jacque to adjust the grip on his weapon. He cocked his head to pop the stiffness in his neck. His jaw tightened and released as he waited, a habit he'd acquired as a young officer when having to wait for the orders to go into a desperate situation.

A dark blur moved through the trees before stopping twenty feet away. It appeared to pivot in their direction.

Neither man spoke, but both raised their weapons slightly higher. The take-no-prisoners mentality took over if things went sideways. The uneven sound of heavy breathing, or maybe it was the sudden breeze that rattled the dry tree branches, compelled each of them to dig in their heels. Without warning, it lunged forward, swinging a long object in its hands and growling.

Both pulled the trigger of their weapons several times before the dark shape changed course and vanished into the trees.

"What the hell was that?" Agent Farrentino gasped as he checked his weapon.

"Maybe a Chaveyo." Jacque replaced the magazine after he'd emptied it into their attacker. "I'm not exactly sure what I saw. But it could move. It had a dark head."

"Tall and hunkered over. Was that a sword he carried?"

Jacque and Farrentino kept talking to establish a list of facts they might have to recall later.

"Did you notice those teeth?" Jacque asked more to reassure himself he hadn't imagined it. "Or was I just scared to death? I'm not sure about that."

"I don't know," Farrentino admitted. "A dark figure emerged from the trees with a growl. It was swinging a stick, a weapon. I'm not sure. Did our imagination get the best of us?"

"No wonder people can't tell us anything. I'm not traumatized, and I can't tell you what I saw."

Jacque held his weapon down at his side, hesitant to slip it in the holster. He stared up at the yellowing sky. "I'm afraid more than ever for Cleo. She doesn't have a chance against that thing."

Farrentino took a deep breath. "Jacque, you need to come to grips—"

"No," he snapped. "I don't want to hear it. She's not dead. Let's go. He's taken her somewhere. We've got to get to her before it's too late." He moved onto the trail. "Wind Dancer is alone. Even his unique skill set won't be enough against whatever is out there."

"I'm calling Perez to let her know where we are and what just happened in case for some reason we don't return." He pulled his walkie-talkie from his backpack.

"I gave Wind Dancer one of those. Try to call him. He knows how to use it."

Farrentino gave him an incredulous look but tried anyway. "Nothing. Sorry." Next, he tried Perez and reached her immediately. He explained their experience and caught up on the latest news that amounted to still trying to locate Tinker's dad and that Mansi had slipped away from the police station.

Perez thanked him for checking in and informed him of other groups out searching. Nothing new on that front. She reminded them to stay together, given what had attacked them.

"I'm waiting here for backup then I'll try to join one of the teams. In the meantime, I'm checking on a lead that might help us with the Tinker murder. I'll fill you in when you come in."

Jacque grabbed the walkie-talkie. "You're there alone?"

"Don't worry. Highway patrol is sending a guy out to help me.

Should be here any time now."

"I don't like it."

"Your concern is touching." The sarcasm came through loud and clear. "Gotta go. A car is pulling in. Need to move them along."

~ ~ ~ ~

When the car rolled to a stop, Perez strolled toward it. The car door opened, and a familiar face appeared. She sighed and put her hands on her hips. "We're a little busy here. Get back in your car and keep moving. I know you've got questions, but I can't deal with that now." He just stood there with a scowl on his face until she inched closer. "Did you hear me?"

~ ~ ~ ~

"Who is it? Perez?" She clicked off, and Jacque handed the radio to Farrentino. "She thinks she's all that, doesn't she?"

"Probably why she's the chief of this end-of-the-world place. Got the feeling she has to do a lot of proving herself here among these macho-guy types." Farrentino continued to survey the surroundings.

"One of us should go check on her," Jacque decided.

"You might be right. Let's just call to see if whoever pulled in got a chewing out and ordered to move along." Farrentino tried the radio with no luck. "I'll try her cell." He handed the radio to Jacque. "You try this again."

Both men did with no luck. Then the radio crackled alive with a deep male voice.

"Hello. Trooper Higgins here."

"Trooper Higgins, this is Detective Jacque Marquette. Can I speak to Chief Perez please?"

There was a pause.

"Trooper Higgins? Are you still there?"

"Yes, Detective. Chief Perez isn't here. I found the radio on the ground. No one else around."

~ ~ ~ ~

Fear gripped Cleo once more as she struggled to pull the hand off her mouth. She dug her nails into the hand and tried to avoid the arm that wrapped around her body before he jerked her hard against his chest. Moving was now impossible. His mouth came down next to her ear.

"Cleopatra. It is me. Be calm."

Cleo froze and twisted around to stare up into the dark eyes of Wind Dancer before melting against him. The struggle evaporated as her arms went around his waist. With a slow gentleness, he removed his hand and rocked her, sliding his hand down the back of her head which was now buried against his chest. Her body shook with sobs.

"You are safe now." He pushed her to arm's length before using his large, dark hands to wipe away the tears. Next, he ran his hands down her arms and checked her ripped clothes. "Are you injured?"

She shook her head and sniffed. "Just scratches, I think. A few bumps and bruises."

He lifted her chin with one finger. "Cleopatra, were you—"

"No. I wasn't raped, Wind Dancer." She again stepped into his arms. "I knew you would find me."

"I heard you call my name." He kissed the top of her head. "I was afraid, Cleopatra."

The warmth of his body surged through her fingers. "I love you so much, Wind Dancer. I thought I might never see you again."

"We must go. The Chaveyo walks near. I couldn't see him, but I felt him."

"The Chaveyo took me. He is terrifying, Wind Dancer. I don't know why he didn't hurt me. I think I made him understand I am a healer."

"Native people have a great respect for medicine healers. For some reason I cannot smell or hear him. I only sense his presence. I'm not sure of that now. Come. We should find Jacque and the FBI man."

"Farrentino is here? And I thought Jacque wouldn't be able to be out here after the attack last night then the accident. That can't be good for his leg," she whispered, knowing their voices might very well carry on the wind. "And you weren't hurt in the accident?"

"I am sore today. Bruised. But okay. I kid Jacque about being weak, but he really strong and wanted to help find you. Worried."

"I'm glad you're okay," she said, adding an embrace. "I worried you might be dead."

They headed down the trail. Wind Dancer took her hand, tugging to keep her moving when she hesitated. "The animals will alert us to the Chaveyo's movements if he comes close. I can trust this. And yes, Jacque is with the FBI man now. They were going to search for you, too."

"Wind Dancer, do you have anything sharp to protect us during the eclipse? It is custom to wear it to protect us. We have to find a place to shelter."

"The moon is halfway across the sun from the way the darkness now moves across the forest. The birds are going silent. We are near a ravine where the trees have grown sideways, like a bridge. We can hide under this. I looked there for you. It remains dry and dark enough to protect us from Chaveyo finding us."

They had to take a slight detour off the trail and then another slippery trek down beds of pine needles to reach it. Once there, Wind Dancer removed a pocket-size flashlight from his vest pocket and smashed it against a rock. He picked up the shards of glass from the globe and stuffed them into his pocket. Gathering Cleo into his arms, he held her tight as an ominous wind swept through the ravine. It lifted debris from the forest floor to swirl upward like a giant ghost hunting for souls to harvest.

Without warning, an avalanche of wildlife thundered down the hillside, crossing the tree bridge, and down into the ravine with a blur of speed. Wind Dancer pulled her as far under their refuge as possible to avoid the animals. Amazed, Cleo clung to him and witnessed all manner of beasts trying to escape, but from what?

An abrupt halt to the stampede and wind brought the awareness of a slow cracking of limbs and the gentle tumble of disturbed rocks.

"Something is out there," Cleo whispered.

Wind Dancer held her so tightly, she thought the glass in his pocket might cut her. Then the appearance of long legs and a saber with a large hand gripping the hilt as it touched the ground appeared in the middle of the ravine. The Chaveyo stopped a few feet from where they hid in the darkness. In slow motion, the feet turned toward them, and the saber lifted out of sight.

CHAPTER 34

Jacque exchanged a bewildered expression with Farrentino before continuing with Trooper Higgins. Tightness settled in his chest.

"She said a car pulled in when we disconnected. Wanted to get them moving. See any signs that someone was there?"

There was a pause again. "Well, there are several search and rescue vehicles here, along with a Sunset Rock police car."

"That belongs to Perez. Should see another one with Colorado plates. Anything else?"

"Hard to say. I was notified there had been an accident here last night, and there are certainly traces of oil on the ground, out near the pavement, along with broken glass. Anyone find that?"

Farrentino shrugged when Jacque locked eyes with him. "No. But the chief did say she had an idea or lead on a murder suspect. Are you up to speed on that?"

"Yes, sir. I am. A lot going on with the eclipse happening. It's almost complete. People get weird during these things. Looks like some of your rescue team is returning. Maybe they know where Chief Perez got to. I'll radio you if they have more info or have seen her. If not, then I'll start a search on this end."

"Check her vehicle. Maybe she left information there. She wouldn't go off half-cocked. Doesn't smell right."

The conversation came to an end, and both men adjusted their backpacks after holstering their weapons. Jacque thought checking on the chief might put Cleo's life in jeopardy if Wind Dancer hadn't found her. Besides, there were now plenty of people there who would know how to sort through the new problems, provided it needed clarification. Troopers were good at that kind of thing and could be counted on to take charge and make sense out of chaos. Maybe it was nothing, but then again, his gut said she was in trouble.

The day turned toward darkness as they pressed on. Jacque didn't like this eclipse nonsense. No wonder a plethora of superstitions revolved around these kinds of events. Should they be taking precautions? Shelter? Do a dance or stand naked in a creek? What? Right now, he'd do almost anything, considering the things he'd seen over the last couple of years.

With coming face-to-face with a living Chupacabra, the night before, he realized it could have easily killed him. Thankfully, Wind Dancer had been able to pull it off him then stab it several times. He thanked his lucky stars, once again, knowing how lucky he'd been Wind Dancer was his partner. Jacque had managed to pull his weapon and shoot the Chupacabra between the eyes when it lunged for his friend, only to have it turn on him. Wind Dancer rolled it off Jacque. It appeared dead as several of the rescue team came on scene, but the beast rallied. That time, they got off several more shots to put it down once and for all.

Were there any more of those beasts lurking about? Did it have a connection to the Chaveyo? He quickly told Farrentino about the beast.

"I thought you were hurt in the accident." He made a sign of the cross. "So, we're out here with not much more than a couple of peashooters against creatures from Hell running rampant in this park. I can tell you this much, nothing like that has been connected with what I've been chasing. If the disappearances I've been studying had been a victim of such an animal, there would be blood splatter and body parts left behind."

"Agreed. From what the locals said last night, rumors of those things have been around forever. Kind of like in the Great Smokey Mountain Park where people go missing from giant wild boars dragging them off. You don't find any blood splatter there."

Farrentino stopped and pulled out a pair of binoculars since they'd reached a scenic overlook area. "Well about that," he said, lifting them to his eyes, "the FBI thinks it's more cases like this one, where people disappear without a trace or are found with no recollection of what happened. More often than not—"

"Let me guess. Found near a body of water. Can't determine the cause of death. Found in an area searched before. No tracks of animals and no sign of being mauled. How am I doing so far?"

Farrentino handed him the binoculars and directed his attention out across a valley. "Sounds like you've run across this before."

"Not until I got here. This place gives me the creeps." He focused through the binoculars.

"You're kind of a spook, you know that?" Farrentino grinned as he took the binoculars. "I bet you sleep with a nightlight, too."

"And I wear garlic and keep plenty of crucifixes on hand."

"I wondered what that smell was. I thought I'd just started craving my mother's Italian cuisine." He elbowed Jacque. "Maybe next time I'm in Chicago, I'll invite you and your comic-relief team for Sunday dinner. She'll expect you at Mass, however."

"I can just see Wind Dancer trying to save Jesus from the cross."

This drew a quiet chuckle from Farrentino. "Okay. Maybe skip Mass. Anyway, did you see movement over there? I think it empties into a ravine. I see a lot of crushed vegetation."

"The stampede went that way?"

"Maybe. But look farther. What else do you see?"

Jacque took grabbed the binoculars then checked the darkening sky before he tried to find the location of the stampede again. "Definitely something down there. We're not that far away." He lowered the binoculars with a jerk then once more lifted them to his eyes. "Whatever that is, it's tall. It's bending down. Wait. People are coming out on the other side of some kind of natural bridge." He looped the strap of the binoculars around his neck and pulled his weapon. "Come on. We've got to get down there."

He was already hobbling down the trail at a speed he'd thought impossible a few minutes earlier. Farrentino caught up and grabbed his arm, pulling him behind him.

"Slow down. You want to injure that leg permanently? What did you see?"

"Wind Dancer and Cleo. The Chaveyo found them."

CHAPTER 35

The noise of feet twisting in gravel moved closer as Wind Dancer and Cleo tried to take cover among moss-covered rocks and fallen tree branches under the natural bridge. The damp smell clung to the air as did the dry debris that constantly shifted in and out from under the bridge. Between the dust and dampness, Cleo could feel her eyes burn, knowing she didn't fare well with mildew. She fought off a sneeze, but it came out anyway, and she buried her face in Wind Dancer's chest.

The Chaveyo bent down to peer under the lopsided nature bridge. When he tilted his head and rolled his eyes, she felt Wind Dancer suck in his breath. She remembered screaming when he came out of the woods and to the car accident, only to be scooped up. He'd tossed her over his shoulder before bending down and picking up his ax and saber with one hand. Now, Wind Dancer's heart raced, along with tightening his grip on her shoulder.

A growl rumbled out the mouth that opened and shut, revealing sharp teeth. They eased backward when he jabbed the saber toward them. Cleo could see the ax dangling from the other hand and wondered if he would use it against them. Emerging from the other side of the bridge prevented the Chaveyo from ramming the saber into their bodies. Outmaneuvering the ogre felt like a better option than outrunning him.

The idea was eliminated when he tossed a few of the smaller logs aside and entered beneath the bridge. Although he hunkered over to navigate through the awkward space, the Chaveyo remained focused on what they were doing. His stare penetrated to her very soul.

Wind Dancer pulled her after him up the bank of the ravine and around the bridge. Maybe they could keep the ogre moving in circles to disorient it. By the time they'd reached the other side, the Chaveyo had figured it out and slipped around to emerge in front of them.

This time he stood close enough he touched the tip of his saber to the ground in front of them. He motioned with the ax for Cleo to move away from Wind Dancer, but he continued to hold onto her.

"No," Cleo yelled as she pulled free of Wind Dancer and held out her hands. "My friend," she said as she pointed to the Pawnee then her heart. She stepped away from Wind Dancer so fast, he couldn't grab her arm. "Please, Wind Dancer," she said through tears rolling down her cheek. "Let me protect you. The kiva is not far from where you found me. I'm sure he wants me to return there."

"I will not leave you." Wind Dancer kept focused on the ogre and stood his ground.

Before he could do anything stupid, Cleo slid down the embankment toward the Chaveyo, catching the wooden hilt of his saber and barely missing impaling herself on the blade. She heard Wind Dancer yell "No," when she pushed at the saber.

"Go." She extended her hand in the direction she thought was the kiva. The ogre let her slide down to the ravine but kept his saber aimed at Wind Dancer until she called to him. "Chaveyo. Come."

When he didn't move, she spoke in the Hopi language, unsure if the words were correct. But the strange words enticed him to turn away from Wind Dancer and follow Cleo who ran down the ravine and then up the side where they had first entered. She turned and glanced over her shoulder several times to reassure herself Chaveyo followed.

Thankfully, Wind Dancer didn't try to intercede on her behalf. He wasn't visible at first, but then she spotted him moving on the opposite side of the ravine and keeping his distance.

More movement from higher up on the ridge where a trail dipped sharply caught her attention. Two men were about to intercept Wind Dancer. One she recognized immediately, by the way he ran. Jacque. He halted and lifted his weapon.

There was no doubt he would hit Chaveyo at this distance. She had already noticed several holes in his body where a white syrupy substance oozed from the wound.

Cleo knew it was an ill-conceived idea, but she shoved Chaveyo behind a tree just as a bullet splintered bark. A growl and snapping teeth, followed by him grabbing her injured hand, drew a scream of pain from deep inside her. He jerked her in front of him. Although awkward, both hurried up to the debris-covered trail, parallel to where she'd spotted Jacque.

She thought he called her name. Tears again flooded her face, but she pressed on, away from the man she loved and the friend who'd go through fire for her.

Chaveyo moved faster than she thought possible. When she lagged behind, he slipped his ax into a sheath and the leather strap attached to the saber around his neck and shoulder. It gave her time to catch her breath. She heard the men moving closer. They would be no match for the ogre. He had no fear, and she doubted bullets slowed him down.

For a second time, he caught her by the bad arm. When she winced, he released it and took the other. She suddenly understood he was trying not to hurt her. Even so, he tugged her after him, and she didn't fight it, fearing his attitude could quickly flip against her. She was buying time for her friends and, hopefully, for herself.

The fear grew that he might put her in the kiva and maybe try to force her into the sapapu. As curious as she was about such things, there was no way she'd survive it.

~ ~ ~ ~

Jacque and Agent Farrentino continued their descent until they met up with Wind Dancer. Jacque's leg throbbed, but he shoved the pain aside until he stumbled and nearly fell. The Pawnee caught him in his arms and held on for a few seconds to make sure he steadied himself. The strength in those arms gave him reassurance. If things continued to go sideways, the Pawnee would be able to finish the job. After all, the man was more like a superhero every day he walked this parallel universe.

"Put your weapons away," Wind Dancer demanded. "They are little use against him, I think. Besides, you might hit Cleopatra. She lured him away to protect me." He shook his head in disbelief. "And he followed her when she called to him. She is in much danger. We must go to his kiva. These are magical places. If he reaches there before us, she might disappear into his world." Even as he spoke, they slid awkwardly down to the bottom of the ravine.

Farrentino pulled out his phone and activated the GPS. "According to the coordinates, this ravine will intersect a trail about a half mile ahead. It's a gradual elevation climb. Maybe we can outrun the creature going this way. It could give us some much-needed time." He examined Jacque from head to toe. "How's the leg? Can you do this?"

"Hell, yes," he quipped then pivoted toward their new destination. He reached toward Wind Dancer who grasped his forearm. They locked gazes with a steely resolve. "We'll get her back."

Wind Dancer squeezed his friend's arm and nodded before releasing him. In seconds, they were on their way again. Jacque set the pace. Although he had stitches in his leg, it didn't keep him from trotting at a pretty good clip. His gait was off, but the stiffness had worked itself out from all the walking. After a few minutes, their speed picked up.

"I go ahead now. I can hear them move. The animals are running. If he takes her inside kiva, I not sure if I can stop the Chaveyo from pulling her to the other world." Before either man could protest, he disappeared down the trail that gradually wound upward.

Jacque and Farrentino stopped for a few minutes to catch their breath.

"There was a time I would have thought someone like Wind Dancer had a screw loose if he talked about parallel universes, sapapu holes, and monsters," Farrentino said while he checked his weapon.

"Ain't that the truth? I have gotten more of an education since I met him and Cleo than I ever had in school."

"You're pretty fond of those two."

At the risk of showing emotion, Jacque picked up the pace. "They're my family. I don't have anyone else."

They'd made it to where the trail leveled off again when they spotted something stomp through the area with plenty of tall brush.

"There." Farrentino raised his chin as they eased off the trail against a gray boulder. "Something big. Different than what we saw earlier," he said incredulously.

Jacque chilled at this new creature as it moved out onto the trail ahead of them, his strides long and hard. "It's another Chaveyo. He's following Wind Dancer."

CHAPTER 36

Perez tried to make mental notes as her captor moved throughout what resembled a workshop. It smelled of grease and metal. Light streaming through an unwashed upper window revealed dust floating in the air. A squeaky ceiling fan wobbled, giving her the sense it could fall at any minute. Half-opened boxes of clutter, consisting of tools, car parts, and hoses, were stacked haphazardly against the walls and workbenches. A refrigerator with a retro-style door had a few rust spots and generated a loud noise when it kicked on. All these things she tried to observe to bring this sick SOB to justice.

Her eyes followed his determined movements. He activated a fluorescent fixture over the workbench by jerking on a dangling cord. The clutter prevented the light from traveling far. Once her eyes adjusted to the dimness, she recognized a late-model truck parked next to the car he'd driven to their location.

No maybes about it, she should have gone with her gut and shot the jerk when she had a chance. You never really expect a person you've seen off and on for years to be capable of committing a crime. Then again, in this day and age, with the Internet, people were able to explore a plethora of macabre activities without having to answer to anyone. Sometimes a once upstanding member of the community acted on those illicit fantasies, gambling he would never be discovered. Was this such a case?

She sat on a wobbly metal chair and, every time she moved, one leg scraped the floor, drawing his attention momentarily. With her hands tied behind her and his dirty handkerchief tied into a gag, all she could do was keep twisting her hands to stretch out the cord. Grabbing her didn't seem like a well-thought-out decision. Maybe it was a spur-of-the-moment action. She remembered him chuckling when he slammed the trunk shut on his car.

When he picked up a hammer and turned her way, his eyes narrowed as if he were deep in thought. Was he trying to talk himself into killing her? She tried her best to calm her rapid heartbeat. Being terrified wouldn't get her out of this situation. It might even excite him. Tilting her head, she batted her eyes and tried to appear vulnerable.

What did he want with her? It had been such a risk to take her. Didn't he understand people would be searching for her? Miss her?

She regretted cutting Jacque off like she did when he showed concern. His macho, I-know-best attitude irritated her, in spite of her being mildly attracted to that very trait. The FBI agent liked flaunting his importance, just like every other Fed she'd met. Threatening to replace her did not endear him to her.

Lesson learned. Don't burn important bridges you might need to cross later. They were out searching for the perky Cleopatra Sommers, thinking a serial killer roamed the woods. And here she was, a victim of the real culprit. If he'd been the one to take Cleo the night before, she most likely was dead. But why? There was always a reason.

He slammed the hammer down, making her flinch. The cap pulled low on his forehead formed shadows on his face. She could still see the grin on his face as he approached. Bending, he tapped her nose playfully then directed the strands of hair away from her cheeks.

"You're a real pretty woman. Why would you want this job? Maybe you want to boss everyone around?"

She tried to talk through the gag but only managed to get it wet with her saliva.

"Talk. Talk. Talk. You women sure can run on about things." He traced his finger down her jawline then her neck. Instinct forced her to lean away. This managed to make him laugh softly. "Let me fix that." Carefully, he pulled down the gag and ran a dirty finger across her lips. "Better?"

She nodded. "People will be looking for me."

"I know. Doesn't matter. They won't come here. Nobody will guess it's me. I'm a pillar of the community." With a heavier hand, he stroked her head. "Beautiful hair. Like silk. Why do you keep it tied up? Makes you look like a man."

Perez took several breaths to hide her fear. "Most men don't think I'm good enough," she lied. Her cops knew she had their back and supported her 100 percent.

"What?" he said in mock astonishment. "Well, I think you do a good job."

She widened her eyes. "Really? I wish you'd tell the mayor that. He's always on my case about something. Wants me to give out more speeding tickets to tourists and even the locals so we can add to the city coffers."

"Shocking," he said drily as he let his hand rest on her shoulder.

"I know, right?" She didn't like the position of his hand so close to her throat. "So, why me? What have you got against me?"

His smile widened. "Nothing. Just thought you were pretty. Kind of remind me of my wife. Well, and wondered if you were softer without that gun and badge. You stopped me a couple of weeks ago, remember?"

"Busted taillight."

"Yep. Let me off with a warning. One of those lame-brain deputies of yours would have given me a ticket. But you were polite and ask me about my wife and business. I thought, now that is really nice. I admit, I've had a crush on you, ever since."

"Maybe you could let me go, then."

"Or maybe I could keep you here to see how things play out."

"Are you going to kill me?"

"Depends." He grinned as he pulled the gag up and tapped her on the nose again. "Better get used to that."

Her reflex was to jerk away and yell threats even though they'd be muffled. There was a gut feeling, again, that would lead to more trouble. It might set him off in a way she'd be the subject of a Dateline episode in the future. So, she sat frozen and quiet until he turned to shut off the ceiling fan.

She made pleading and whining sounds. He paused and listened, as if he were enjoying the situation. Strolling to the workbench nonchalantly, he pulled the string for the fluorescent light, bathing the room in darkness. He returned to the door and left the building. The door rattled a bit when he slammed it shut. There was a jerky sound on the door once or twice, checking to see if the door locked, she guessed.

Now. How was she going to escape?

<h1 style="text-align:center">CHAPTER 37</h1>

Cleo experienced both curiosity and trepidation at the Chaveyo's willingness to follow her earlier in the ravine. His guttural growl mixed with that raspy breathing and the snap of his jaws continued to keep her fixated on those razor-sharp teeth. When she slowed and grabbed at large rocks to steady herself, he stopped and took stock of their surroundings. It only took a few minutes for him to be ready to keep moving.

The area grew familiar since she'd escaped this way earlier. How far was the kiva? She wasn't sure, but it couldn't be far. She had to keep him slowed down for help to come. How would she be able to keep from going into the kiva once more? All she wanted was for the beast not to hurt Wind Dancer. She couldn't imagine his powerful body being able to match this supernatural creature.

"I have to stop. Tired." She took big exaggerated breaths and bent over to hold her knees. It was yet another tactic to give the three men a chance to figure things out and rescue her. If she had stayed behind, they would have run the risk of being killed. Whatever oozed from his chest wasn't blood, but the holes did resemble gunshot wounds. She'd seen plenty of those as a trauma doctor in the ER in Chicago.

She patted her chest then pointed to his. "Hurt?" Creating a gun

206

with her finger and thumb then pretending to shoot drew a growl from his chomping mouth. "Hurt?" she said softly then winced and touched her chest again. Slowly, she stepped closer to him, keeping an eye on his flexing muscles and chomping mouth. "Let me look."

He let her peel away his chest covering to examine the problem. She gasped.

She moved closer and spread the fabric wider to see multiple gunshot wounds, no doubt, from Jacque and Farrentino's guns. A white gravy-like substance oozed out, carrying a smell resembling smoke. A kind of ash appeared to grow around each wound.

"Are you in pain?"

He stared down at her but shifted on his feet while his head tilted from side to side. She gently closed the fabric, which was remarkably clean, except for the ooze. She laid a hand on his forearm. With each second, he grew more restless.

Closing her eyes, Cleo raised her chin toward the darkening sky and prayed in a loud voice. It was something she'd seen tribal medicine men do when she traveled with her father. In awe, she'd watched as children thought dead would be raised to live another day. Women in the throes of childbirth relaxed, soothed by a healer's words. Bloody wounds that shouted impending death miraculously failed to rob a person of life with the care of a medicine man. That was the whole reason she'd gone into medicine. She wanted to heal people.

So, she chanted in the darkness that fell around them as the moon crossed the face of the sun and turned the day to night. The sound of the chanted prayer gave her strength. Words thought forgotten now rushed back to her tongue. A strong breeze, refreshing and cool, stirred up the pine needles. Tiny leaves floated across the path and spun around them like magical dancers. In seconds, she was lost in the power of many healers that came before her, encouraging her to continue.

She laid her hands on both his arms and took a chance to observe him. He stood close enough for her to be startled by the grotesque head covered in black fur that caused her to stutter her words. The Chaveyo rolled his eyes down to watch her but finally stopped chomping his jagged teeth. She swallowed hard then slowly withdrew her hands and let them hover over his arms for a few seconds.

"Taawa. Muuyaw." *Sun. Moon.* Using her hands, Cleo pantomimed what was happening in the sky. A Hopi Proverb swam up from her memories with her father who'd taught her so much concerning the Southwest tribes. She didn't know the Hopi words for this and prayed he'd understand the English version. "Inside your heart is a tiny place where all knowledge and wisdom reside."

He nodded. His mouth moving side to side, he gritted his teeth as he turned his eyes skyward. Cleo knew staring at the eclipse was dangerous, but she pretended to follow his example, closing her eyes tightly. When she felt him shift his body, she opened one eye to see him staring at her. He used his saber to direct her attention down the trail, followed by a loud, demanding grunt for her to get going.

"No. It is not my time. I have done nothing wrong, Chaveyo. I am not the one you desire for today. Release me now."

She realized that idea wasn't going to work when he took his free hand and shoved her backward then touched her chest with the point of the saber.

"Okay. Okay. Can't blame a girl for trying," she mumbled. She slapped the saber away, hoping an attempt at bravery would make a better impression. "Naki!" She pointed to herself and prayed she'd pronounced the correct word for *friend*. She had a fleeting thought about the cartoon version of Beauty and the Beast and wondered if she broke out into song, this whole scenario might change. Considering her singing voice resembled a frog croaking, she quickly put the idea on the back burner of just-in-case-this-doesn't-work-I'll-try-it. Either way, she had a whole new respect for the girl, Belle, in the movie version. That chick was tough.

In that split second of indecision, Cleo ducked so fast, she fell to the ground as Chaveyo swiped the saber at her throat. She crab-crawled away from his giant steps but couldn't avoid him when he grabbed the front of her shirt and yanked her to her feet. This time, he took her arm and pulled her after him toward their ultimate destination. When she twisted and resisted, he would only go faster. Once, she tripped and fell to her knees. It didn't slow him down. It wasn't until sounds of dry branches breaking that he stopped and released her, allowing her to claw her way to a standing position.

The darkness lifted, and the forest trail brightened to its normal color. A breeze swept through, as if offering a moment of much-needed refreshment. Fortunately, she'd managed to protect her injured arm. Whether the ogre purposely grabbed the good one was unknown. The damaged wrist throbbed as she gently lifted it in hopes the adjustment would free her of some of the pain. Closing her eyes, she raised her face to the breeze and sun, drawing strength from the chance to rest.

The grunt forced her to open her eyes and gaze into the face of the ogre. He pointed to her wrist.

"Hurt," she whispered. She stroked the bandage and let her lip tremble for effect.

Chaveyo slipped the leather strap attached to the saber around his neck and reached into what might have been a medicine bag. He pulled out greenish-brown leaves torn in small pieces then offered it to her in the palm of his grotesque hand. When she tried to decide if it might have a paralyzing effect so she could no longer resist, he grew impatient and shoved it into her mouth. Even though she tried to spit it out, he just jammed more in, holding her head steady. When it was all gone, he stepped away. There was nothing to do but swallow.

Her tongue felt a little numb, but the remarkable thing was that in less than a minute, her wrist stopped hurting. Dragging her sleeve across her mouth, she frowned up at the ogre.

"Thank you." Nothing. She switched to Hopi to express her gratitude. "Askwali."

Touching his chest where she'd examined the wounds, he then pointed to her wrist. She understood he was returning the favor. Had he also taken the strange leaves earlier to reduce his own pain?

This wasn't a crazy, unhinged beast, but something capable of understanding and reason. Was he lonely? Could this be why he hunted for humans? The stories she had been told were of the Hopi oral tradition where when the people of the village behave improperly, their chief sought help to end their evil ways. The Chaveyo took care of those kinds of problems.

The problem today was that people found it difficult to believe anything beyond themselves. What would the world say about

Wind Dancer and the love between them that crossed time and space? She'd believed from an early age that Native People knew and experienced things the rest of civilization discounted as belonging to backward people. Many times, her father had led her to spiritual and tribal elders who taught and nurtured her beliefs and soul.

Chaveyo's days were numbered in this time. Did he have the power to unleash a kind of chaos no man could survive? Or was he the definition of one of the FBI's most wanted and now had been exposed? She envisioned him ending up with other strange artifacts at Area 51, studied, dissected, and preserved in a macabre test tube then stored away from the world of unbelievers.

Once more, she expressed her gratitude. "Askwali." And laid her hand on her heart and smiled. "Askwali." She pointed to him then to herself. "Naki?" Friend?

"Naki," he finally said. It sounded like he spoke through a tin pitcher, but the feeling of elation washed over her that she'd been able to communicate with him. The idea of learning from him sparked excitement rather than fear. Could she save him?

CHAPTER 38

Jacque and Agent Farrentino caught up with Wind Dancer, who hunkered down behind some rocks. He was keenly aware the Pawnee was focused on something they couldn't see. They had lost sight of the second Chaveyo, forcing both men to constantly check over their shoulders in case the thing circled back for them. How could he disappear like that? Was it joining the other one to help with Cleo or maybe take her for himself?

As they neared Wind Dancer, he motioned for them to get down and be quiet. When they dared sneak a peek over the top of the boulder, they could see Cleo talking to the Chaveyo.

"I caught up with them because Cleo slowed him down," Wind Dancer whispered. "She very tired."

"Doesn't look like he's hurt her. Wait. What is he feeding her?" Jacque asked in alarm. "Poison?"

"No. He take from his medicine bag."

Jacque watched, ready to limp toward the ogre with the speed of a wounded turtle, if need be, but Wind Dancer placed a hand on his shoulder to stop him.

"I got news for you, buddy, the stuff people use today in their medicine bags is most likely illegal and will trip you to kingdom come."

Wind Dancer turned to check on Cleo and the Chaveyo. "I do

not know this kingdom come place. Maybe, when this is over, we can all go."

"I'm going to pretend I didn't hear that, and I'm certainly not going to try explain," Agent Farrentino moaned. "What's the plan, Wind Dancer?"

"We wait to see. She is making friends. I hear her speak a language I do not know. She knows many words from these tribes. Her father teach her their ways. If we go now, the Chaveyo might force her into the sapapu."

"The what?" asked Farrentino.

"It's a hole in the floor of the kiva." Jacque recognized bewilderment on the agent's face. How many times had he himself taken on that pinched brow gaze of unbelief? "Never mind. Cleo can explain after we rescue her." He elbowed his partner. "Let's hear your idea. We already know that bullets don't do squat."

"Why would you squat? That will not help, Jacque."

With a heavy sigh, Jacque noticed the FBI agent cover his mouth, most likely to suppress a chuckle. He felt his nostrils flare in irritation as he narrowed his eyes at the agent. "Don't start with me. This is what I deal with all the freakin' time. One of these days you're going to find me a slobbering mess on the floor from everything he puts me through."

Wind Dancer leaned back on his haunches and nodded at Agent Farrentino. "It is true. When he drinks with the man called Jack Daniels, I find him in that position. It is not…" He paused and focused on Jacque. "What is the word?"

"Dignified."

"Yes. He is not dignified."

Jacque opened his mouth to speak and decided it might delay them longer.

Wind Dancer continued. "I think we near the kiva. I can find my way faster if alone and cut them off so the Chaveyo has trouble getting her into the kiva. You two come from behind. When I confront him, you can grab Cleo." He shook his head and stared at the ground.

"What's wrong?" Jacque asked. "We've got your back, buddy."

"I am not afraid for me." He lifted his chin toward where the Chaveyo and Cleo walked away. "She friends now to the Chaveyo. Healers want to know more than they should. Cleo wants to know what her father could never find. Her trust will take her to a place we cannot see. If that happens, it will be forever." He cocked his head toward Jacque. "And I will go after her, my friend."

"I'm not going to let that happen," he said in a quiet voice.

Farrentino weighed in. "We'll take care of Cleo. They're on the move. Get going before Jacque starts crying like a baby." He grinned.

Wind Dancer slipped away like a breeze lifting a fallen leaf. In seconds, he'd blended into the surroundings.

"Want my hanky, Jacque?" Farrentino sniffed and pretended to dab at his eyes.

"Want my foot up your ass?" Jacque growled. "I'm thinking I'll grab Cleo and shove you to Chaveyo. How about that?"

The agent smiled and followed Jacque up onto the trail.

~ ~ ~ ~

Chief Perez continued to twist her hands and stretch the cord around her wrists. He hadn't done a very good job at securing her bonds since she could now easily wiggle her hands out of it. Instead of dropping the cord on the floor, she studied it before shoving it in her pants pocket.

There remained enough light in the shed for her to select a large pipe wrench mounted on a pegboard at the end of the workbench. When she lifted it off the hook, it slipped and hit the floor with a loud ping. Grabbing it up, she tripped over the clutter on her way to the door. If he returned, she'd use the wrench to club him in the head.

The string for the overhead light remained out of her reach. Since the workbench was packed with junk, she opted not to climb up to try and reach the string. One false move and she'd tumble off, maybe injuring herself.

She waited. Listened.

When nothing happened, she tried to ease the door open, only to find it secured from the outside. Even when she put her shoulder to it and shoved, it didn't budge. The clink suggested there was a chain and probably a padlock. The cloudy window at the far end of the shop was partly blocked by stacked furniture and boxes. A small amount of light had squeezed around the obstructions until the eclipse robbed her of that security blanket. After a few minutes, the light returned, aiding her as she picked her way through the mess.

Most of the boxes were empty or filled with what she regarded as garage-sale rejects. Moving them took a few minutes. The furniture was a combination of old kitchen chairs, a few bicycles, a small chifforobe missing a leg, and an aluminum Christmas tree that had several branches bent in half. This took longer to move out of the way than she planned.

A family of mice skittered out from the chifforobe when the door swung open. It startled her so she fell against a music box, shaking it enough to begin playing a song so slow, it reminded her of bizarre background noise for a carnival fun house.

After she managed to calm herself and picked the pipe wrench up from one of the chairs, she wiggled in through the path she'd made to the window. A box of discarded towels would make it possible to wipe the grime from the glass. The hope had been to knock out the glass and squeeze through, but up close, it appeared it might be too small. Hopefully, her captor was gone, and she could determine where exactly he'd hidden her and how to escape once outside.

With the glass pane partially cleared, Perez took a moment to peer outside. Before she could get her bearings, a man stepped in front of the window to stare eye to eye with her.

CHAPTER 39

The sudden appearance of a man in the window frightened Perez enough to jump back and fall over the boxes she'd moved. When the face pressed against the glass, she eased out of her precarious position on the floor and rolled behind the chifforobe. Enough grime remained on the outside of the panes to make it impossible to see who now came calling. One thing was clear,s it was not the man who kidnapped her.

Did he have an accomplice?

She heard the crunch of gravel moving along the wall that led to the door. The thought of trying to escape out the window before the new person came through the door encouraged her to give it a try. She scampered up and stumbled to stand in front of the window only to realize it had been nailed shut A few of the rusty nails were bent as if someone had tried to pry them out. A new white ribbon of heavy caulk sealed over several places. Had someone else tried to escape? Her other option was to use the pipe wrench to shatter the window. The crash would draw this new person to check things out.

The door rattled several times. Perez's heartbeat increased as she decided to confront this new menace. The sound of metal against metal slammed against the door. With a stealth approach, she heard a chain, being dragged off of whatever lock had been put in place. She readied herself as the creak of the lever-like door handle lifted, followed by the moan of rusty hinges of the door opening. The light momentarily blinded her, except for the silhouette of a man stepping inside, then stopping.

With a burst of adrenaline, she rushed him, swinging the pipe wrench at his head. He managed to dodge the blow by jumping to the side but lost his balance and fell against the doorframe. When she raised the wrench over her head for a second chance, he held his hands up in surrender.

"Wait," he begged. "It's me. I won't hurt you." She stopped with her weapon in midair and did a double take in unbelief at the man before her. When she stepped closer and prepared to swing the pipe wrench anyway, he tried to move, only to land lopsided on the floor. "We need to go."

She lowered the wrench and jammed her boot in his chest. He tried to straightened to a sitting position, but she applied more pressure on his chest.

"Mansi? Why aren't you at the police station?" she growled.

"I escaped. No one came to check on me, so I walked out." She withdrew her foot and stepped away just far enough for him to right himself.

"Get up," she ordered. "So, help me, if you try anything, I'll knock your head off."

He raised his hands again and nodded. "I won't. I came to help. Honest."

"How did you know where I was?" She dared take a peek outside the door then snarled at the man who was one of her prime suspects up until this happened.

He rolled to his knees then grabbed the doorframe to pull himself up.

"My son called me."

"Alo?" Another suspect.

"Yes." He stepped outside and motioned for her to follow. "Come on. I parked off the road. He didn't see me when he left."

She motioned for him to take the lead but waved the pipe wrench to urge him to take her seriously. His gait reminded her of a penguin as he moved quickly down a dusty road. Looking over her shoulder, she saw only the building where she'd been held prisoner: a garage. The wooden garage doors had been secured with a long flat piece of wood. A vintage camping trailer resting on blocks, nearby, caught her attention. An awning flapped gently in the breeze. Considering it had the appearance of one of those restored campers that was all the rage, stirred up a lot more questions as to what it might be used for out here in the middle of nowhere.

"Wait. I want to take a look inside the trailer."

"Are you crazy? He could come back any minute."

She reached out and grabbed his arm and forced him around. "How did Alo know I was here? Maybe Alo helped him."

"No," he insisted as he turned to stare nervously down the road. "He didn't."

"How did he reach you?"

"I still had my phone." She thought she'd taken it at the station but remembered she'd left it in the room with him, thinking they'd be right back. "He saw you out by the road. He found Dr. Sommers. He discovered she got off the right trail and was coming to get help when he dragged you into the trunk."

"Why didn't he help me?"

"It happened so fast. I asked the same thing," he fumed. "Now, come on." His gait turned into a quick jog, something she thought impossible for him, considering his weight. "And he saw him pull a gun. After he locked you in the trunk, Alo ran into the park. No way he would follow. He went back to help Dr. Sommers."

That may have been the most embarrassing part. Not only did he have a gun, he'd shot it in the ground around her. He'd made her pick up the casings so there wouldn't be any trace of what he'd done. After handing them over, he smacked her upside the head with the gun.

"Do you still have your phone?"

He nodded.

"Give it to me." They had reached Mansi's car, hidden off road and covered with piles of brush. He started dragging it off as she punched in the station's number. "Where is this place, Mansi? I'm lost." He gave her quick directions, which she repeated into the phone. "There's several buildings. One is a trailer. Be sure to check it out. Got that?" she ordered into the phone. Slipping into the front seat, Mansi joined her and fired up the car. "Yeah. We're on our way back to the scene." With the seat belt buckled, Perez pointed down the road for Mansi to get moving. After reassuring the desk clerk she was okay, she clicked off.

"I'm fine. Pull whoever you can and meet me there. I don't know who else is still searching. Get that info to me ASAP. We've got those two guys from Chicago on the search, and an FBI agent. Try and reach them. They have a radio. I have a feeling they are in serious trouble."

~ ~ ~ ~

The forest opened up to a meadow, alerting Cleo the kiva was about three hundred yards away. The trail ended, and the ground became dotted with scattered basketball-size rocks, sparse vegetation, and stunted trees. Hills looming in the background gave the illusion of touching the sky. Any other time, she would have admired the scenery and taken pictures. Now it felt more like a nightmare she couldn't climb out of.

She had to convince the Chaveyo not to take her down into the kiva. How many others had found they were out of options? Why did a few survive, like the little boy? Then there were others who were found dead with no sign of what had killed them.

Maybe fear killed them.

Maybe their heart just stopped.

Maybe they escaped and were never found because animals removed any evidence of their existence.

Or maybe it was a random killing or kidnapping. So much of that these days. A person at the wrong place at the wrong time. People did all kinds of stupid things because of the belief nothing would happen to them. Yet the fact remained, these kinds of incidents had gotten the attention of the FBI.

Besides trying to lead Chaveyo away from the three men in her life, she hoped to lead Farrentino here to help with his investigation of other cases with the same characteristics. Were there openings that allowed beings to enter this world?

Wind Dancer had found his way to her by entering from a parallel universe. He had showed her there were holes to these places everywhere. Some were no bigger than a cell phone and others, like the one Wind Dancer walked through, were big enough to drive a truck. They opened and closed at will. There was no rhyme or reason to when this would happen.

If the kiva was a permanent opening into another world, Agent Farrentino needed to know.

There was no way of knowing if anyone could explore that sapapu. She was sure no sane Pueblo people would try it, but studying the Chaveyo would be much more interesting. However, she also knew, this would be impossible and could only lead to a horrible death or imprisonment in a place like Area 51. If Chaveyo had spiritual powers, then heaven help anyone who tried to stop him.

Chaveyo stopped two more times and surveyed the surrounding area, adding a growl for an unnerving effect. Deep inside, she knew Wind Dancer grew closer. He would never leave her to be a victim and would fight to the death to save her if the ogre turned on her or tried to pull her into the sapapu.

In minutes she spotted it, the kiva. Time to stall. But how?

She flopped down on the ground and wiped her brow. "Kuuyi." Water. He stopped and stared at her with those huge rolling eyes. Did she mispronounce the word? "Naki, kuuyi." Friend, water. This time she pantomimed drinking. Did he understand humans needed this? Hadn't several of the missing people later found been dehydrated?

She repeated the action, and this time he nodded and strode off their course.

"Cleopatra." Wind Dancer emerged from behind a wall of rocks and pulled her to her feet. The touch of his hands collapsed her into his waiting arms. He kissed her deeply so that her knees nearly buckled with relief at the wave of protection that engulfed her. "We must go before he returns."

"Jacque?"

"Not far. I can hear them."

A booming growl of discontent alerted them, and they spun around to face the Chaveyo a few feet away.

CHAPTER 40

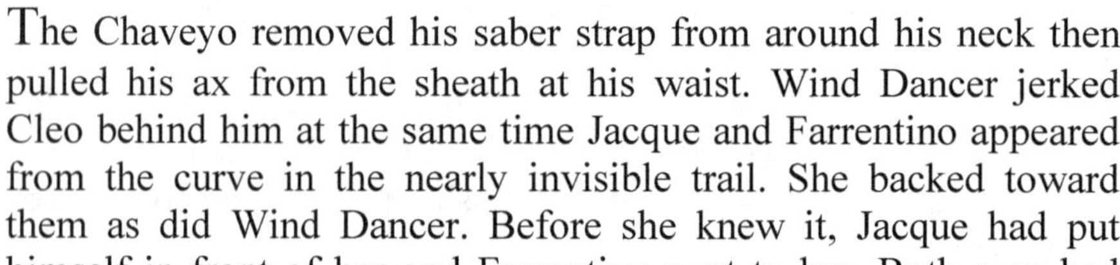

The Chaveyo removed his saber strap from around his neck then pulled his ax from the sheath at his waist. Wind Dancer jerked Cleo behind him at the same time Jacque and Farrentino appeared from the curve in the nearly invisible trail. She backed toward them as did Wind Dancer. Before she knew it, Jacque had put himself in front of her and Farrentino next to her. Both men had their weapons drawn.

Wind Dancer spread out his arms to block the other three from stepping closer. He began speaking in his own Pawnee tongue. Cleo wondered if such a creature could understand all Native tongues since the ogre stopped swinging his saber. He took a fighting position as he rolled his head from side to side.

Without warning, the Chaveyo let out a scream and charged Wind Dancer who had just enough time to grab a fallen branch and lift it. The ogre split right through the branch with his ax then twirled it, only to let it go toward Jacque who managed to dodge the attack. Farrentino tackled Cleo, landing on top of her.

Chaveyo threw down his saber then picked up Wind Dancer and tossed him against a tree at the side of the trail. The Pawnee grunted in pain and tried to stand. The ogre now moved toward the other two men, making ungodly noises that would have frightened a poltergeist.

He first loomed over Jacque who didn't get a shot off before the ogre kicked the gun out of his hand. Reaching down, he lifted the detective and tossed him at Wind Dancer, knocking them both to the ground. Farrentino rolled off Cleo and lifted his gun. He did get a shot off, but it went askew when the monster landed a kick in the agent's side.

The ogre bent over Cleo, grabbed the front of her shirt, and lifted her in slow motion until they were eye to eye. He brought her up to his chest then slipped his other arm under her legs to carry her body easily. Before he moved toward the kiva, he landed another kick to Farrentino's gut, eliciting a pained moan.

Wind Dancer and Jacque threw rocks at his legs and his head, but he shoved past them. Cleo felt paralyzed with fear and, once she got her wits about her, squirmed enough to make him stop.

"Put me down," she demanded. "Down." She spoke forcefully and glared at him. They stood at the opening of the kiva, and he slowly lowered her to the ground and backed away. "Askwali," she thanked him.

The ogre turned toward the three men charging forward.

Chaveyo now had no weapons, only his brute strength. Farrentino could barely walk but circled around so that the beast studied him ominously. Jacque limped to the opposite side, drawing his attention to yet another direction while Wind Dancer approached from the front, proud and tall.

The Pawnee attracted the most focus from the ogre who clicked his sharp teeth and hunched his back, taking on the bristled appearance of a wild animal ready to attack.

Wind Dancer used the words of his own people in a threatening tone. Then he chanted, softly at first then with each word, he spoke louder until the Chaveyo threw up his hands and covered his ears. Finally, he became so enraged that he charged Wind Dancer and tried knocked him down. Wind Dancer stood his ground in an effort to slow him but was knocked down. Without much obvious effort, the Pawnee jumped to his feet and landed a gut punch to the ogre, only to be tossed against a rock that caused him to gasp for air.

Jacque reached for his gun on the ground where he fell. Farrentino had also lost his weapon and tried to stop Cleo as she ran for the detective's. She picked it up and raced to stand in front of Wind Dancer just as Chaveyo reached for him.

"No. My naki." *Friend.* She patted her chest and leaned against Wind Dancer as he straightened, still trying to suck air into his lungs. She could only imagine what kind of angry expression he might be leveling. "Naki," she insisted.

The Chaveyo once more grabbed her by the collar and dragged her toward the kiva. Jacque and Farrentino tried to stop him but got knocked to the ground with little effort. Wind Dancer ran up and took the arm that held Cleo and bent it so he had to release her, followed by a terrifying scream. His monstrous hand went around the Pawnee's throat and lifted him off the ground. Jacque and Farrentino tried to intercede, but Chaveyo shoved both men with such force, they spun facedown in the dirt. He continued to squeeze Wind Dancer's throat.

"No. Please. Chaveyo. Naki. Naki." Cleo circled the ogre's waist and cried, "Nu' umi unangwa'ta." *I love you.* Immediately, she felt him drop Wind Dancer, who coughed and gulped air. The ogre turned to face her, his jaws snapping and eyes rolling. "Nu' umi unangwa'ta" she repeated. She took his hand and led him away from Wind Dancer.

Before she understood what was happening, the Chaveyo kept stepping toward her, causing her to walk backward.

"Cleopatra, stop." Wind Dancer's breathless shout enough to make her glance behind her to see she was about to step into the hole of the kiva.

She dug in her heels and shoved against the ogre's chest. It felt like attempting to move a brick wall. "No, I cannot go, naki."

"Chaveyo," came a new voice from the other Chaveyo that had helped her escape. Alo. He emerged from the underbrush near the woods. Alo picked up the saber from the ground then pointed it at the ogre. "Let her go. My naki, too."

He pivoted and bolted toward this new threat. But Alo met the charge with his own and held the saber up to ram it into the gut of the ogre. Unfortunately, he was too slow, and the Chaveyo snatched it away like a bully stealing a toy. He tossed the saber into the brush and stomped toward the kiva. Wind Dancer struggled to breathe but managed to jump onto the ogre's back as he passed.

Farrentino reached Cleo, who had been cut off from them until

Wind Dancer tried to slow the ogre down. He edged her away from the kiva opening as Jacque ran up to the Chaveyo and fell down on his hands and knees. Wind Dancer managed to force the Chaveyo off-balance causing him to fall across Jacque who then was pinned beneath the long legs.

Alo ran to block the kiva opening. "Take me, Chaveyo. I have no life here. Please."

The Chaveyo slowly rose to his feet and snatched Cleo away from Farrentino before shoving him to the side.

"Let her go," ordered Chief Perez. Everyone including the Chaveyo turned to see the chief and Mansi. The chief raised her weapon when Cleo heard another shot fired, hitting the chief in the shoulder. In that split second when blood began to pool on her shirt, she dropped her weapon. Mansi caught it and nearly dropped it as he fumbled to hold it correctly.

Floyd Miller, owner of the mechanic shop, stepped out into view, holding a rifle. "Should have figured you'd get in my way, Mansi. Your boy there"—he nodded toward Alo—"was always following me. Messin' in my business. The freak. Who's that?" He leveled the rifle at Chaveyo. "Another freak like your son?" He gave a sarcastic cackle.

"Just put the rifle down. I'm sure you're here to help out," Jacque said, easing toward Perez who covered her wound with a bloody hand.

She struggled to rise but fell again. "I have people everywhere looking for you, Floyd. Some are right behind me."

The Chaveyo's deep rolling growl got the mechanic's attention, and he turned the rifle on him. When he advanced, Floyd pulled the trigger. He'd managed only one shot when the ogre grabbed the gun away from him and clubbed the man's head with the stock.

Cleo pulled free of Wind Dancer and gently took the rifle. "Alo, do you speak Hopi?"

"Yes."

"Tell him he must return to his world without me so that I might heal Chief Perez. It is my duty. She is a good woman."

Alo circled carefully until he stood in front of the ogre. He told the Chaveyo Cleo's words several times before the beast focused on Perez lying on the ground then on Cleo.

He extended his hand to her, and she took it. Feeling its massive size close around her fingers she, smiled up at him. Without fear, she placed his hand on her cheek and whispered, I love you, friend, in Hopi. "Nu' umi unangwa'ta, naki." She laid a hand on her heart. "Askwali." Grateful. She then motioned to the kiva and walked, leaning him gently toward the opening. Pointing to the inside, Cleo whispered, "Goodbye."

Wind Dancer retrieved the saber and ax then handed them off to the ogre.

The Chaveyo hurried to the opening and jumped inside, bypassing any need for a ladder.

Other officers swarmed into the clearing, along with several EMTs.

Farrentino edged to the opening in the kiva and hesitantly peered into the depths of the darkness. Jacque came alongside him and also glanced into the hole.

Cleo watched the two men as Wind Dancer gathered her into his arms. She then went to assist the EMTs to make sure Chief Perez was stable. They called in a helicopter to transport her to Santa Fe, but she insisted the hospital in Sunset Rock would be just fine.

"Don't listen to that hard head," Jacque said as he came up alongside the gurney. "You've got a lot of explaining to do, Chief Perez."

She grinned. "Maybe I'll tell you over dinner."

"You buying?"

"I have an expense account."

"I was thinking maybe the Signature Room in the Hancock Building."

"That's in Chicago."

"Exactly. We don't have creepy stuff there."

She tried to chuckle but ended up wincing. "I'm not sure my expense account will cover all that."

"You pay for dinner, and I'll do the rest." She gave a thumbs-up and let the rescue team head toward the open meadow where they were to meet the helicopter.

They made their way to where Farrentino and Wind Dancer stood guard over the kiva opening. Alo was there, mask off and talking to them. Mansi stood at his son's side and stroked his arm. Cleo could hear the FBI side of Farrentino had kicked in and was conducting the first of many interrogations. He passed both men off to the state police to get them to Sunset Rock. The sound of the helicopter landing then taking off again brought other things to mind.

"Cleo, I've asked the state police and a few of the locals here to keep watch over the kiva until we can get down there and check things out." Farrentino motioned for several of the men to come and take up positions. "We need to get down there ASAP."

"He is gone," announced Wind Dancer.

"You don't know that," Farrentino insisted.

"If he says he's gone…he's gone." Jacque put his hands on his hips and peered down into the hole. "Wind Dancer knows more about the boogeyman than you ever will, so get over yourself. Let's cover the hole and get out of here."

It didn't take long to secure the scene with so many people onsite. Cleo knew if Chaveyo wanted out, there wouldn't be much they could do to stop him. After an hour of standing around, she'd had enough.

"Can we just go?" Cleo begged. "I'm dirty, hungry, and—"

"Horny?" Wind Dancer asked, brow creased.

"I was going to say tired." Cleo smiled.

"Buddy, that was an inappropriate question to ask her with all of us standing around." Jacque sighed and rubbed his neck.

"Oh." He took Cleo's hand and pulled her up next to him. "I am sorry. I must remember that much of what Jacque teaches me is inappropriate. Jacque says when I speak these words, I will not be lucky."

"No. I said you would not get lucky," Jacque corrected.

"I do not understand the difference."

Cleo took a deep breath. "Guess I'll have to show you later, Wind Dancer."

Jacque shook his head and strode away as Agent Farrentino burst out laughing.

EPILOGUE

Jacque stared at the distant mountains and wondered what other mind-blowing secrets the world held because of the lack of understanding and fear man held. The air was so clean and sweet here, he found himself filling his lungs at every opportunity then releasing it slowly, to hold it in as long as possible. For a city guy, this felt a lot like a drug. Maybe he could get used to a place like this. He twisted around to see a pueblo mural on the side of the hamburger restaurant in Sunset Rock about the same time a teenager rode his horse down a side street.

"Nope. Not for me."

"What's not for you?" came a feminine voice.

"Chief Perez, you are looking down right fetching this morning," he said, opening the passenger side door of his rental. His car had been destroyed in the fire, so this would have to do.

"I had no idea wearing a sling and having a bruise on my cheek would make me such a head turner. Guess all that makeup, expensive lotion, and new cowboy boots I bought to impress you were a waste of money." She slipped into the passenger seat and gazed up at Jacque who couldn't resist a grin.

"You don't have a gun hidden in that sling, do you?"

"No, but that's a really good idea." Her black hair, straight and shiny, fell down to her shoulders. A pair of jeans and a plaid shirt gave her a less-threatening appearance than her usual work attire.

"How's the shoulder? Heard you tried to tell the doctor how to do his job."

"He was an idiot. Kept trying to tell me jokes while I was bleeding all over myself. I finally had to tell him I'd be doggin' his every step from now on if he didn't shut up and get to work."

"Good thing I'm not intimidated by that sass."

"I'll work on that." She cocked her head and smiled while batting her eyes, like she'd done at Agent Farrentino a few days ago. Only now it was at him, and he felt inclined to think the flirting was exactly what he needed. Leaning closer, he buckled her in and caught a whiff of the lotion she claimed to have bought.

He shut the door and hurried around the other side to climb in and start the engine. Before he put it in drive, she reached over and laid a hand on his arm. "Thanks for all your help. This could have been a big mess without you."

"Sure." He pulled out onto the road and waited a few minutes before getting into detective mode. "Care to help me put all the pieces together?"

"No problem. Floyd Miller was an angry man. There have been complaints about him being a tough boss. Apparently, his much-younger wife liked to go to see her mother pretty often, leaving him to fend for himself. He made all kinds of remarks about her lousy cooking and often said she was trying to poison him."

"And the truth of the matter?"

"She liked those young men who worked for him a little too much. He caught her with Tinker, that young mechanic we found in the tow truck. Floyd told everyone his wife was gone to some baby shower, but he'd actually killed her. Found her in that trailer I spotted on his property on the other side of town."

"That's where he took you?"

She did a slow nod in a moment of reflection. Being a captive could really do a number on your head. He wondered how'd she'd fare with the trauma.

"He thought Cleo had seen him after he'd hidden his wife's car down the road. Cleo remembered his cowboy boots, more evidence against him. Abby showed up. He overheard her say she'd run out of gas, so he called Tinker away from a job to meet him there. Cleo was running for dear life, from who knows what. He thought she'd seen him leaving the cab of the truck."

"But it was Abby's dad chasing her."

"Right. When the ranger showed up, he hiked to his wife's car and hid it in that garage he took me. He knew where Tinker kept his truck, so he took it to crash into you guys. He thought she was a loose end."

"Hadn't expected a policeman and us to be tagging along, I'm guessing."

"Not likely. He's been charged with the murders of his wife, Tinker, and my officer." She shook her head. "What a waste. I tried to keep him safe until he could retire."

Jacque reached over and took her hand and squeezed. She held on tight. "When I went to get him, the car was completely engulfed with flames."

"I remember. And, although, later I thought Floyd had taken Cleo—"

"It was actually the Chaveyo."

"Yes. He didn't stick around and didn't know what happened to her, only someone else was there. He thought it was Alo, since he'd been following him."

"And why was that?"

"Like Tinker, Floyd was an abuser when it came to anyone different. Name-calling. You know. Bully stuff. He worked in Kewa Korner and liked to visit the coffee shop where Abby worked. Her statement said he flirted a lot, and she found him creepy. Apparently, she and Alo had become secret friends and would often walk along that city trail. She mentioned it to him. Abby is such a good kid who is nice to everyone. Wasn't anything romantic."

"When she went missing, Alo went to find her."

"He didn't know for sure if Chaveyo had taken her until he found her climbing out of the kiva."

"That's why she kept mentioning his name after we found her."

"Exactly. Except we didn't understand Alo had also become a follower and friend to Chaveyo."

A sign had been posted, warning there was road construction ahead, although both of them knew it was just a way to slow people down and not be surprised at all the equipment and state police presence.

"He wondered if Chaveyo was involved which is why he went to the kiva to make sure she wasn't there, but of course she was. He helped her escape, just like Dr. Sommers, I mean Cleo. Unfortunately, Abby fell and hit her head. He carried her as far as he could manage then went for help, covering her with pine boughs in hopes Chaveyo wouldn't find her."

"Why didn't he come forward?"

"You've seen him. Would you have believed him? The little boy, Tonya—they would have identified Alo, not some mythical Chaveyo."

"All he could do was wait and hope things worked out." Jacque shook his head. "Poor guy."

"After the car crash, Chaveyo was close by and took Cleo. I'm sure you already know what she went through and how things turned out there."

Jacque pulled into the parking lot. "Do we know if Floyd was the one who killed the girl, Karla? The one you showed us the first day we were here?" He helped her out of the car and guided her to where Abby's father waited with a golf cart. He would take them to the kiva site.

"Floyd had a solid alibi that whole week. He wasn't responsible."

"So maybe Chaveyo?"

"Agent Farrentino thinks so. Has all the signs. Cause of death couldn't be determined. Found in a spot that had been searched the day before. Missing shoes but feet were clean. Rescue dogs whined and refused to work near the location when they finally found her near a creek. She wasn't a risk-taker when it came to hiking. Very responsible."

"Meaning, she had other people with her."

"Until the last hour or so when they parted. She promised to join up with them later."

"And what about that Chupacabra beast? What will become of it?" Jacque rubbed his leg then touched his side, remembering the power in those muscles that easily overcame him.

"My zoologist friend brought some colleagues with him and, next thing I knew, it was gone. My friend wasn't happy because someone from the FBI must have showed up and took it away.

Probably in a giant test tube some place."

Jacque hummed the Twilight Zone theme song.

They sat in silence as Abby's father drove them to the hidden kiva where several grad students were helping an archeologist secure the site. Farrentino was listening intently then walked over to call down into the entrance hole.

Catching sight of Jacque and Chief Perez, he motioned for them to join him. After he introduced the archeologist, he went to give the grad students further directions.

"Where's Cleo and Wind Dancer?" Jacque asked. He'd dropped them off a couple of hours ago before going to pick up Perez.

Farrentino pointed down the hole. "They insisted on being there when the hole was sealed."

"No sign of the Chaveyo?" Perez asked.

"Not so much as a footprint. I'll never understand how he could just disappear with all of us standing around. I had plenty of security."

"You've got a lot to learn about Native People." Perez grinned. "You just don't understand."

"I'm going down there and see how things are progressing. You be okay up here with this hotshot FBI Agent?" Jacque asked.

"I'll be fine."

"Get them to hurry it up." Farrentino stepped aside to let him enter the kiva.

~ ~ ~ ~

Cleo watched Jacque hop off the bottom rung of the ladder then stop, blinking. She spent the last few days recovering from her ordeal and then yesterday went with Wind Dancer and Jacque to take down their camp.

There had been a great number of jokes and insults concerning Jacque going out in the wilderness to camp. He tried his best to convince them it was for the best, considering they both had suffered injuries.

"What is that wet stuff in the hole?" Jacque asked.

"Cement. Just on the top two feet or so. There are rocks below that." Cleo's voice hinted at regret.

"How deep is it?" Jacque squatted down to get a better look.

Wind Dancer kneeled down next to him. "The archeologist said they didn't find the bottom with the probe. It did narrow."

"How in the world did that huge guy get through there?" Jacque stood.

"Magic. This will not hold the Chaveyo." Wind Dancer stood and led Cleo to the ladder. "We go now. It is time."

Once outside, a steel screen was welded into place so curious hikers wouldn't try and enter. It would be protected then studied at a later date. For now, it was secured with cameras and light sensors.

When the group of workers, students, and archeologist hiked out, Chief Perez and Jacque got in the golf cart. The ranger said for Wind Dancer and Cleo to use the other one when they were ready.

As they drove off, Wind Dancer climbed behind the wheel. "I try driving now. Okay?"

Cleo smiled and agreed. "I think I left my phone on the rim of the kiva. I'll be right back."

She ran to the kiva and paused one last time to gaze into the exit hole, now covered with a steel screen. The sound of the ladder moving drew her closer.

A long finger, covered in wet cement, eased up through the screen and waited.

Wind Dancer was busy examining their new ride.

She reached down and touched the finger with her own and whispered, "Naki, Chaveyo. Naki."

Then he whispered the words back. "Friend."

THE END

ABOUT THE AUTHOR

Tierney James decided to become a full-time writer after working in education for over thirty years. Besides serving as a Solar System Ambassador for NASA's Jet Propulsion Lab, and attending Space Camp for Educators, Tierney served as a Geo-teacher for National Geographic. Her love of travel and cultures took her on adventures throughout Africa, Asia and Europe. From the Great Wall of China to floating the Okavango Delta of Botswana, Tierney weaves her unique experiences into the adventures she loves to write. Living on a Native American reservation and in a mining town, fuels the characters in the Enigma and Dark Side series.

After moving to Oklahoma, the love of teaching continued in her marketing and writing workshops along with the creation of educational materials and children's books. Try some of her other books to bring a little adventure to your life. Visit her website at tierneyjames.com Speaking at book clubs, school functions, church and community groups are a few of the things Tierney enjoys doing when not writing her next adventure. She also helps beginning writers in their quest to becoming a published author through her workshops and classes. Family, two adopted dogs and gardening fill her life with plenty of laughter to share with others.

Tierney has been an Amazon #1 Best Selling author and won

awards at the Annual Ozark Creative Writer's Conference as well as the Sleuths' Ink Mystery Writers.

OTHER PUBLICATIONS BY TIERNEY JAMES

Enigma Series
1.   An Unlikely Hero
2.   Winds of Deception
3.   Rooftop Angels
4.   Kifaru
5.   Black Mamba
6.   The Knight Before Chaos
7.   Invisible Goodbye

Children's Books
1.   There's a Superhero in the Library
2.   Zombie Meatloaf
3.   Mission K9 Rescue

Marketing for Authors
1.   How to Market a Book Someone Besides Your Mother Will Read

Education
1.   African Safari – A Teacher's Guide

Stand Alone Books
1. The Rescued Heart
2. Dance of the Devil's Trill
3. Turnback Creek

Dark Side Series
1. Dark Side of Morning
2. Dark Side of Noon